"Jennifer Mathieu masterfully explores how families break, how siblings survive, and all of the ways that love can hold us back and let us go."

—Robin Benway, National Book Award–winning and *New York Times*–bestselling author of *Far From the Tree* and *Emmy & Oliver*

"*The Liars of Mariposa Island*, with its richly layered exploration of the complicated love and lies that attend familial bonds, reasserts Jennifer Mathieu's standing as one of young adult fiction's most skilled storytellers."

—Jeff Zentner, Morris Award–winning author of *The Serpent King* and *Goodbye Days*

"In this tenderly told novel with a rich sense of place and time, Jennifer Mathieu unravels one immigrant family's secrets. Thanks to shifting narrative voices, readers grow in compassion for all three characters, flaws and all, and her masterful storytelling invites us to do the same."

—Mitali Perkins, author of *You Bring the Distant Near*

★ "Mathieu masterfully invests readers in the characters' origin stories, emotions, and motives. Her descriptions of the various settings over time and space are vivid and pulsating, immersing the audience in the psyches and nostalgia of each narrator."

—*Booklist*, starred review

"An emotional, sensitive, and heartbreaking story about one dysfunctional family's survival and unhappiness . . . . Quietly powerful."

—*School Library Journal*

"Mathieu empathetically delves into thorny questions of identity, trauma, abuse, choices, family bonds, and the lengths people will go to keep a measure of control in their lives. With a touch of romance, this gentle, multilayered novel comes with a dash of the unexpected thanks to the deeply unreliable nature of its narrators."

—*Kirkus Reviews*

"These stories intertwine and reflect one another with luminous intensity; Mathieu makes Caridad's story as compelling and thorny as that of her children without sacrificing their centrality or letting her off the hook."

—*The Bulletin of the Center for Children's Books*

THE
LIARS
OF
MARIPOSA
ISLAND

THE LIARS OF MARIPOSA ISLAND

JENNIFER MATHIEU

SQUARE
FISH

ROARING BROOK PRESS
NEW YORK

SQUARE
FISH

An imprint of Macmillan Publishing Group, LLC
120 Broadway, New York, NY 10271
fiercereads.com

Our books may be purchased in bulk for promotional, educational, or business
use. Please contact your local bookseller or the Macmillan Corporate and
Premium Sales Department at (800) 221-7945 ext. 5442 or by email at
MacmillanSpecialMarkets@macmillan.com.

Library of Congress Control Number: 2019932711

ISBN: 978-1-250-10424-3 (paperback) / ISBN: 978-1-62672-632-1 (ebook)

Originally published in the United States by Roaring Brook Press
First Square Fish edition, 2020
Book designed by Elizabeth H. Clark
Square Fish logo designed by Filomena Tuosto

3 5 7 9 10 8 6 4 2

For the Canales sisters
Graziella, Georgina, Maria Elena,
and especially my mother, Maria Teresa

Las mentiras tienen las patas cortas.

(Lies have short legs.)

ELENA FINNEY

MARIPOSA ISLAND, TEXAS

1986

CHAPTER ONE

MY BROTHER JOAQUIN KNOWS THE CALLAHANS ARE
back on the island just by the look on my face. And there's no
doubt he's pissed about it.

Squatting on our screened-in porch in front of our door,
working to repair the loose doorknob Mami has been after
him about, he glances up at me and he knows. He just does.

Good, noble Joaquin. Always trying to do the right thing
for Mami and never winning. His efforts end in explosive ar-
guments or him cursing her later behind her back, working
himself up into such a frenzy he needs to listen to music on his
Walkman at top volume or guzzle a Budweiser to calm down.
Such a waste of energy if you ask me. Better to ignore her.
Hide from her. Agree with her even if you don't. It isn't that
hard to do, really. Not if you do it often enough.

I don't even have to say anything to him and he figures out

the Callahans are back. After all, school ended last week. It's been just a few days since Joaquin walked across the auditorium stage at LBJ High School in a rented burgundy cap and gown, and later Mami, Joaquin, and I enjoyed a celebratory dinner at El Mirador, compliments of Joaquin's boss, Carlos. The Callahans always show up a week after school lets out. It's been that way since the summer after I finished seventh grade.

"Hey," Joaquin says, lifting the bottom of his white T-shirt to wipe the sweat off his face. He squints up at me.

"Hey," I answer back. "I have a babysitting job tonight."

Joaquin stands up, arches his back. He flips the screwdriver he's holding in his hand over once. Twice. Both times he catches it without even looking. He keeps his gaze on me.

"It's so hot, Elena," he says. "Why the hell do the Callahans come to Mariposa Island every summer? Why don't they go to, like, the coast of Maine?"

I shrug. "Who can understand the ways of the rich?"

"Fine," he says. "But I have a shift at the restaurant tonight. So I hope you won't be home too late. Someone has to be here to pour Mami into bed."

I roll my eyes. First of all, it's almost always me who pours Mami into bed. He knows this. And secondly, any chance he gets to go after Mami, he does. One time in middle school, he brought home pamphlets about alcoholism from the school nurse and started marking Mami's bottle of Bacardi with a black magic marker. That lasted about two weeks. Honestly, he can be so dramatic sometimes.

4

"Mr. and Mrs. Callahan are just going out to dinner," I say as Joaquin resumes his squat and peers at the front doorknob like he and it are about to engage in hand-to-hand combat. "I have to get the kids into bed, and I'll probably be done by ten or so. Maybe ten thirty."

"How old are those little brats now, anyway?" Joaquin asks, jiggling the doorknob, his brow furrowed.

"Jennifer is eight and Matthew is four," I answer. "At least Matthew's out of diapers. And they're not brats. They're sweet kids. I mean, a little spoiled, yeah. But they like me. They never give me any trouble."

"A regular Mary Poppins you are," Joaquin says dryly.

"Are you going to let me in or not?" I ask, one hand on my hip.

Joaquin jiggles the doorknob one more time, and rocking back on his heels, he opens the front door and wordlessly lets me enter. I'm pretty sure the accompanying slam is meant for me.

I have an hour until Mami gets home from work, so I hunt through the pantry until I find an almost-empty bag of potato chips. I'll finish them and Joaquin will have another reason to be pissed at me, but at least he gets a free meal every shift at work. And El Mirador is better than Mami's dinners. With her it's always *ropa vieja* or mac and cheese or overcooked burgers for the five millionth time.

Taking the kitchen phone off the hook, I stretch the cord as far as it will go and slide onto the floor behind my bedroom door.

Michelle answers on the second ring.

"Hey, it's me," I say.

"Hey," she responds. "So can you make it out tonight? To the party?"

I crunch down on a chip and lick salt off my fingers. "Yeah, I should be able to make it." The Callahans are often home sooner than they say.

"What about your brother?"

"He has to work."

"Shit."

"God, Michelle, don't be gross."

"How am I being gross?" she asks. "I literally just said *shit* to express my disappointment that your brother isn't going to make it to the party."

I cram a handful of greasy potato chips in my mouth and talk through my crunching, little explosions of chips flying from my lips. "It's gross because . . . you think my brother . . . is cute."

"You're the one who's gross, eating and talking at the same time," Michelle answers. "And your brother *is* cute."

I swallow and shout into the phone. No words, just a loud, sustained yell.

"Jesus!" Michelle cries, and I burst out laughing. "Fine, I won't bring up your brother again."

I slide down my bedroom door farther until my chin is resting on my chest. Madonna stares down on me from the poster on the wall, her eyes killing me with confidence. I wonder how long before Mami makes me take that poster down. I need to make sure I keep my bedroom door closed more often.

"My brother never does anything fun anyway," I say. "He just suffers."

"I'm not even going to respond because I'm afraid you're going to shout again," Michelle answers.

"Let's move on to other boys I'm not related to," I say. "Namely, Jimmy Paradise."

It's ridiculous this could actually be someone's legal name, of course, and that this person could be as hot and cool and amazing as his name suggests, but Jimmy Paradise is a real person, and he's had that very real name since he moved to Mariposa Island this past school year, in the middle of tenth grade. In the five months he's been here he's had one suspension and two girlfriends, and every time he walked into my Spanish II class I wanted to die. I let him cheat off me on every verb conjugation quiz. Señora McCloud doesn't know I'm almost fluent, but Jimmy figured it out. After every A he made, he flashed his paper at me and winked.

"I'm sure Jimmy Paradise will be there," Michelle answers. "Honestly, I don't know what you see in him. Too many muscles for my taste."

"What?" I shriek, savoring my last chip. "You have *no* taste. That's your problem."

"Oh, please. Whatever."

She may sound annoyed, but I know she's not. Michelle

and I have been best friends since second grade. Or maybe third grade, I'm not sure. I just know I can't remember a time when we weren't slipping notes to each other during class or trading scented erasers or going through our freshman yearbook putting dots next to the names of all the kids in our class who we were sure had done it.

We talk and talk, and before I know it, an hour has slipped by and I hear the front door open and then shut. I feel my chest tighten.

"My mom's home," I say. "I gotta get off."

"Elena, you're going to break the phone with that stretching! I've told you one million times!"

Michelle laughs. It's not her mother, after all. All she says is "Jesus, I can hear her from here."

"I'll bet," I say. "See you tonight."

"Okay. I just wish you could spend the night after."

"You know I can't."

"Elena! The phone! Hang up!"

"Trust me, I know you can't," Michelle says, and I don't even say goodbye, I just stand up and open my bedroom door.

• • •

Everything about Mami has a weight to it. Her words. Her movements. Even her thoughts. Really, even the things she doesn't say or do have a weight.

When I was little and In Trouble, I would go into her bedroom at night to hug her and find her tucked into one side of

8

the bed as if someone else was going to take the other side. Lying there on her stomach reading a celebrity magazine she'd brought home from work, her dark hair jumbled up and pinned to the top of her head like a storm cloud, she would turn to me as I entered, quiet as a cat, to say good night. To say, *I'm sorry*.

"Good night," she would say, stiffening as I placed my arms awkwardly around her. Sliding away from me as if I were toxic. "Sleep well."

The hug that was not a hug had a weight. The words that were not words had a weight.

But I could shrug off the weight if I ignored it. Move on and play nice. Something Joaquin has never learned.

"Elena, I've told you a million times not to stretch the phone cord," Mami says as I emerge from my bedroom. She sets two large paper bags from Belden's on the kitchen counter and begins unpacking them. "I mean, literally one million hundred times." She runs a hand through her shoulder-length dark curls that are now only dark because of a box of hair dye she splurges on at the drugstore every once in a while and hides in the cabinet under the bathroom sink. I pretend not to know this.

"I'm sorry, I just forgot," I say, placing the phone back in the cradle where it belongs.

"Who were you talking to?" she asks even though she knows. Still, I play along.

"Michelle," I answer.

My mother's nostrils flare, and her mouth turns down at

each end. She places bananas and apples in the fruit bowl and slides it into its place over the permanent mystery stain on the pink Formica, a stain that's been there since before we rented the place. Mami's frown is the first invitation to debate her, followed by a second in the form of a loud exhale. I do not engage, just dig my hands into one of the paper bags.

"Here," I say, "let me help."

"You know how I feel about her," my mother starts in, since I haven't taken the bait.

"Yes, Mami."

Michelle's mother is on her third husband. Michelle's older sister used to work at the Pink Pussycat before getting pregnant out of wedlock. Michelle's father, who is not even her father, can't keep a steady job.

Basura.

Mami doesn't say anything else and neither do I, and we finish putting the groceries away in silence until Joaquin walks in, his wrestling match with the faulty doorknob apparently over. The weight in the kitchen immediately feels even heavier.

"Did you fix it?" Mami asks, straining to shut the last of the boxed mac and cheese in one of the top cabinets. Her blue patterned top hikes up over her khaki slacks, and after she puts the food away, she tugs down the top and smooths it out carefully.

"Yeah," Joaquin answers. "I mean, yes."

"Good. Elena, leave that meat to thaw in the counter. I want to use it for dinner."

"*On* the counter, Mami," Joaquin corrects her. "Leave it *on* the counter."

"God, Joaquin, let it go already," I say, setting the ground beef out. "You're always going after her on those little phrases that she's never going to get right anyway."

"I love it when my children talk about me like I'm not here," says Mami. "So respectful." For a second I hold my breath, but then she turns away from her bag of groceries and gives us a half grin, so I know it's okay. *"Debería hacer que ustedes hablen español, y luego verán quien suena cómico."*

I push out a laugh, but Joaquin says, "Maybe if we'd practiced more as kids, our Spanish would be better." He looks down at the screwdriver in his hand when he says this.

"Like you wanted to practice Spanish?" my mother says, her voice crackling just the slightest bit. "You complained enough about your name." I have to feel for Joaquin on that. How many teachers on the first day called roll for a Joe-a-kwin? At least my name can be Americanized into Uh-lay-nuh. The way some of the teachers at the high school say it, I sound like a wealthy Southern debutante instead of the daughter of a Cuban refugee turned doctor's office manager and single mother. I kind of like it.

Joaquin doesn't answer Mami's remark about his name, just wanders over to the kitchen drawer where he keeps his tools and dumps in the screwdriver and a few loose screws.

"Elena's got a babysitting job tonight in case she forgot to tell you," he says suddenly, shutting the drawer and heading

11

down the hallway, walking past without looking at me. It's a look that is not a look. "I'm going to take a shower before work." A few beats later I hear his bedroom door shut more loudly than normal. In a couple of moments his stereo will turn on. That weird-ass moody Jesus and Mary Chain tape again. All that guitar feedback and distortion. Gag.

My mother folds the paper bags from Belden's and places them in the space behind the garbage can. She glances at her wristwatch before taking out a glass tumbler, opening the refrigerator, and pouring herself a drink. The *plink plunk* of ice, the *hiss pop* of a can of off-brand cola, the *glug glug* of the big jug of Bacardi. I could write lyrics to this music, I know it so well. While she makes her cocktail, I stand barefooted in our kitchen and wonder how much Matthew and Jennifer have grown since last summer.

"So as far as the babysitting, is Mr. Callahan here or is it just the mother and children?" Mami asks, sipping her drink. As she swallows her cocktail her shoulders drop just a millimeter or two, a distance only Joaquin and I would be able to measure.

"Mr. Callahan is down for the weekend, but on Monday he goes back to Houston for work, same as the other summers."

"And she doesn't get bothered?" Mami asks, arching one eyebrow. "Her husband always away like that?"

"Well, someone needs to earn the money to get a house on Point Isabel," I argue. "It has the prettiest views of the ocean."

My mother flares her nostrils again. "The ocean," she remarks. "You mean the Gulf of Mexico. There's a difference."

The waters off Mariposa Island will never rival those my mother grew up next to in Havana, something she reminds us of every chance she gets.

"Right, the Gulf of Mexico," I answer. "Anyway, they're going out to dinner and then to see a movie. So I'll probably be home by ten thirty. Maybe eleven." I look down and scratch an imaginary bug bite on my leg. When I look up, Mami is pursing her lips the same way she pursed them three years ago when I found the flyer Mrs. Callahan had posted for a mother's helper on the community bulletin board at Belden's. *Mother's Helper Needed for the Summer! Two sweet kiddos, ages 1 and 5, like story time, trips to the beach, and playing dress-up!* It's the same tightly wound face Mami makes every summer when the Callahans come back and she finally gives me permission to leave the house like a regular person.

"What are they paying you?" she asks, taking another sip. A gulp, really. The glass is half empty.

"Three dollars an hour," I say. "Plus sometimes tips. It's more than any other girl I know gets."

My mother opens the fridge and pulls out the jug of Bacardi. She calls it freshening up her drink, the same way she freshens up her makeup after work even though she never goes anywhere.

"Do they rent out their house during the off-season?" Mami asks, topping off her glass and screwing the cap back on the jug. I've answered this question before, but she's either forgotten the answer or just likes hearing it again.

"No. They have someone who comes in once a month or something to check on the place and keep it clean. Or maybe it's twice a month." Mr. Callahan must bring in a ton of money. Most families who own homes on Point Isabel at least rent out their houses when they're not using them.

"They must be very wealthy," says Mami, in a voice equal parts admiration and envy.

"I guess," I answer.

Mami takes another sip from her drink and looks out the front window that sits over the kitchen sink. The window that stares at another saggy clapboard house staring back at us. She scowls at some imaginary spot on the windowpane and is soon attacking it with a paper towel and a bottle of glass cleaner, her drink temporarily forgotten on the counter.

"So . . . I can babysit, yes?" I ask. I hold my breath. Her hand swipes furiously back and forth at the spot on the glass.

"Yes, fine," she says, not turning to look at me. "But you know what?" Her voice is thick with certainty. "I bet that man cheats on his wife. I bet when he goes back to Houston during the week it's one big party for him. Remember, Elena, that most men are not to be trusted."

I exhale. "I bet you're right about Mr. Callahan," I answer, ignoring the part about not trusting men, and I head back to my bedroom and shut the door.

CHAPTER TWO

MICHELLE AND I ARE HEADING TOWARD THE PARTY ON the beach, a six-pack of Budweiser swinging from Michelle's hand. The gritty sand under our feet is still warm because night has only just fallen, and the stars are starting to peek out and say hello like shy toddlers. I think about my babysitting charges, Matthew and Jennifer. How at the beginning of the summer they're always a little bashful, and Mrs. Callahan has to coax them out from behind her legs with the promise of Oreos.

"Oh, you remember Elena, don't you?" she always says on my first job of the season, her singsong, honey-sweet voice always so understanding. Always so patient. Then again, maybe mothers are just more patient when they have lots of money and time to themselves. I swear Mrs. Callahan gets younger and more in shape each year. She says she has a tennis pro in Houston named Antonio who keeps her honest.

"First party of the summer," Michelle says, and she shimmies a bit with anticipation. "Three months of no school. And a six-pack of beer. Yes, please."

I smile, but as my eyes take in the large crowd down by the surf, my heart pounds. I don't get out much during the school year. Michelle spends every weekend all year long at some kegger since her mother doesn't lose her shit just because she wants to have fun sometimes.

"Do you see Jimmy Paradise yet?" she asks.

"God, shut up."

"Elena, we're still, like, a million miles away. He'd never hear me."

"Just shut up anyway," I say, and then I spot him. He's got on shorts and a Polo and is off to the side with a bunch of other guys kicking a soccer ball around. As Michelle and I get closer, I can hear they're all swearing at each other, and in the middle of it Jimmy stops to finish his beer, crumple the can, and toss it to some guy in the circle.

"Catch, asshole," he says, and then he laughs. The other guy laughs and tosses the beer can back.

"No, *you* catch, you dick."

None of the boys look at Michelle and me. I try to appear disinterested with the whole scene. Just then we hear a familiar voice.

"Hey, come sit by us."

It's our friend Tara with a few other girls we know. They're sitting on a ratty quilt, smoking cigarettes. Tara pats the blanket, and Michelle and I drop down to the sand and kick off our flip-flops and open some beers.

16

"Is that really you, Elena, out in the land of the living?" Tara says before taking a deep, slow drag on her Marlboro.

"Can I bum one?" I ask, dodging the question. Tara tosses me her pack and her lighter, and then Michelle asks for one. Soon we're sitting back on the quilt, watching the boys kick around the soccer ball and gossiping about the various couples who break off and head down to the surf's edge, melting into each other like it's their last night together on earth. It's a big party—maybe sixty or seventy teenagers from LBJ High— and every time I turn around, some more are walking up to the perimeter, six-packs in hand. Sometimes whole coolers. There's a boom box playing, turned up to top volume.

"I hope we don't get shut down," Michelle says. "That would suck."

"Totally," says Tara.

"Yeah," I add, trying to track Jimmy Paradise as he breaks out from a group of guys and walks up to the surf, his back to me. A beat later some tiny blond girl darts toward him, jumping up to wrap her arms around his shoulders for an impromptu piggyback ride. She jumps sure in the knowledge that she weighs next to nothing. She jumps sure in the knowledge that Jimmy Paradise would want nothing more than to have her appear out of nowhere with her arms around his chest, her legs around his waist, her face buried into his neck. She yelps in excitement as he grabs her legs and spins around, but she's cute about it, like a newborn puppy or something.

I can't tell in the moonlight, but I can guarantee she has shell-pink nail polish put on by a professional, perfect, gleaming white teeth, and sweet green eyes the color of jade. Oh, and her name is Ashleigh or Siobhan or Vanessa, and when she gets home in the evenings her mom is always up waiting for her and the two of them curl up on the living room couch and the mom grins at how much Ashleigh Siobhan Vanessa reminds her of her own girlhood, full of beauty and popularity and everything good.

Sigh.

Michelle catches me watching all of this and what happens after, too, which is that Jimmy Paradise and the girl slide down the coastline and into the inky blackness of night, becoming one of those melty couples. I finish my cigarette and dump it into the empty Budweiser can in the middle of the quilt that everyone's using for ashes and butts. Michelle leans against me and puts her head on my shoulder for a second before she presses a quick kiss on my cheek. She smells like Love's Baby Soft and cigarette smoke and she's my very best friend, so she doesn't need to say a single word.

"Anyone want another beer?" asks Tara, digging into the cooler.

"Yeah," I say, "and I want to go put my feet in the water for a sec, too."

"Want company?" asks Michelle.

"In a little bit."

I take the slick wet can from Tara and walk down to the gulf, sinking my feet into the water and letting the small waves rush back and forth until I'm ankle-deep in sand. When Joaquin and I were little and Mami would take us to the beach, I remember I would stand by the edge of the water and wonder how long I would have to stay there before the sand would cover my knees and then my waist and then my face. I take a swallow of Budweiser and wish I liked the taste more. Mami's Bacardi and off-brand cola would be better, probably. Not that I would know. But at least cola is sweeter.

"Hey, Elena."

I startle and almost drop my beer. It's Miguel Fuentes, a classmate of mine since forever. He jumps back a bit.

"I didn't mean to scare you."

"No, it's okay," I say and take a swallow. "I didn't see you come up."

"I wasn't sure it was you," Miguel says. He shoves his hands into the pockets of his shorts. "You hardly ever come out." We glance at each other and then switch our focus back to the dark, rippling gulf. I wrinkle my nose at the fishy stink that Mami says she never had to endure on the beaches in Cuba.

"My mom's better about me having a social life in the summer," I say. I check my wristwatch. Nine thirty. I have an hour at least before I have to be home, and I quietly give thanks that Mr. and Mrs. Callahan got back early, just as I'd hoped they would, leaving me more time to hang out.

"I guess she thinks you can relax a little more since school's out, right?" Miguel asks.

"Yeah," I answer.

He takes his hands out of his pockets and cracks his

knuckles, then shoves them back in his pockets again. I wish he had a cigarette or a beer or something so he would have something to do with his hands.

Miguel Fuentes likes me. He has since the eighth grade. I mean, he's never said it, but I'm pretty sure it's true. My experience with guys is more limited than I want to admit, but I'm pretty sure there are only a few ways for a teenage boy to show you he likes you. Like waiting by your locker to say hi or offering to let you copy his notes when you've been home sick or telling you he likes your hair even though it's brown and boring and nothing special. All of which are things Miguel has done. Why would a guy be nice to you if he wasn't also hoping that maybe one day he could get in your pants?

"You ready for junior year?" he asks me, his eyes still trained on the water.

That's the other thing that makes me think he likes me. He always asks the most obvious, rehearsed questions.

"I guess," I answer, taking another swallow of beer. "What about you?"

Miguel's eyebrows pop up, like maybe he wasn't expecting me to ask the question back.

"Screw junior year," he says at last, and I have to laugh.

"What? Did that amuse you?" He's pleased with himself, obviously.

"A little," I tell him, and Miguel grins and it's quiet between us, but it's okay. We stare out at the water, the shrieks of our classmates filling the sticky summer night behind us. Miguel scratches at a mosquito bite on his arm, his fingernails cutting across his skin. He is *puro indio*, Mami would say, rolling her eyes when Joaquin would then tell her how racist she sounds. Miguel is the kind of brown that people on Mariposa Island think of when they think of Hispanics. Dark skin, dark eyes, Spanish last name. The funny thing is his grandparents were born in Texas, so his family's been in the United States a lot longer than mine. And I know for a fact he can't speak Spanish for shit. Who would ever guess fair-skinned Elena Finney knows more of our mother tongue?

"So," Miguel starts, his eyes still focused on the water. He swallows. I look away because I know what he's going to say. I just know it. "If you're allowed some freedom this summer, maybe you could let me take you out?"

Sometimes he comes to school with stains on his shirts. His bushy black eyebrows grow too close together into the space above his nose. Once in geometry class I swear he farted during a test.

I cannot get excited about Miguel Fuentes.

"Um . . ." but I've already crushed him by waiting too long to answer. I can tell by the way he looks away from me and down the shoreline that he's hoping a beached whale might turn up to end this conversation.

"Forget it," he says. "You're probably busy."

I wince a bit. Maybe Miguel isn't Jimmy Paradise, but he's still a nice person.

"No, I mean, it's just . . ." I can't look at him anymore, so I stare at the sea in front of me, like the right words might float in on a raft to save us both.

"Hey, you hogging my friend here?"

Okay, so maybe it's not a raft, but Michelle will do.

"Hey," I say, sliding my arm around her shoulders. "There you are."

Miguel exhales. I think he's relieved Michelle has shown up, too. I picture both of us hours later—him in his bedroom and me in mine—only he'll think of me and cringe and I'll think about Jimmy Paradise and cringe and we'll both be depressed because neither one of us got what we wanted.

Mami is right about one thing. *La vida no es justa.* Mami always says those words in Spanish, not English. Like maybe that makes them extra true.

"How's tricks, Miguel?" Michelle asks. Miguel rubs the back of his neck and sighs.

"The usual," he says. "Another Mariposa summer. Tourists overtaking everything, and nobody can find a freaking parking spot by the beach. But at least there's more money in tips." Miguel works at El Mirador with Joaquin, but as a busboy, not a waiter. Even I can admit my brother can turn up the charm for a job serving customers directly. Miguel just doesn't have what it takes in that area.

"I need to go hunt down a beer," he says, giving up at last. "See y'all."

"Take care, Miguel," I say, feeling like a real jerk.

Michelle and I link arms, and she tugs me down the

shoreline. The waves lap at my feet. "I could tell he was asking you out," she says.

"I really don't want to talk about it." I find my eyes searching the night for Jimmy Paradise and that girl, my ears listening for his deep, sure-of-itself voice. Then I glance down at my feet and kick at the sand hard, watching the tiny grains spin up and collapse back down. It feels good to kick it, so I do it again and again.

"You need another beer," Michelle suggests, stopping me by tugging me back up the beach toward Tara's quilt. And for my last hour of freedom this is how I spend the first real night of my summer, drinking cheap beer and smoking even cheaper cigarettes, surrounded by the gossip of girls and the heat of the Texas night as it holds us in its tight and all-too-familiar grip.

CHAPTER THREE

PLEASE LET HER BE ASLEEP.

She isn't. Of course.

She's up, watching the tail end of the local ten o'clock news in the den off the kitchen, curled up on the couch on her side, with her head propped up on a throw pillow and an empty tumbler resting by her breasts. The news anchor on the television blabs on about the annual Miss Crawfish Boil pageant.

"Look at those girls," Mami says, stabbing her finger at the air in the general vicinity of the television. "Walking around in their underwear. *Fea. ¡Sucia!*"

"Definitely," I say as I watch girls that look a lot like Jimmy Paradise's latest fling flouncing around on the boardwalk in string bikinis, not underwear. Not that I correct Mami. Instead, I reach for the glass she's been drinking from that's too close to the edge of the couch for my comfort. "Here, let me get that."

"Wait," she says, her hand suddenly on mine, her grasp stronger than I would have imagined it would be by this hour of the night. She sniffs and I freeze. "You stink of cigarettes, Elena." She lets go of my hand and hauls herself up to a sitting position, inhaling again. "Yes, that's cigarettes." Her bleary eyes sharpen. She grimaces.

"It's Mr. Callahan, Mami," I say, walking the glass a few feet to the kitchen sink and taking enormous pains to rinse it out over and over, trying to extend the distance between us so she can't smell me up close again. "He smoked in the car when he was bringing me home. He's just . . . stressed from his work, I think."

I put the glass in the dish rack and turn toward my mother, leaning my back against the sink.

Mami's eyebrows tug together. "Why is he stressed with work? Or do you think it's something else?" She tips her head to the side.

"I really don't know. He just seemed stressed. He said he had a lot on his plate, and he was so grateful that I was able to help out Mrs. Callahan this summer since he was going to be gone so much." He really had said that, even if he hadn't smoked a cigarette. He's like Mrs. Callahan, sort of a health nut. He plays racquetball, too. And in college at Northwestern he played soccer. Mrs. Callahan always finds a way to mention that to me, like that's more impressive than him being a big-time oil-and-gas guy or whatever it is he does. I think it's so cute that his soccer-stud background means more to her than his fat paycheck. I know she must really love him.

"I'm telling you," Mami says, thrusting a finger toward me, "he's stressed because he's keeping up one family in Point Isabel and another back in Houston." Her words are slurry. Lazy. She's had a few for sure. "I hope they know you come from a fine family, where that kind of behavior is frowned upon."

"I'm sure they know," I say, filling a clean glass with water and heading toward Mami's bedroom off the den. She has the biggest bedroom in our dollhouse-sized house. Joaquin's bedroom and my bedroom are really one room with a fake wall the landlord put up to charge more money. Once inside Mami's room, I turn down her sheets, plump up her pillows. I put the water on her nightstand, right by her collection of old romance novels. She keeps them with the covers facedown so we won't see the bodice-ripping pictures, like we're still little kids.

I glance around for her nightgown but can't find it. Finally, I recover it hidden all the way at the foot of the bed in one wadded-up lump. With a quick flick of my wrists, I air it out and lay it on the bed for her, pearl buttons and lace front-side up. When Mami was a little girl in Cuba, her maid, Juanita, used to put clean sheets on her bed every night and brush her hair and help her bathe and change clothes, even when she was a teenager. Honestly, Mami was a little spoiled when she was younger, so sometimes it's easy for me to see why she is the way she is. I don't know why Joaquin can't understand it. Especially considering that it's me who helps Mami get into bed most nights anyway.

I walk back into the den. Mami is curled up on the couch, lightly snoring. I turn the television off and think briefly about leaving her there, but the one time I made the mistake of doing that, she woke up in the middle of the night panicking and not sure where she was. She jumped up in such a rush that she knocked her favorite lamp off the end table. She loved that lamp, too. It was pale pink with white piping and it cost a whole five dollars at Goodwill. Afterward, I had to give up a lot of my Callahan babysitting money to pay her back for it.

"Mami?" I say, shaking her shoulders gently. She grunts. Her thick foundation looks cheap this close up, buried into the fine lines around her eyes. "Mami, you should get to bed."

Her eyes pop open. She sits up as if she's been poked by something hot. "Okay!" she says. "Okay, I'm going." She stumbles off to the bathroom, and I can hear water splashing around and the sounds of her muttering.

Finally, she heads into her bedroom. "Good night, *preciosa*," she calls out from inside her room. Before I can answer, she's shut her door. I hear loud footfalls and finally the squeaking sigh of her mattress as she collapses onto the bed and falls asleep.

• • •

When Joaquin gets home, I'm fresh out of the shower and towel-drying my wet head, trying to stop the replay in my mind of my awkward conversation with Miguel Fuentes. I pull my nightgown over my arms and peek out of the bathroom

27

to see my brother hanging his keys on the hook by the front door. He glances around the living room and kitchen area for a moment, like maybe he expected it to transform itself into something nicer while he served people cheese quesadillas at El Mirador all night.

"Hey," I say, my voice a whisper as I step out to meet him. I hold a finger to my lips.

"She asleep?"

I nod.

"Good mood or bad?"

I shrug. "The usual, I guess." Joaquin shrugs back, then rolls his eyes a little bit. I swear, if he keeps waiting for a good mood like the one he wants, he's going to be waiting for the rest of his life.

I curl up on the edge of the couch. I had sort of planned to watch the late movie on television, but Joaquin would probably make fun of me for it. I miss the days when we liked the same things—the same Saturday morning cartoons, the same cheap candy bars from the Stop-N-Go down the street. I pull my arms and legs inside my nightgown and hug my knees up to my chin. Joaquin gets a beer from the refrigerator.

"Remember the time you were a kid and you sat like that?" he asks, motioning to me before sitting down on the recliner with the cat scratch marks back from that one year that Mami let us have a cat. "Only you fell off the couch and you couldn't catch yourself, and you chipped your front tooth on the coffee table? God, was Mami pissed about that dentist bill."

I give him a dirty look and drag my arms out through the sleeves. "Happy now?"

Joaquin takes a sip of beer. "Hey, you're old enough to do whatever you want."

"What planet are *you* living on?"

Joaquin ignores me and pulls a cassette tape out of his jeans pocket, flipping it over a few times.

"Anything good?"

"Someone at work gave it to me," he answers before he slides it back into his pants pocket. "It looks like it could be good."

"I hope it doesn't have any of that music-to-get-depressed-to on it." I motion like I'm gagging.

"Well, I hope it doesn't have Madonna on it," he tells me, then fake-chokes himself until he pretends to pass out, slumping deeper into the recliner. When he sits up, I laugh but I'm not sure what to say next.

There have been times when I've felt like I would die for my big brother and do anything for him, and sometimes it feels like we're just playing out the parts somebody wrote for the stupid brother-sister sitcom that we're on, and we barely have anything real to say to each other at all. Lately it's been more the second one.

Outside, we hear the roar of an engine followed by another, like rockets taking off.

"Drag racers," I say. They might even be some of my classmates post-party. I picture Jimmy Paradise and Pretty Blond

Girl sliding wildly down Esperanza Boulevard, Pretty Blond Girl's hair whipping in the wind like party streamers.

"Yeah," Joaquin says, swallowing the last of his beer. "Hope they don't wake Sleeping Beauty." He nods over his shoulder toward Mami's bedroom.

"I'm sure she's out," I say, stretching. I'm not in the mood to dissect her, and I hope he's not, either. He almost always is though.

"So how was your babysitting job?" he asks, surprising me by changing the subject.

"Fine," I say, standing up and turning away from my brother to tidy up the already-tidy kitchen. Just in case Mami missed something. She won't like waking up to anything misplaced. I grab Joaquin's empty beer can to throw it away.

"The Callahans paying you the same as last year?" Joaquin asks my back. "Or are they giving you a raise?"

"Same," I say, moistening a sponge and wiping down the counters and the refrigerator handle.

"You don't deserve a raise after all these years together? I thought they were supposed to be loaded."

I shrug and put the sponge away, turning my attention to straightening the magnets on the refrigerator. One in the shape of the Cuban flag. One in the shape of the Texas flag. One in the shape of a banana that has *I'm Ah-PEEL-ing!* printed on it. Joaquin gave it to Mami as a Christmas present one year when we were small.

"Seems to me like you'd want to make more money,"

Joaquin says. God, why is he harping on this? Three dollars an hour is pretty good even if the Callahans could definitely afford more.

"Maybe," I say. "But I'm lucky to have the job at all."

"You mean you're lucky Mami lets you have it."

I finally turn to face Joaquin. He's not looking at me. Instead, he's taken out the cassette his coworker gave him and is turning it over and over in his hands.

"If you're worried that my babysitting job is going to cut into me being here to help Mami, stop, okay?" I say. "I proved you wrong on that tonight."

Joaquin takes a deep breath. "It's not that, Elena." He so rarely calls me by my name. It sort of makes my throat ache with sadness when he does.

"Then what is it?" I demand.

Joaquin stares out our front windows, silent. I notice Mami forgot to shut the curtains, so I walk over and pull the blue fabric tight, making sure the edge of the good curtain is lying over the edge of the curtain with the uncleanable stain.

"Forget the babysitting and listen to me for a second," he says to my back. When did we start having so many conversations where we can't look at each other?

"Yeah?" I ask, squeezing the curtains briefly in my hands until the veins pop out of my knuckles.

"I'm not going to live here forever, you know," he says. "I'm thinking about moving out at the end of the summer. Of leaving the island."

"Okay," I say, still not turning around.

"I mean, I'm done with high school. I've been saving up my money. And there's really nothing for me here." He pauses between each sentence, like he's practiced this little speech. Knowing Joaquin, he probably has.

Silence sits between us, but I finally manage to shoot him a look over my shoulder. I can feel my mouth turning into a frown.

"There's nothing for you here? Gee, thanks."

"Elena," he starts again, only this time when he says my name it makes me feel like a little kid, like a dumb baby. "Elena, you know what I mean."

Facing him completely, I ask, "Where are you going to go? Why can't you stay and take classes at MICC?" Please don't cry, I tell myself.

"I don't want to spend money on community college classes when I'm not even sure what I want to do with my life," he says. "I'm thinking I want to travel for a little while. Maybe head out to California."

"Oh, where *he's* supposed to be?" I fire. I realize my hands are on my hips, but I don't remember putting them there.

"It's not about that," Joaquin says, lowering his voice. "It's not about him."

"Yeah, right it's not," I shoot back with a roll of my eyes. Hasn't it always been about him a little bit? At least for Joaquin? The mystery of our father has always been more important to him than to me. Why anyone would want to meet an asshole who abandoned his family is something I can't understand.

"Don't be so loud!" he urges, standing up from the recliner. He glances at Mami's door again.

"She's not going to wake up," I tell him. "Stop worrying about it. If you can't handle waking her up, I don't know how you're going to handle telling her you're going to move out and leave us." It's a low blow and I know it. I don't care.

"Enough," says Joaquin, holding up his hands. "Let's just . . . look, it may not even happen. I may not be able to save enough money to leave anyway."

I pout for a moment, chewing on my bottom lip.

"You probably will," I say at last, my voice resigned. "Save enough, I mean."

"Maybe, maybe not. I shouldn't have even said anything. I don't want to worry you. I mean, I just graduated last week. It's a long summer."

"It's okay," I say, anxious to relieve him of guilt even while hoping he feels guilty as hell.

"I'm going to take a shower and go to bed, okay?" he asks. "I'm working a double tomorrow." He pauses and stares at me. "Are we okay?"

"Yeah," I say with a nod even though we both know we aren't.

"Hey," my brother starts, making a move toward me. We're not a hugging family. Mami doesn't hug us much, so I guess we never learned. Now Joaquin sort of puts his arm around

33

me, leans in, and squeezes me. He smells of Tex-Mex. His squeeze is surprisingly strong. "Look, it's going to be okay. And you know what? If I leave, one day you can leave, too."

That's easy for Joaquin to say. He's the oldest. He's the boy. He can leave and know I'm still here on Mariposa Island with Mami. If I leave, she's left with no one.

"Yeah, maybe," I say, just to finish this conversation.

"Hope you have a good sleep," he says, heading for the bathroom.

"You, too," I answer.

I stand there until I hear the rush of the shower start, then I tiptoe down the hall to peek in on Mami. It reminds me of how I peeked in on the Callahan kids tonight to make sure they were safe in their beds. The door squeaks just a bit as I open it a crack and peer in. Mami's a motionless lump. I wait until I glimpse her body rise and fall once, twice, and then I quietly shut the door and head back to my own room.

CARIDAD
DE LA GUARDIA

MIRAMAR, HAVANA

CUBA

1957

She was fourteen years old and her life was perfect. It was easy to count all the ways.

First, she was blessed with dark hair, full lips, a lovely figure, and sweet blue eyes the color of the water off Varadero Beach, where as a little girl she had walked hand in hand with her grandmother, who had doted on her as any *abuela* would, especially an *abuela* with only one grandchild to spoil and coddle and love.

She lived in a lovely home in one of the nicest neighborhoods in Havana, whose name, Miramar, meant *look at the sea,* because when you lived in Miramar that's what you could do, anytime you wished. Look at the sea stretching out in front of you like one enormous bolt of blue velvet. Look at it and imagine all the good things in your life falling into place like a row of perfectly placed dominos.

At her all-girls academy run by the Ursulinas, Caridad was a favorite of the strict Catholic nuns, who would offer up rare smiles at her masterful recitations and perfectly executed papers. Her pencil bag was always neatly organized, full of pencils sharpened to a fine point and smooth rubber erasers her father would bring home from his office. Caridad loved the clean, queer smell of them. Her school uniform, ironed each morning by her maid, Juanita, was a soft pink that contrasted so nicely with her dark, wavy locks. Her shoes were never scuffed.

After school she and her best friend, Graciela, would head over to Caridad's house in Miramar and sit in the *salita* and drink pink lemonade that matched their school uniforms, and they would gossip about Ricardo, the boy down the street, whose dark eyes and swoony good looks reminded them of the singer Pedrito Rico. Ricardo's parents and Caridad's parents were good friends, and Caridad was sure that her mother and father were anxious to pair them off one day. How lucky for her to be matched with someone so handsome! During those sunny afternoons in the *salita*, Caridad and Graciela would dream of their upcoming *quinces* at the club and what they would wear and how they would dance and what songs the band would play, certain that when the night was over, they would be transformed into women at last.

And after Graciela went home and Caridad had finished her homework, she would go into the kitchen where Juanita would be preparing dinner, filling the house with the rich, delicious smell of pork chops or *papas rellenas*, potatoes stuffed with ground beef and olives and onions. When Juanita chopped the onions, first she cried and then she laughed at her tears, and Caridad would laugh, too, and then she would beg Juanita to make rice pudding or *dulce de leche* with *galletas* for dessert, and Juanita always would. Caridad would linger in the kitchen after the meal was ready, watching Juanita clean up. Juanita always finished with a careful wipe-down of the kitchen windows, never leaving behind the slightest streak.

And then her mother would come home from her shopping or her before-dinner drinks with her friends at the club, and her father would come home from his office, and Caridad would admire them both—how beautiful both of them were. How they could have been Hollywood stars in one of the American magazines she loved to flip through, even if she couldn't understand the words. Striking and poised, both of them had that lovely combination of dark hair and blue eyes. During dinner they would remind Caridad of all the ways she was special and pretty and clever and charming, and when they slipped into the *salita* for after-dinner cigarettes and cocktails, Caridad went to take her bath.

And in her bedroom in that lovely house near the sea, Juanita would pull back the comforter, revealing clean white sheets that were put on fresh each day, and after her bath— even though she was getting too old for it, really—Caridad would wrap herself in a fluffy pink towel and balance herself on the stool in front of her vanity and wait patiently for Juanita to work out the tangles in her long, dark hair before she perfumed it with a splash of *agua de violetas* cologne as she had every night for as long as the teenage girl could remember.

And as she fell asleep it was as if she could hear the ocean roaring and singing outside. She couldn't, of course, but if she opened her bedroom window, she could smell it, and she would be filled with good memories of walking along the water at night with her *abuelita*. She would remember how her *abuela* would tell her that when the moon came out was when the sharks would come to shore to feed, and as they walked, Caridad would grip her grandmother's hand, filled with the delicious feeling of being scared and safe at the same time.

And after the memories of her *abuelita* had faded and she had drifted off into a sweet, restful sleep, she would wake up and do it all again the next day.

Yes, when Caridad de la Guardia was fourteen years old, her life had been perfect. At least this was how she remembered it.

ELENA

CHAPTER FOUR

EVER SINCE I TURNED NINE AND MAMI DECIDED I WAS old enough to stay home by myself during the summer while she went to the doctor's office where she works, she's had a system for making sure I'm accounted for. Every hour or so, but not exactly *every* hour, she calls home, and I'd better be around to answer the kitchen phone.

"What are you up to?" Mami always asks, not even bothering to say hello.

"Just the chore list," I always answer, even if I'm watching television. Even if I'm watching television and eating Doritos. Even if I'm watching television and eating Doritos and getting orange Dorito dust all over the couch, which I'll have to clean up later.

"Okay, good, but don't forget about the baseboards," she says. Or under the couch. Or behind the refrigerator.

"I won't, Mami."

"All right, I'll talk to you soon."

And she will. Maybe in forty-five minutes. Maybe in two hours. It's not exact because that would make her system too easy to get around, but she *will* call, and if I'm not here to answer the phone, it's not okay. Not that I don't like to tempt fate every once in a while. Not that I don't sometimes hang up the phone after one of her calls and run down the street to the Stop-N-Go, just because it's somewhere to go. Somewhere to get the *Mariposa News* free weekly paper or a wrapped peppermint from the complimentary dish Mr. O'Rourke likes to leave out. Somewhere to *be*. But then it's back home, and if I bring the *Mariposa News* with me, I'd better hide it under my bed so Mami won't wonder where it came from.

I've only missed Mami's call once, the summer I was twelve, and after that, I didn't go to the Stop-N-Go for the rest of the summer or even dare to look in its direction when we drove by in the car.

It isn't so bad to be home all day if Michelle can come over and keep me company and manage to stay quiet during Mami's check-ins and not crack me up by whipping off her T-shirt and dancing around in her bra or something while I try to answer questions about dusting and mopping. But Michelle started working at the beach this summer doing umbrella and chair rentals, so that means less time with her.

And it isn't so bad to be home all day if Joaquin's around, but Joaquin has his job at El Mirador, and anyway, Joaquin has never had to do Mami's check-ins, which is brutally unfair if you ask me. Once when I was younger and helping her with the dishes, I dared to ask why Joaquin could go out with his friends during the summer. Mami lifted a juice glass out of the sudsy water and smacked it with her bright pink sponge.

"This is a good girl," she said, slapping at the glass, flecks of steamy water hitting my face. I blinked. "And this," she stepped back and let the glass fall to the ground where it shattered into dozens of see-through slivers, "is a bad girl." I yelped and jumped back, but Mami didn't flinch. Later, as I picked up the slippery shards of glass and dropped them carefully into a paper bag, I figured out what Mami meant, even if I'd probably already known the answer all along. Boys who go outside scrape knees or wreck bikes or get cursed at by irritated neighbors and store employees. But worse things can happen to girls. Especially when there are boys around.

"What are you up to?" Mami asks as I pick up the phone for the third time that morning. I look at the kitchen clock. Ten fifteen.

"I just finished folding the laundry," I tell her. "But remember, I have a babysitting job after lunch. I'll be home by the time you get back though."

"Where is that mother going now?" Mami asks. In the background I can hear her stapling papers for Dr. Sanders. *Cha-chunk.*

"I think she's getting her hair done and maybe a late lunch

or something with some of her girlfriends? She really didn't say."

"So sad when a mother doesn't want to spend time with her own children." *Cha-chunk.*

"I know, it really is. At least I can make the kids happy while I'm with them." Mrs. Callahan is an amazing mother, so patient and kind with her kids. So patient and kind with me, too. But of course I don't say that to Mami.

"You need to get another picture of them," she says. "I want to see how much they've grown." *Cha-chunk.*

"Okay, I will," I say.

"Be home when I'm home. *Besitos.*"

I hang up. Mami hasn't ever wanted to meet the Callahans. She's weird around strangers, which for Mami is most everyone, so I guess it makes sense that she's satisfied with the one picture I have of us, the Polaroid that Mrs. Callahan took of Matthew and Jennifer and me on the beach last summer. When Mami saw it, she glanced at Jennifer's sweet tummy and muttered, *"Gordita."*

I take the stacks of clean clothes Mami and I washed at the Laundromat yesterday and distribute them to Mami's room, then my room, and finally to Joaquin's. His folded jeans go on the top shelf of his closet and his neatly rolled socks in the top drawer of his dresser. My brother's room is all lines and right angles, all neatness and order, from the Joy Division poster tacked on the back of his door to the alphabetized records in a milk crate at the foot of his bed.

The cassette he brought home from work the other day is on his nightstand, perfectly centered on top of a stack of science fiction novels. I pick it up and read the spine: *xoxoAmy*.

I wonder if *xoxoAmy* knows my brother is planning on ditching her and us by moving to California at the end of the summer. In the same breath I wonder if maybe she can make him stay.

I scowl at no one and push the thought out of my mind, putting the cassette tape back on the nightstand, but a little crooked this time. It's bitchy and I know it, but I don't care. Damn Joaquin for wanting to leave.

Then I call Michelle and tell her I have a babysitting job so maybe I can come over after and visit her at work.

"You don't want to bring the kids down to the beach?" she asks.

"In the heat of the day? No way. Those kids burn so easy."

"Yeah, Mrs. Callahan might have your head if they turn up with a sunburn," Michelle says.

"Yup. And I need this job," I say, even though Mrs. Callahan would never get mad at me for an accident. To tell the truth, it's hard to picture her getting mad at all.

"Tell me about it," says Michelle.

• • •

My summer job is babysitting, but Michelle's summer job basically involves getting paid to get tan. Families and couples show up in the morning and pay her cash, and she hauls umbrellas and chairs to wherever they want them on the beach and then sets them up, and at the end of the day she comes back and packs everything up for them. We haven't been out of school a week, and she's already brown as toast and looking a little more fit than she did at the end of May.

"You know, I think some of the dads are staring at my ass when I stake the umbrellas," Michelle says, taking a drag on her cigarette.

"They probably are, but blow that the other way, would you?" I ask, digging my feet deep into the sand. "My mother gave me all kinds of shit the other day for coming home smelling like smoke. I had to say it was Mr. Callahan."

"Oh, so he's a smoker now?" Michelle asks, peering out at the expanse of Mariposa Island sand in front of us. She takes another drag, and I notice that somehow she's managed to keep her pink frosted lipstick on all day long.

"No, he's a health freak, but I had to come up with something," I answer. Steps away a little girl and her mother are building a sand castle with a tiny yellow bucket and pail. Now that the sun's worst rays are behind us, it feels good out here.

Suddenly, something ice cold slides down my back. I yelp and jump in shock, then twist back to discover it actually is ice—and sticky soda—draining down my back all the way to the green-and-white-striped beach towel I'm sitting on.

"Oh, shit, I thought you were Michelle."

The voice belongs to a guy I've never seen before. Trim, tan, with a flop of black hair drifting into his brown eyes. Orange-and-white-checkered board shorts. He looks like a skater from the neck up. From the neck down he's a beach bum.

"Jesus, J.C., be careful," Michelle says, taking her towel from under her butt and blotting my back.

"I'm really sorry," says this mystery boy, pulling out a pack of Camels and sitting down next to me. He doesn't seem all that sorry, honestly. But he sure is hot. He's older than me, definitely. Maybe older than Joaquin.

"J.C., this is my friend Elena," Michelle says. "Elena, this is J.C. He's Jack's nephew." Jack is the guy who runs the umbrella and chair rental place that employs Michelle. Sort of an old-guy version of J.C., with a potbelly where J.C.'s six-pack is.

"Hey, Elena," J.C. says, looking at me and nodding, a hint of a smile on his face. He lights a cigarette.

"Hey," I say, careful not to let my voice warm up too easily. After all, he did just spill a soda on me on purpose, even if he thought I was Michelle. The sticky residue feels gross on my back, and I'm glad at least that I'm wearing a dark shirt. I'm also glad I'll get home before Mami so I can change and not have to think up a story to explain away the stain.

"You work with Michelle?" J.C. asks, exhaling a long, straight stream of cigarette smoke toward the sea. I feel my cheeks pink up. He is *cute*. Even though I most definitely am going to go home smelling of cigarettes.

"No, I don't," I answer. "I babysit mostly."

J.C. nods, then shoots us both a big grin.

"So . . . you guys wanna go back to my place and smoke a joint?" His eyebrows jump up and he shrugs his shoulders apologetically, like maybe he just asked us to a movie or even to church.

"What?" Michelle shrieks, cupping a handful of sand and tossing it toward him. "You're fucking crazy, J.C. I'm working."

"So after?" J.C. asks.

"No, J.C.," Michelle says, rolling her eyes. "Your uncle would fire me."

"Aren't you off the clock in, like, half an hour?"

"Whatever, J.C."

At J.C.'s remark about the time, I check my wristwatch. I have about an hour before Mami will be home.

"What about you, Elena? Wanna go burn one?"

I shoot J.C. what I hope is a world-weary look and in my best bitchy-girl voice I say, "Uh . . . no?" So far as I can tell, it's the voice that wins you points with boys. Maybe it works, because J.C. cracks up and shines such a beautiful, adorable smile in my direction that I get dizzy. My breaths start coming a little more quickly. I look away, sure I'm blushing.

Michelle isn't paying much mind to J.C. After a few more moments of silence, she dusts sand off her body and announces that she has to go start collecting umbrellas and chairs from customers.

"I guess I'll go, too," I announce, half of me eager to get away from this weird hot boy and the other half of me desperate to impress him any way I can.

"You need a lift?" J.C. asks, jumping up. He extends a hand and I reach for it. Once I'm standing, he holds on to me for two more seconds than he needs to. I swallow hard. God, he's good-looking. A weird pressure starts building up from the center of me.

"I was gonna walk or take the bus," I say, "but yeah, I could use a ride." I can feel the weight of Michelle's gaze behind me. I don't turn around to look at her.

"We'll talk later, right, Elena?" she says, her voice laced with something that's maybe concern and maybe judgment.

"Yeah," I say, not turning back, and before I know it, I'm following J.C. to a bright yellow VW Bug in the parking lot, its back windshield covered in Grateful Dead stickers.

"You're into the Dead?" I ask, just to be saying something.

"Yeah, I followed them for most of last year. My favorite show was at this outdoor place in Maryland last summer. We danced our asses off." We slide into the car, the hot black seats briefly burning the backs of my thighs.

"How old are you anyway?" I ask as J.C. starts up the engine. I just got into a car with a strange boy. Maybe a strange man. It sure beats being a teenage shut-in. For once I feel like the main character in a movie.

J.C. laughs. "I'm nineteen. Why, how old are you?"

"Old enough," I say, because I think that sounds smart. Maybe even a little sexy. But also maybe a little bit stupid, so I immediately follow it by saying, "I'm just messing with you. I'll be seventeen in October." That sounds better than saying sixteen.

"Okay, Miss Seventeen in October," he says, and he grins again.

With my heart thudding inside my chest, I manage to tell J.C. how to get to my house, already planning on having him drop me off by the corner of Esperanza and Fifteenth just in case.

"So you're going to be, what . . . a junior?" he asks, sliding a cassette into the tape deck. I recognize Jerry Garcia's voice from beach parties and kids playing the Dead at school. The guy always sounds like he's trying to catch his breath while he's singing, but J.C. bobs his head along as he pulls out onto Esperanza Boulevard.

"Yeah, a junior," I answer. I notice J.C. doesn't have any shoes on. The smile on his face grows as Jerry's voice aims for the high notes. I wonder what it must be like to take a year off to follow your favorite band all over the country. I can't even picture it, really.

"I'm really sorry I spilled that drink on you," he says. "I was just fucking around."

"It was no big deal," I say as we pass clumps of tourists trudging down the main drag, their arms full of striped umbrellas and beach chairs and beach bags straining under the weight of too many plastic beach toys. It seems like way too much work for a vacation.

"No, it was kind of a dick move," he insists, "which is why I really wish you'd taken me up on my offer of a joint. I owe you."

I wonder what J.C. would say if I told him I've never smoked pot, not even once. But of course I would never admit this. It would be totally embarrassing.

"Maybe next time," I say, and then I motion toward the corner. "You can drop me off here."

"I do door-to-door service, you know."

I grin and shake my head. "No, this is good. I like to walk."

"Okay, but I still owe you," J.C. says, sliding his car toward the curb.

I want to get out and run away. I want to keep driving with him all the way to Houston and beyond. I want to never have to talk to him again because he makes me feel like a tongue-tied girl. I want to slip under my bedspread and think about what it would be like to let him kiss me on the neck.

"I promise I won't forget about that joint," I say, already realizing that I will replay these words over and over in my head later, trying to figure out how stupid I sounded when I said them.

J.C. grins at me. I shut the passenger door, and when I turn around, I find my older brother pulling up on his ten-speed.

For the tiniest second it feels like I've been caught by Mami, because Joaquin has Mami's bright blue eyes. But her eyes bore into you, and Joaquin's just stare.

As J.C.'s VW drives off, all Joaquin has to say, in a not unkind voice, is "So, *hermanita*, who the hell was that?"

CHAPTER FIVE

MAMI SLIDES THE BOWL OF SPAGHETTI ACROSS THE table and it skids to a stop. Then she drops the pasta spoon back in the pot with a clang. Judging by the amount of abuse the dishes are taking, Joaquin and I are in for a long night.

"Thanks," I say, trying to brighten my voice but not too much. Otherwise, she'll think I'm sassing her.

"I think it's undercooked." She puts both hands on her hips and frowns at the spaghetti.

"I'm sure it's fine," I say, then recalculate. "I mean, I'm sure it's great."

Mami sits down with a thud. She's not a big woman at all, but she's capable of moving with great heaviness. The kitchen chair squeaks underneath her. She sighs. Joaquin doesn't say anything. He just reaches for a takeout container from El Mirador that's been sitting on the counter and shoves it toward me.

"Leftover nachos," he offers. I catch his eyes, and he smiles broadly.

Mistake number one.

"Nachos," Mami announces, like she's the leader of a small country, which in a sense is true. Only the citizens of the country are just me and Joaquin. "Nachos are tacky."

Joaquin laughs out loud.

Mistake number two.

"How can a food be tacky?" he asks. Then he doubles down. "That's absurd."

Damn, Joaquin.

"When I was a little girl, my maid, Juanita, would have never served me something like nachos," Mami says, wrinkling her nose. She turns and stares out the kitchen window. My heart picks up speed. Joaquin says nothing, but I can hear his response in my head. *She probably wouldn't have served you spaghetti, either.* I pray he doesn't say it.

I twist up a huge pile of Mami's noodles onto my fork and shove it in my mouth. It is undercooked.

"This is good, Mami," I tell her.

"Mm-hmm," she says, still staring out the window. Then she takes a sip of her rum and Coke.

"How was work, Joaquin?" I ask, trying to move the dinner train forward to a more pleasant stop. Or at least a more tolerable one.

"The usual," says Joaquin, jumping up for a second and grabbing a beer from the fridge. It opens with a sharp *fizz pop!* He takes a slurp and then reaches for the nachos, biting down on one and chewing enthusiastically.

"These are excellent," he says. "Excellent nachos."

Here we go.

Mami gets up, knocking over her chair in the process, then dumps her entire bowl of spaghetti into the trash can in the corner. *Clash! Bang!* Then she tosses her fork into the sink. *Clatter!* Then she grabs her drink and stomps off to her bedroom. *Slam!*

I take a deep breath and push the spaghetti away. I wish I had a dog I could feed it to. I wonder if Mami will check to see if I threw mine away, too.

"Thanks a lot," I say to Joaquin.

"Oh, come on, Elena. Just eat the nachos." He rolls his eyes at me, but he glances in the direction of Mami's shut bedroom door with something like regret. It's like he can't stop himself sometimes.

I give in and slide a chip into my mouth. It's not excellent, but it's better than Mami's spaghetti.

"I wonder how long I'll get the silent treatment for this one," Joaquin mutters. He drains his beer. He acts like he doesn't really care how long it will last, but I know he does.

"If you didn't want the silent treatment, you should have just eaten your spaghetti," I say. "You knew she was in a mood. You pushed it with the nachos."

You pushed it when you wore that T-shirt.

You pushed it with that comment after Mass.

57

You pushed it with that look you gave her when we were driving home.

You pushed it when you brought up our dad.

You pushed it, Joaquin.

"Yeah, I did," Joaquin says with a sigh. "Sorry I screwed up dinner."

"It's okay."

Neither one of us is really hungry but we make it through most of the nachos. Joaquin helps me clean up, including fishing Mami's bowl out of the trash can. I wonder what she's doing in her room. That rum and Coke was her third. Maybe her fourth. It's hard to tell because she's always freshening up her drinks.

"So are you going to tell me about the guy in the VW or what?" Joaquin asks, wiping down the stovetop. I spy some spots he's missed and take care of them.

"I did tell you. He's just a friend of Michelle's and he was giving me a ride."

Joaquin takes my serving of spaghetti and heads for the trash can.

"Hold on," I say, and after I take it from him I lean against the counter and force down a few bites. Joaquin rolls his eyes.

"So this friend of Michelle's is into the Dead?" he asks.

"I guess," I say, handing him a half-empty bowl. "Like I said, he was just giving me a ride."

"The Dead suck."

"Okay," I say.

"What, you don't think they do?"

"I don't have an opinion on the Grateful Dead," I say. I don't tell him that when I got home this afternoon I went into my bedroom and found the one Dead cassette I own—*American Beauty*—and listened to that song about sugar magnolias on my Walkman over and over again. It's pretty, honestly.

When the kitchen is finally clean enough for Mami's standards, Joaquin and I walk the few steps it takes to get to the living room and flop down, Joaquin in the recliner and me on the couch. Joaquin clicks through the channels but there's nothing on. I pick at my fingernails and think about Mami in her bedroom on the other side of the living room wall. It's like her presence is pulsating through the Sheetrock. Is she sleeping? Stewing? Ready to come out at any moment and lay into Joaquin? Or me?

"I'm going to go see how she is," I say at last. Sometimes it's better to defuse things early on.

"Okay," says Joaquin. "Better you than me."

He's right about that.

I push Mami's bedroom door open just a crack. I see the lump of her on the bed, curled up on her side. One of her romance novels is open in front of her. Her rum and Coke is drained down to nothing. Even the ice cubes are gone.

"Mami?" I ask, my voice soft.

"Yes?" she answers, not looking at me but at the book. That's not a promising sign.

"I'm just checking on you," I ask. "Are you okay?"

"I'm fine," she says.

"The spaghetti was good. I finished mine."

"That's good."

"Can I get you anything?"

"No, thank you."

At least she said thank you.

"I'll get the glass for you," I say. I walk to her nightstand and take the tumbler, its sides wet with condensation. Mami shifts and flips the page of her book as soon as I get close. Only Mami can turn the page of a paperback novel and make it the loudest sound on earth.

I hear the phone ringing in the kitchen. Mami doesn't move.

"If it's for me, tell them I'm not here," she says to her book. We both know it's not going to be for her because it never is. Other than the occasional call to confirm an appointment or try to sell her something, no one ever calls Mami. Especially not on a weeknight.

"I will," I say. The ringing has stopped. Joaquin has picked up.

After I shut the door behind me, I walk into the living room and see Joaquin standing by the kitchen phone, his hand pressed over the receiver.

"I think it's Grateful Dead guy," he says, raising an eyebrow. "Asking for you."

I'm not sure how I don't drop Mami's glass.

"What?" I ask.

60

"Like you didn't hear me," says Joaquin, snorting. "Grateful Dead guy is on the phone for you."

Since I make no movement, Joaquin walks toward me, takes Mami's glass, and hands me the phone. It feels heavy and electric in my hand.

"I'm going to watch television, so take it into your bedroom," he says, gently turning me and pushing me in the direction of my room.

A boy has never called me before. Not ever in my life. If Mami knew it was a boy on the other end of the line, she'd rip the phone from my hand and slam it into the receiver. Then she'd demand to know what nasty thing I'd done to make a boy call me in the first place.

My heart hammering, I stretch the cord and step inside my bedroom, shutting the door and sliding to the floor.

"Hello?" I ask.

"Hey," says the voice on the other end. I'm used to the bubbly, dizzy voice of Michelle. Or the thick, pressing voice of Mami. J.C.'s voice sounds deep. Deeper than it did at the beach or in his car. It isn't really a boy's voice. More like a man's.

"How did you get my number?" I ask. I wince immediately. It's kind of a stupid thing to say right off the bat.

"Michelle," J.C. says. "I hope that's okay."

"Yeah, of course," I say. My heart is hammering even faster now. The inside of my mouth is dry.

"You doing okay?" he asks.

"Yeah, I just finished dinner. Spaghetti." Why did I just say that?

"Was that your brother who answered?" J.C. asks.

"Yeah, my older brother."

"Cool," he says.

Silence. As I scramble for what to say next because it's my turn to talk, J.C. says, "So . . . about that joint."

"Wow, you really get right to it," I answer, pleased with myself for my quick comeback.

"Ha," says J.C. "Seriously, I was just wondering if you wanted to hang out tonight?"

I tug at the cheap tan carpet underneath me, twisting it anxiously. Through the door I hear Joaquin watching some game show. Muffled sounds are punctuated with forced cheers and claps. I glance at my watch. Seven o'clock.

"Like hang out and . . . ?"

J.C. laughs, but it's a kind laugh. "Hey, we don't have to get high," he says. "We could just hang out or whatever. You know. Nothing too intense or anything."

I remember his dark eyes and black hair. I remember the way he wouldn't let go of me after he helped me up off the sand. I remember his infinite hotness.

But I've never gone on a date with a boy. Not for real. My few kissing experiences are limited to stupid summer beach parties with random boys after we each had a few beers, and once we're back at school we ignore each other. But now this nineteen-year-old wants to spend time with me. The thought that races through my mind at first is that nineteen is really close to twenty, which sounds impossibly grown-up to me.

But he wants to go out. With me. Away from the four walls of my living room. Away from slumping, sighing, scary, page-turning Mami. Out. Somewhere. Anywhere.

"So what do you think?" J.C. asks again. He coughs. I wonder if he could actually be nervous. The idea seems ridiculous.

"You know . . ." I take a breath. I listen to the game show. I picture Mami in her bed, shut up for what will probably be the rest of the night, unless she stumbles out for another cocktail. I hear my voice saying, "Okay, sure."

"Cool," says J.C. "Want me to pick you up in, like, half an hour or so?"

"Yeah," I say, and now my heart is running so fast I think it might give out. But I keep talking. "Just pick me up on the corner where you dropped me off this afternoon."

"Seriously?"

"Yeah. It's better that way. You could say I have, like, an overprotective mom or whatever."

"I've heard of that type," J.C. says. "My mom's the opposite."

"Like she didn't care that you followed the Dead?"

J.C. laughs. "Seeing as I haven't talked to my mom in five years, I don't think so."

"Oh," I say. "I'm . . . sorry?"

"Don't be," says J.C., and the way he says it I know he's

done talking about it. "Okay, so I'll pick you up in half an hour?"

"Okay, cool," I say, and before I know it we are saying good-bye and I am sitting on the floor of my bedroom and I am grinning and nauseated all at once.

• • •

Joaquin is standing in my bedroom. I've motioned him inside because I can't risk having this conversation in the living room. It's weird to see my brother in here. After I started wearing a bra and putting posters of Ralph Macchio on my walls, it was like he didn't ever want to come in here.

"You want me to say you have a babysitting job?" Joaquin says. "Why not just say you're out with Michelle?"

"Shhh . . ." I say, as if Mami could open the door any second, which she could. She's so small and sneaky you never hear her coming. "You know I can't just go out with Michelle," I answer. "I can't believe you would even suggest that." I check my wristwatch again then glance at my reflection in the full-length mirror on the back of my bedroom door. Ugh, I look like shit.

"You never even ask if you can," Joaquin says. "You just assume."

I slide open my closet doors and pick through my limited options. "I'm assuming right and you know it," I say, pulling out a light blue top and tossing it onto my bed. I'm on edge and need Joaquin to help me out right now. "You don't know

64

what it's like because you can go out anytime you want. You can see Amy whenever you feel like it."

Joaquin jumps a little. Frowns slightly. "How'd you know about her?"

"I saw it on that mixtape."

"What were you doing, spying on me?"

"I was just putting your laundry away, so calm down," I say as I squat and dig through the bottom of my closet for my best Keds.

"Okay," he says.

I find the shoes. Success. When I turn around to face Joaquin, his mouth is twisted up in thought.

"Hey," I say, taking a breath. "Please, if she comes out of her room or wonders where I am, just tell her the Callahans had an emergency and they needed me? That's who was calling on the phone? And I didn't want to disturb her? Please, Joaquin. I never get to do anything." The way it comes out makes me sound pathetic, I realize. But it isn't that far off from how I really feel.

"What time will you be back?" he asks. "And are you sure this guy is okay?"

"He's the nephew of Michelle's boss," I say, and I realize my breathing is a little shallow. Nerves.

"The nephew of Michelle's boss?" Joaquin asks, incredulous. "So he's essentially a stranger, right? How old is he?"

"Seventeen," I lie. "And he's really nice."

Joaquin scratches at the back of his neck. He exhales, loudly.

"I have to get changed," I say.

Joaquin nods, his face still lost in thought.

"That means you have to leave," I say, spelling it out for him.

After he finally does, a flurry of activity follows, but everything from my hair to my outfit to my makeup feels like it's coming out wrong. I wish I had time to call Michelle. For her first date our freshman year, her mom did her hair in a French braid and let Michelle wear some of her Chanel No. 5 behind her ears. I briefly imagine calling Mrs. Callahan and asking her for advice, but that would be way too weird. We've never spoken on the phone about anything but babysitting. Still, for a moment I can picture her sweeping blush over my cheeks and smiling at me with reassurance, making me feel like the most beautiful girl on the island.

I listen for Mami but there's nothing.

Please, God, don't let her come out.

I need at least five minutes to walk down to the corner where I'll meet J.C. I can't rush or I'll get all sweaty. Taking a breath to calm myself down, I check my lipstick in the mirror. It's a soft pink color called Gum Drop. I purse my lips together one more time to even out the coverage. I frown. It's not a hundred percent perfect, but it's going to have to do.

I step out into the living room, my breath held, bracing myself for Mami. She's still in her bedroom.

I think I'm going to pull this off.

"Let me give you some cash," says Joaquin, getting up from

the couch and digging his beat-up leather wallet from his back pocket and pulling out two wrinkled bills. Tips from El Mirador.

"Here's ten bucks," he says, straightening the bills out neatly before folding them up and pressing them into my palm.

"Thanks, Joaquin," I say, grateful. I slip the money into my jeans.

"So you're really sure this guy is okay?" he asks, his eyebrows sliding toward each other in concern.

"Yeah, I really am," I say. *He's a cute pothead who followed the Dead for a whole year,* I think to myself. I wonder what Joaquin would do or say if I told him that. I think he wouldn't let me go, more because of the following-the-Dead thing than the pot thing.

"Well, I'll cover for you if she comes out," he says, nodding toward the back bedroom.

"Thanks," I say. Suddenly, we hear a cough over the sound of the television. She's still awake. My eyes grow big.

"You should probably go," says Joaquin, lowering his voice. "Just . . . be careful, all right? And don't be too late. And . . . call if you need me. I'll come get you. No questions asked."

I smile, and for a moment I feel a bit of the same closeness we had as kids when we would wake up early to watch television on Saturday mornings, slumped together on the couch while Mami snored through a hangover.

"I promise I'll be careful," I say. "And I won't be too late." And then, before my nerves or my mother can stop me, I'm opening the front door and slipping out into the dusk of early evening, skipping down the porch steps, my heart thudding inside me, my mouth turning into a hesitant smile, the word *freedom* spinning over and over in my mind on some frantic, endless loop.

CARIDAD

1958

When she stepped out onto the ballroom floor, her hair perfect, her dress gorgeous, she was sure she would feel like a princess.

That was what Caridad wanted for her *quince*. It was what she had always wanted, but Caridad's father was not so sure.

It was too dangerous, he said. The rebels were in the mountains, but it seemed each day as if the fighting was getting closer. The headlines in the newspapers loomed larger. Caridad's friend Graciela had a little cousin who lived on the family's *finca* in Santa Clara. Graciela had told Caridad that one morning when she was leaving for school, her cousin found her two dogs, Johnny and Daisy, slaughtered by the rebels, gunshots to their heads and blood seeping out of their skulls into the fresh green grass. Most likely the rebels had come down to the small stream on the property for water, and Georgina's dogs had barked too loudly. *Pop* had gone the guns and then the dogs were dead.

Caridad wasn't supposed to have overheard her parents discussing that story, but she did anyway, hiding in the kitchen one evening eating crackers with Juanita.

"*Ay, mija*, your parents would be angry at me if they knew you were listening," Juanita had said when the voices of Caridad's parents drifted in from the *salita*. "You need to go get ready for bed."

"Are the rebels truly as scary as they sound?" Caridad had asked, trying not to picture the little girl's crushed face when she found her pups.

"They say Batista is worse," Juanita said with a shrug. "They say he keeps jars full of the eyeballs of his enemies in his office."

Caridad wrinkled her nose. "That's a lie."

"Yes, probably," Juanita had said. "But some people believe it. Maybe that's why they have hope that the rebels will bring good things."

Maybe Juanita was right, Caridad believed. Maybe they would bring good things. And maybe it hadn't even been the rebels who killed the dogs. Maybe it had just been an angry neighbor, drunk and unhappy. Caridad settled on that explanation because it made her feel better. And that explanation made her more convinced than ever that there was no reason why she should not have a *quince* after all. Still, she did not ask for it. Her parents didn't like it when she whined.

Fortunately, Caridad's mother still wanted the party, too, and she took on the task of trying to convince Caridad's father.

"I don't know, my dear," her father had said when the topic came up toward the end of dinner one evening. Both her parents puffed over Pall Malls even though their plates were still mostly full. Lately, they had been smoking more and eating less. Caridad was a little surprised that they were having this conversation in front of her. They rarely allowed for Caridad to be a witness to any tension.

"Ay, Joaquin, we only have one child and it's a daughter," she said, grimacing. "We've waited all these years to really show her off." Caridad tingled with pride and watched as her mother brushed back her dark hair and tucked it behind her ear. A diamond earring twinkled merrily, and Caridad took it as a good omen. She was right because the next words out of her father's mouth were, "All right, then. She can have her *quince*."

And so it was that four months later Caridad was wrapped in pink French chiffon that swallowed her up and made her look like a little tea cake, dainty and pretty and sweet. It had been made by a fussy woman who had studied under the finest dressmakers in Paris, and she had tugged and pulled and pinned and hummed to herself and in the end she had made Caridad look more beautiful than ever.

Caridad and Graciela and some of the boys from good families had practiced the waltzes in the party room at the club. Ricardo was there, with his swoony dark eyes and shy smile, and even though Caridad knew her parents were responsible for making him her dance partner, she thought from the way he looked at her that he, too, was glad for the arrangement. Caridad's mother had hired the daughter of a famous composer to choreograph the complicated dances, and whenever Ricardo's hand touched Caridad's, she felt a shiver of possibility run down her spine.

Nearly three hundred invitations had been delivered, complete with dance cards tucked inside, and Caridad had seen them in stacks on the dining room table, ready to be addressed by a calligrapher her parents had hired. In the days leading up to their delivery, Caridad had slipped on her white gloves so as not to risk fingerprints, then picked up the thick, creamy card stock and flipped the invitation over and over, relishing the dark cursive font: *Joaquin y Elena de la Guardia . . . el honor de invitar . . . los Quince Años de su hija . . .* They were perfect.

The afternoon of the *quince* felt dizzy and dreamlike. Caridad had munched on crackers, but she'd been too nervous for much else. Her mother had dabbed Arpège behind her ears before cupping Caridad's face in her hand and smiling, her expression wistful now that Caridad was too old for *agua de violetas*. Juanita had shaken her head as the hairdresser brought in for the occasion had hovered above Caridad, and she'd finally stepped in to arrange Caridad's dark locks herself. That night, Juanita would watch from the kitchen with the rest of the help. She promised Caridad she wouldn't miss a minute.

After the sun set, Caridad was whisked away with her father in a luxury car to one of the fanciest hotels in downtown Havana. Caridad clutched his hand and willed herself to absorb every moment into her mind for safekeeping. This night would never happen again. There would be other magical nights, she knew that intuitively. But not *this* night. This night would always stand alone.

"Papi," Caridad had said, looking up at him, squeezing his large hand with her small one, "I'm so happy." And her father had looked down at her and smiled, and Caridad had known without him saying so that he was happy, too.

There were society reporters and photographers waiting to take pictures outside the hotel, and Caridad had tilted her head just so, finally debuting the smile she'd practiced for so long in the mirror, demure but authentic. Innocent but sophisticated, too, somehow. The flashes left bright white explosions in her eyes for a moment, and when she was finally out of the range of photographers, she shut her eyes tightly in an attempt to adjust to it all.

And then as she walked inside toward the ballroom with her father, she could hear the light strains of Barbarito Díez's band, the violins swelling more loudly and sweetly the closer they got. As they entered the ballroom, she took in everything in one wild rush. The men in their white dinner jackets, the women in their long dresses, the palatial birthday cake—pink and white—on a special table in front of the band stage.

And there was Ricardo hovering on the edges of the crowd, his eyes looking right at Caridad, his eyebrows slightly up, his face full of a pleasantly shocked expression that Caridad had to believe meant that she was the most beautiful girl he'd ever seen.

"You've got to smile, *hija*," Caridad's father reminded her, his own eyes crinkling at the sides as he grinned, pulling Caridad into the center of the dance floor and beginning to waltz with her. *"Te quedas como una piedra."*

The words made her relax a bit at last, and she must have smiled, too, as she was led on the dance floor by her father, executing the moves she had practiced with him. Barbarito Díez's voice sounded more beautiful in person than over the radio, that was for certain. As her father spun her, she caught a glimpse of her mother, her hands clutched under her chin, her face about to crack in two from happiness. If only Caridad could see Juanita.

It was then that it happened. A loud blast accompanied by shattering glass. She felt the hardness of the dance floor under her. Caridad could not remember landing there. She only knew that she could not breathe. She turned over onto her stomach, placed her hands firmly on the floor underneath her, and tried to push herself up, but she couldn't do it. She willed herself to breathe, but the more she did, the tighter her chest became. She was seized with a cold panic.

Her ears were ringing, and the smell of something rancid and burnt seared the insides of her nose. Someone grabbed her from under her arms, hoisted her up. Perhaps it was her father. The good news was she could still stand, and somehow her lungs started working again. Then someone was moving her, pushing her toward the ballroom doors. Her ears rang so loudly she could hear nothing else. Caridad briefly wondered if she was dead, and if this was the afterlife—a chaotic, hellish place. *Hadn't she been good enough to deserve better?* she wondered. As the stranger behind her maneuvered her outside, her mind rested dumbly on the birthday cake. She wondered if it could be saved.

And then she was outside on the street, the sounds of wailing sirens growing closer and closer and overtaking the ringing sounds in her head. In the same spot where moments before Caridad had smiled for the photographers, guests from her *quince* milled about, crying and staring at each other, their eyes wide and their mouths hanging open. One man clutched a white handkerchief to his forehead, and Caridad watched, stunned, as it turned bright red.

"*¡Caridad, preciosa! ¡Qué horror!*" It was Caridad's mother, her dress ripped, her dark hair in a loose frenzy. She grabbed Caridad in her arms and clutched her, hard. Caridad opened her mouth to speak, but she discovered she was mute. She brought her hands up to gently pat her mother's back, to comfort her, but her mother was crushing Caridad in her arms so tightly Caridad was worried she would feel that same sick loss of air like she had in the ballroom.

She saw her father then, racing up to them, his face smeared in soot. The emergency vehicles had arrived. People were shouting, screeching for help.

"I knew it was a mistake," her father said, breathless, approaching his wife and daughter, his eyes wild. He looked at the injured guests, the broken glass, the slick pool of someone's blood spreading on the sidewalk. "I knew I should never have agreed to this."

"Joaquin, not now," Caridad's mother had snapped, and then she had burst into tears.

Years later, Caridad would recall the horrors of that evening with unwanted regularity, as often as other people might look back happily on something pleasant. The night of her birthday party would become woven into the fabric of Caridad's mind, and it would enter her dreams at random and unwanted intervals, like a virus. But all of it was private. Hidden. She talked about the *quince* as it had actually happened only once, with Juanita—who survived—unlike Ricardo, who did not. And once she left her island home and her parents behind, once she had climbed the metal steps into that airplane and held her breath as she was lifted high up into the sky, Caridad would never speak honestly of that evening ever again.

ELENA

CHAPTER SIX

THE LIGHTS OF ESPERANZA BOULEVARD MAKE THE streets of Mariposa Island feel magical and romantic, like Paris. Or maybe it's just J.C. that makes it feel that way.

"I thought maybe we'd go to my place and get a drink, then maybe walk along the beach?" J.C. asks. His gaze drifts from the road for a moment, his dreamy, dark brown eyes fixing on me.

Go to my place. It sounds like something a guy would say in a silly made-for-TV romance, but tonight feels very serious and real. My body thrums with excitement.

"Yeah, that sounds good," I hear myself saying. My very first date and it's not to the Cinemark or Gino's Pizzeria or any of the places kids in my class go, but to a guy's place. A guy who doesn't even live with his parents.

Well, Elena, you might as well go all out when you finally get the chance.

I don't talk the entire drive to J.C.'s place, which I worry makes me look like some sort of high school dork, but J.C. doesn't talk, either, so maybe it's fine. He keeps the radio tuned to some rock station. I want to say something about liking the song that's playing, but I don't know what the band is, and if he asks me too much about it I'll sound stupid. Better to just stay quiet.

My mind slides back to my house. To Mami holed up in her bedroom and Joaquin keeping guard, ready to lie for me if need be. *Hopefully* ready to lie. I say yet another prayer that I don't get caught. It all feels so reckless and weird but also like I can't stop myself and don't even want to try.

Finally, J.C. pulls up near the spot on the beach where Michelle rents umbrellas. Wordlessly, I follow him up the steps to the second floor of a run-down, two-level complex of cheap apartments that rent out for the month or the season. Chipping seafoam-green paint covers the entire building, and empty planters line the perimeter, any plants they may have held long since dead and gone. A sad-looking wooden sign with the words *Once Upon a Tide* is tacked up by the main entrance.

"Once upon a tide?" I ask incredulously, glad to finally be able to say something.

"Yeah, it's hella corny, isn't it?" J.C. says, unlocking the door. "I actually have a roommate, but he's working tonight. Go ahead and take a seat."

It's a tiny apartment, full of a sweet smell that I think might be incense mixed with pot. I sit down on the one couch in the living room, some scratchy plaid number that must have come with the place. It's dusted with sand, making it even scratchier.

"You like bourbon?" J.C. asks, taking two glasses out of one of the cabinets in the adjoining kitchenette.

"Sure."

He drops the ice cubes in the glasses one *plink plunk* at a time. I watch Mami make cocktails every day, of course, but I've never had hard liquor. Joaquin always says stick with beer because it's safer. But before I know it, J.C. is handing me a tumbler and I'm taking careful sips and trying not to raise my eyebrows.

How does anyone drink this shit?

"Let me put some music on," J.C. says, moving to the stereo on the other side of the room. He has to shift a pile of guy clothes in order to fiddle with the dial. I want to put down my drink, but the coffee table is littered with Styrofoam cups from Whataburger and a half-filled ashtray. Honestly, the whole place is cluttered with mess except for the pale blue walls, which are mostly empty, except for one painting of a little girl collecting shells on a beach that looks a lot nicer than the coast of Mariposa Island. The painting clearly came with the apartment and was intended for very different tenants.

"So . . . you got the job here because of your uncle?" I ask as J.C. makes his way back to the couch, drink in hand. He sits down next to me but not creepy close. I try to settle in and make myself look natural, forcing myself to take another sip of my drink.

"Yeah, I did," J.C. says, dragging his hand through his hair. I wonder if he knows how hot that makes him look.

"So you're not from Texas?"

"California, actually," says J.C. "Los Angeles. My Uncle Jack and my mom grew up out there, but my uncle followed a girl here like a million years ago and then never went back. Seems weird to trade L.A. beaches for this shitty place, but I'm here now, too, so I can't judge, I guess."

"It *is* a shitty place," I say, even as I feel like a traitor for disparaging my hometown. I wonder why the urge to defend the place of your birth is such a natural thing for people to do. To stand up for the place where your parents happened to have sex one time.

"I mean, it's not so bad," J.C. says, putting his drink down on the floor and leaning for a pack of Camels on the coffee table. "It's cheaper than L.A. for starters." He points the pack of cigarettes at me. "Want one?"

"I'm okay," I say. I'm so anxious I'm afraid my hands will shake or I'll cough too much. I can barely handle the bourbon.

"But you don't mind if . . . ?"

"No, go for it," I say. I manage another sip of my drink. Maybe soon the alcohol will numb my mouth and I won't be able to taste it anymore.

"So . . . are you so over high school?" J.C. says before

taking a long drag. I know smoking is terrible for you and it causes cancer and yellow teeth and whatever but something about a hot guy smoking a cigarette is enough to make me melt. It just is.

"I have two more years left at LBJ High," I say. "I hate it." I don't actually hate it, but I think that's what I should be saying.

"I fucking *hated* high school," J.C. says, taking a sip of his drink. More like a swallow. "It was such a drag. I barely finished."

"I'll be lucky to finish, too," I say, rolling my eyes. In truth, I have a B average, but sometimes I wonder if this is because I'm smart or because LBJ High is a joke. I don't even have to try that hard to make Bs.

"So what are you going to do after school?"

I shrug. "I'm not sure," I say. "Maybe some classes at the community college. I don't know." Now I am being honest. Mami wants me to become a nurse because she thinks that's a good job for a girl to make decent money. Actually, I think she wants me to marry a rich man and never work a day in my life just like Mrs. Callahan, but that seems like a highly unlikely career path for a working-class girl from Mariposa Island.

"Well, take it from me," J.C. says, letting the rest of his cocktail slide down his throat, ice cubes and all, "you've got time to figure it out. It's a long fucking life."

"Unfortunately," I say, sneering, and J.C. laughs. I'm pleased I said something funny even though deep down I feel stupid. My life is sucky in some ways, but I want to be living it. It is, after all, my life.

"So it's you and your mom and . . . ?"

"And my older brother. The one who answered the phone. Joaquin. He just graduated. I think he's going to abandon me at the end of the summer though." I wince a little inside at the thought.

"Joaquin?" J.C. says, frowning a little. "Isn't that a Spanish name?"

"*Claro que sí,*" I say, smirking. "*Sabes que puedo hablar español.*" I love pulling this little trick out of my pocket, mostly for the shocked expressions I get.

"What the hell!" J.C. says. "You don't even look Mexican!"

"I'm not from Mexico!" I say, laughing. "I'm Cuban. I mean, at least on my mom's side."

"But you're white," J.C. says, confused.

I roll my eyes like he's dumb, but I'm enjoying myself. I have something clever to talk about at last. Something that maybe makes me worth being the kind of high school girl you take back to your apartment. "You can be white and Hispanic," I say. "You can be black and Hispanic, too, you know."

"Huh," J.C. says, wrinkling his brow. "Well, I learned something today, I guess. Hell, that's cool. So you speak Spanish?"

"Yeah," I say. "I mean, I'm not totally fluent, but I can get by."

J.C. grins at me. "That Spanish makes you even cuter, you know."

I blush and stare at my drink, but I manage to say, "*Gracias, chico.*" J.C. knocks into me playfully with his elbow and I die.

"So what are you?" I ask. "I mean, like, your ancestors."

J.C. stubs out his cigarette and laughs. "Irish or some shit. My last name's Keller so, like, I think maybe German. You know . . . just a boring American mutt."

I giggle a little and take one more sip of my drink. I'm feeling warm and a little relaxed. Maybe the bourbon is starting to kick in a little. At least I hope it is. There has to be some payoff for the nasty taste.

"So if your mom is Cuban, what about your dad?" J.C. asks, getting up to go to the kitchenette to refill his glass.

I take a breath, not sure how to answer. But to my surprise the words just tumble out.

"He lives in California," I say. "I mean, I think so. I think he was an American mutt, too, but I'm not sure. He took off when I was a baby, so I don't have any memories of him. I think that's one reason my brother wants to abandon me at the end of the summer. I think he wants to go find him, maybe?" For the first time I'm grateful for my screwed-up backstory. Weirdly, I think maybe it makes me sound more interesting. More mature. More something.

"That fucking sucks," J.C. says, making his way back to the couch. This time when he sits down, he's so close our knees touch. I feel floaty and golden and warm.

"Yeah, it sort of does," I say, although does it really? I can't miss a man I never knew. In the few snapshots that Mami begrudgingly showed us when we were small, I saw grainy images of a so-so-looking guy with Joaquin's nose and my lanky build. Mostly we'd inherited Mami's features. Truly, we were fortunate, because Mami was a beautiful woman when she was younger, and it's a good thing her genes are stronger than our father's. Of course, Joaquin was the lucky one who inherited her blue eyes.

"I had the opposite thing happen," J.C. says. "My mom took off when I was in junior high. So it was just me and my dad."

"God, she waited until you were in junior high?" I say. I've never known anyone whose mother left them. Taking off when your kid is a teenager seems almost criminal somehow.

"Yeah," J.C. answers, lighting another cigarette. "But she was always sort of checked out, to be honest. She moved to Taos to find herself, I think. For a while she sent me Christmas cards and shit. But then I told her to knock it off because it was all bullshit."

Something about this speech makes me want to throw a raincoat over J.C. and protect him and also kiss him for a hundred years. I look down and my glass is empty. I feel good. Safe. Happy.

"I guess we're both fucked-up people then, huh?" I ask. A little thrill runs up my spine when I swear.

"Maybe a little fucked-up," J.C. says, bumping his knee into mine completely on purpose. When he gets up to refill my drink, I manage to promise myself I'll only drink half. And soon I'm realizing what Mami gets out of all that Bacardi and off-brand cola. Suddenly I feel very smart and sophisticated and fascinating. And J.C. and I start talking and it's not as hard as I feared it would be. We talk about the people who come to Mariposa Island for vacation ("They couldn't afford a real beach?" J.C. asks) and about Michelle ("She's been my best friend since forever") and we talk about whether or not the Russians will ever drop the bomb ("Back in California I think I saw *Red Dawn* five times in the theater"). Finally, two drinks in for me (and three for J.C.), he asks me if I want to go for a walk on the beach.

"Sure, why not?" I ask, checking my watch. It's only nine thirty. By now Mami is probably asleep. I think about making up an excuse to call home and check in with Joaquin, but I'm scared the ringing will wake her up if she is down for the count, and if she isn't, she might get curious and venture out of her cave and then not believe Joaquin's story that I'm at the Callahans'. Better to just cross my fingers and hope for the best.

I have to use the bathroom—which is so boy-gross I hover over the seat and skip washing my hands because the sink seems dirtier than any other part of the bathroom—and when I walk out, J.C. is leaning up against the little breakfast bar that separates the kitchenette from the living room, inhaling hard on a small pipe. A cloud of sweet-smelling smoke fills the air.

"Hey," he says, then coughs once. He holds the pipe and a lighter out toward me. "Interested? It's totally cool if you're not."

"I'm cool," I say, shrugging. I feel light-headed enough

from the drinks, but I do notice that it's odd how my brain is deciding which lines to cross tonight. Sneak out of the house without telling Mami? Sure. Go to the apartment of a strange boy who is really, for all intents and purposes, a man? Okay. Drink liquor? Fine. Inhale marijuana? Now hold up there, Elena.

I don't have to wonder if crossing some lines makes it easier to cross more in the future. I know the answer to that already.

The beach is mostly empty. Lights from the parking lots and crappy beachfront hotels cast a spooky, yellowish hue on the sand. The moon is out, too, which is nice, at least. Nicer than parking-lot fluorescents. I see a few kids around my age sitting on one of the tipped-over lifeguard chairs, drinking beers. They probably go to LBJ, so I keep my head down. I don't want to talk to anyone but J.C. tonight, and I don't need the word to get around that I was out with some strange older guy.

I left my flip-flops back at the apartment, and at this hour the sand is actually cool under my feet. Little baby Gulf Coast waves crash lazily along the shoreline.

"You should see the waves in L.A.," J.C. says, raising a hand high up over his head. "Like as tall as a two-story building."

"Really?" I ask, trying to picture something like that. But instead my mind flashes on Joaquin standing all alone on a California beach at night, getting swallowed up by some gigantic wave. I squeeze my eyes shut for a moment and push the picture out of my head. *God, Elena,* I think to myself, *it's really good you didn't smoke that pot.*

I'm focusing on clearing my head when I feel J.C.'s hand slip into mine.

"Is this cool?" he asks, glancing at me.

"Yeah," I answer, my entire body electric. "Totally." *Ugh, why did you have to say* totally *like some cheesy girl.*

My chest is tight. I'm trying to burn every sensation into my mind, like the fact that J.C.'s hand feels rough but warm. Strong but not crushing. I hope my hand feels nice to hold. Not too sweaty or anything. He's probably held hands with lots of girls before. Honestly, he's probably done lots more with lots of girls before. He's nineteen, after all. And I'm just sixteen-year-old Elena Finney, with only a few clumsy make-outs on the beach at parties during the summer to my name. Kisses that were mechanical and boring, and under-the-shirt gropes that reminded me of an eager puppy trying to jump into my lap.

We walk in silence for a bit. J.C. motions toward the next tipped lifeguard chair.

"Want to stop there?" he asks.

"Yeah."

When we get there, J.C. pushes the chair upright and we climb up, my hands scraping against the peeling white paint and rough wood.

"These chairs look like they've been here since the fifties."

"They have!" I answer. I think about when Michelle and I

were in junior high and we would rate the lifeguards by their cuteness, categories one through five, just like hurricanes.

J.C. reaches for my hand again. We stare out at the ocean— the *gulf*, Mami would remind me.

"So you're here for the whole summer?" I ask. "Or what?"

"At least the summer. Maybe more. My uncle wants me to take some classes at some community college around here in the fall. Try to get my act together or whatever." At this he half rolls his eyes.

"Oh, yeah, Mariposa Island Community College," I say. "Everyone just refers to it as M-I-C-C," I say, spelling out each letter.

"Okay," says J.C. "My uncle wants me to take classes at M-I-C-C. Now I won't stick out too much since I know the island lingo. Thanks."

"My pleasure," I answer, smiling.

J.C. squeezes my hand a little tighter. I might be imagining it, but I think he scoots a little closer, too. He's still wearing those same orange-and-white board shorts from earlier today. It sounds ridiculous, but I can't help but notice how much hair he has on his legs. I wonder if he has hair on his chest.

I'm so weird.

"What would you study if you went to school?" I ask.

"I honestly have no clue," J.C. answers. "I can't really picture myself doing that. I keep agreeing to it so my uncle will relax. I mean, you wouldn't think a guy who runs a beach rental outfit would be so uptight, but he fucking is, man."

"So come fall you might leave?" I ask. Just like Joaquin. It must be nice being a boy.

"I guess I'll have to see what the summer is like," J.C. says, and I'm not so sixteen and naïve that I don't notice a shift in the sound of his voice. I'm not so naïve that I don't know the meaning behind those words. And soon, before I even have a chance to process that it's happening, J.C.'s mouth is on mine and I'm trying to keep up. He is not without kissing experience, it's obvious. He kisses with purpose. With focus.

My whole body feels like it might implode. Or is it explode? I don't know, but kissing J.C. is literally the best thing I've ever done with my lips in my whole entire life.

"Is this okay?" J.C. says, his voice husky. He's hovering right by my mouth when he asks, like he knows it is but he's trying to be polite.

"Yeah," I say, barely able to get the word out. I feel a warmth spreading over my whole body, and suddenly, out of nowhere, my mind flashes on Mami dropping that soapy glass and it shattering all over the floor. This is what happens to ruined goods, Mami would argue. This is what happens when you trust boys.

I shake my head a little in protest at the thought, enough that J.C. pulls away for a moment.

"You okay?" he asks, breathless.

"Yeah," I say, and as if to prove it to myself, I lean back in, and soon thoughts of Mami fade away, thank God. J.C. and I kiss some more and the good feelings come back, and in my mind I wonder how two people even decide to stop kissing, but eventually we do, somehow, and J.C. grins.

"That was nice," he says, almost like he's shy about it.

"Yeah," I say again. It's the only word I can manage.

"So this is obvious, probably, but it would be cool to hang out again," J.C. says. His knee bounces up and down a bit, like maybe he's nervous. It's absurd to think he could ever be nervous around me.

"Yeah, it would," I say, finally able to say more than one word. "Just . . ." I hesitate. I don't want to sound like I think we're supposed to be boyfriend and girlfriend now just because we kissed on a lifeguard chair.

"What's up?"

"It's just . . . it would be better if I call you. My mom doesn't want boys calling the house." *Or anyone, really.*

"Damn," J.C. says, his eyebrows raising briefly. "But yeah . . . I get it. No phone calls. I mean, you better call *me*. But nothing in reverse. I get it." He winks and I die.

A few moments later we are kissing again, and I think I could kiss all night, really, but finally, a little after ten, we both agree we should walk back, and I mention I should be heading home. I get my flip-flops from his apartment, and when we get to his car, J.C. digs around a bit until he finds a piece of paper and a pen, and he writes down his phone number. I slide the number deep into my back pocket, thinking about which hiding spot in my room is the best place for it.

On the ride back up Esperanza Boulevard, I try to process

everything that's happened to me tonight, but it's too over-whelming, so I just close my eyes briefly and allow myself the teeniest, tiniest smile.

• • •

I make my way down the sidewalk, replaying J.C.'s goodbye kiss on my lips, but as I approach our house, the image fades. I climb our front steps and cross both sets of fingers and toes before I slide my key into the front door. I open it a crack and hold my breath.

"It's fine," Joaquin's voice says, and every molecule in my body relaxes.

"She never came out?" I ask, my voice a half whisper as I step all the way inside and shut the door behind me.

"Once," says Joaquin, glancing up at me from his slumped position on the couch and then staring back at the television. "Just to go to the bathroom and then back to bed. I never even saw her. Just heard her."

"Okay, that's good," I say. I got away with it. I can hardly believe it.

"Did you have fun?" he asks.

"Yeah," I answer, sliding off my flip-flops.

"What'd you do?"

"Went to the Cinemark."

Joaquin nods. I realize the trap I've just walked into, but he doesn't even ask what movie we saw. I've got to get my head back on straight.

"Hey, I didn't need the ten bucks you gave me," I say, sliding his El Mirador tip money out of my pocket. "He paid for everything."

"Wow, a real gentleman," answers Joaquin.

"Are you being a dick or serious?" I ask, irritated. "He was actually very nice." I toss Joaquin's money onto the coffee table.

"You think you're going to go out with him again?" he asks, ignoring my question.

"Yeah, probably," I say. Talking about me and boys is more than uncharted territory for me and my brother. It's an entirely new universe.

"Okay," says Joaquin.

"Don't worry, I already told him he can't call here," I say. I think about the slip of paper with J.C.'s phone number on it. Just picturing it makes me feel giddy again.

"Elena, it's your life," Joaquin says, and he really looks at me at last, his face set and serious, his words filling this weird space between us.

"Okay, I'll try to remember that," I say, half rolling my eyes but not really because, hell, he's the reason I was even able to go out tonight. My irritation softens a little. "Anyway, thanks for covering for me. I'm going to bed."

I don't make it three steps before Joaquin calls me back. He picks up the two crumpled five-dollar bills and hands them to me.

"Keep it," he says, his eyes back on the screen. "For next time. For an emergency. For whatever."

"Joaquin, you don't . . . ," I start.

"Just take it," he says.

"Seriously?"

"Elena, take the money."

I do.

"Thanks. You didn't have to."

"I know," says my big brother. "Now get to bed."

"I thought it was *my* life," I say, my smirk breaking into a full-blown smile.

"Good night, *hermanita*."

"You know that nickname is so annoying," I say, my smile turning into a fake pout. But my brother just laughs softly and I do, too, and it feels okay again between us. And once inside the safety of my room, I hide J.C.'s phone number in the good hiding spot in the closet and I put Joaquin's money in the back of my nightstand drawer and I pull out my Gum Drop lipstick and paint my lips as dark as I can before blowing sexy kisses at my reflection in the bedroom mirror. And when I finally slide under the covers, I find myself pressing my fingers to my lips as if my fingertips could somehow find proof there that finally, at last, my life had started for real.

CHAPTER SEVEN

I'M GIDDY WITH RULE-BREAKING, AND I EVEN HAVE A car to do it in.

Mami almost never lets me borrow our old Honda—I'm still sort of stunned she even let me get my driver's license. But it helps for the times she's too tired or too angry or too something to do whatever errand she has on her list. Then I'm sent into the land of the living all by myself, and I don't even have to have a job lined up with the Callahans to do it.

This morning when she asked me to spend the better part of Saturday running by Kroger and Walgreens, I jumped at the chance, rushing to finish the breakfast dishes and get ready.

"You can pick up your brother at the end of his shift," Mami says from her position on the couch, her feet up on a pillow, a mint-green wet washcloth on her forehead. Maybe too much rum last night. Or maybe just an opportunity to get the house to herself.

"I'll call and tell him I'm coming," I say.

"That's good," she says, pulling the washcloth down over her eyes. In a minute I can hear light snoring.

As I pull out onto Esperanza Boulevard, all I can think about is J.C. It's still early, so I'm not sure he'll be at the beach, but there's a chance. He was there the last time I showed up unannounced after a morning spent taking the Callahan kids to the Mariposa Island library for story hour, which Jennifer is really getting a little too big for but Matthew seems to like. When I arrived at the place where Michelle rents umbrellas, there he was, smoking a cigarette and talking to her. I hesitated for a minute. It had been only two days since our date, and I hadn't worked up the guts to call him. But when he saw me making my way across the parking lot, he grinned at me so widely I knew it wasn't a mistake that I had shown up out of nowhere, and I was even more sure of it later when we walked down the coastline and he pulled me under the boardwalk and kissed me and everything fell away until it was just the two of us pressing into each other. When we crept out from under the boardwalk and my eyes adjusted to the brightness of the sun and my ears to the piercing tweets of the lifeguards' whistles, it was as if I was landing back on Earth after a trip to some other universe. My legs had even felt a little wobbly.

Just thinking of it as I pull into the parking lot by Michelle's stand makes my heart start racing. I check my lip gloss in the rearview mirror, squeeze my cheeks a bit to make them extra pink. But when I make my way toward Michelle's chair, I realize J.C. isn't there.

"Hey, lady, surprise," I say, approaching Michelle. I try to act like I'm not even looking for J.C. I don't want to hurt her feelings.

"He's not here," she says immediately, glancing up at me with her hand over her eyes to block out the sun. I drop down on the sand next to her, trying to act like I'm not crushed.

"Who says I was here for him?" I answer, rolling my eyes.

"Oh, please, you think I took moron pills this morning or something? Cut the bullshit." But Michelle laughs when she says it, kicking a little sand at me at the same time.

"Okay, fine, maybe I was hoping he'd be here," I say, looking away so she can't see my blush of embarrassment. "But you're acting like I don't want to see my best friend, too."

"Well, he still might show up," Michelle answers, digging through her green-and-white-striped beach bag for her brown bottle of sunscreen. "So how come you're out? Babysitting gig? The Callahans get home early?"

"No," I answer. "She actually let me out on my own to get some shopping done for her. I even have the car."

"No shit," Michelle answers, squirting on the lotion and rubbing it in on her body. She holds an arm out and studies it. "I thought by this point in the summer I'd be browner." She frowns.

"You look good to me," I tell her. "Next to you, I look like a ghost."

"And you're supposed to be the ethnic one," Michelle says with a snort.

"*Ay, chica, me estás volviendo loca,*" I shoot back, arching one eyebrow. Michelle loves it when I break out my Spanish, even when I'm telling her she's driving me bonkers.

A family comes up and asks to rent some umbrellas, leaving me to sit alone and stare at the weak Gulf Coast waves that roll up lazily onto the sand. Just when I decide I have to start my errands, I feel a kiss on the back of my neck.

"Hey!" I say, with a little shriek that I instantly hope sounds more cute than scared.

"Hey, back," J.C. answers, sitting down next to me on the sand. He offers me a lopsided grin. I notice the rims of his eyes are red, but I don't have time to get a good look because he leans in and kisses me right on the mouth. I used to roll my eyes at PDA, but with J.C. it's like nothing else exists when his mouth is on mine. When he pulls back, I have to catch my breath.

"You're so pretty," he says. He's giddy. Silly. And almost certainly high. It's only ten in the morning, I remind myself. But whatever. It's the summer. Isn't he allowed to have some fun? Plus, he called me pretty. I play those words in my mind over and over. *You're so pretty.*

"So, you can hang out all day, right?" he asks, nuzzling my neck again.

"I'm sorry," I say, carefully watching his face for disappointment. "I have to do a bunch of errands for my mom."

"Shit," he answers, and he reaches out and takes my hand in his. "But what if I never let you go? What if I just don't let you get up from this beach?" He opens his mouth like some sort of Muppet and then shuts it before he starts cracking up. I've never seen him so wired, and I can't decide if I like it or not. But it's J.C., and he's so cute, and he likes me—so I should like it, I think.

"Well look what the tide washed in," Michelle says, making her way back to us. "Are you actually here to, like, work for your uncle for once?"

"I took an afternoon shift," J.C. says. "And hello to you, too."

Michelle is looking us over carefully, eyeing my hand wrapped in J.C.'s, then letting her gaze rest on J.C.'s face. Finally, she plops down on the other side of him and glances sideways in J.C.'s direction. "A little wake and bake, huh?" she asks, not too loud but loud enough that I can hear it. My stomach knots up a bit. It's one thing to suspect my boyfriend—or whatever he is—is high, but it's different to have Michelle say it out loud. Riskier, somehow. And maybe even a little more exciting, too, which is probably absurd and definitely dangerous, but I find myself squeezing J.C.'s hand even tighter.

"Jeez, Michelle, relax," J.C. answers, squeezing my hand back, which makes my heart race faster. "You'd think this was a real job and not just, like, chilling on the beach."

"Screw you," Michelle says, her voice skating carefully along the line between being playful and being annoyed. "All I'm saying is don't be late for your shift." She hasn't made eye contact with me since she sat down.

We sit in silence for a bit, and I try to think of the right words to cut it, but all I can come up with is that I probably have to get going, which is the truth. I try to catch Michelle's gaze. She doesn't look mad or anything, but the way she's staring straight ahead, I think maybe she is.

"You know, I really gotta go and get started on this shopping for my mom," I say, and J.C. lets go of my hand. Once I'm standing up, I'm reluctant to leave, even if Michelle might be mad at me and I don't know what to make of J.C. when he's high. I offer up a tentative smile in Michelle's direction and she looks up and smiles back—a small smile, but a smile, at least—and then she says, "Hey, call me tonight? After your mom has locked herself in her cave or whatever?"

"Yeah, of course," I answer. My smile grows even bigger and I feel like a dork. But Michelle and I are best friends and we never get annoyed with each other. Not over anything major, anyway. Certainly not over a guy.

J.C. takes my hand again and tugs me toward the parking lot. "I'll walk you to your car," he says.

"Bye, Michelle," I say in the general direction of her back as J.C. slides an arm around my waist. Michelle holds up her hand and waggles her fingers at me, but she doesn't turn around.

J.C. and I head toward the Honda, passing families straining under the weight of beach bags and towels and whining toddlers. When we get to my car, he pulls me toward him and says, "Can you get out tonight? Come over or something?"

I say yes before I can stop myself. The last time I babysat for the Callahans, Mrs. Callahan mentioned they were heading back to Houston for the weekend for a family birthday party, so they won't need me. But Mami doesn't know this, so I could always tell Mami I ran into them on my errands or something, and they asked me to babysit. I try to think of some frivolous thing they might go to at the last minute that would really make her feel superior to them as a parent.

"Just come get me on the corner around eight? I'll figure out a way to meet you."

"Awesome," J.C. says, his voice soft, tender even, the giddiness from a few minutes before gone. He reaches up and runs his fingers through my hair and tucks some strands behind my ear and I melt right there, leaning against my Honda, careful not to burn the backs of my thighs against the hot metal. Before I know it, I feel his lips on mine, urgent, searching. I kiss him back, not caring who sees, until I hear a little boy's voice say, "Ew, those teenagers are kissing!"

I pull back and spot him, dressed in green swim trunks and matching flip-flops. He looks a little bit younger than Matthew Callahan. I blush a bit and glance down at my feet, but not before catching the boy's mother grimace, obviously convinced I've corrupted her son's innocence. I peek up at J.C. and grin, and he grins back. He kisses me again even though the little boy hasn't gotten very far, and the kiss is even sweeter since we're being a little bad.

"Okay, okay, I've really got to go now," I manage, pulling out of his arms and sliding into the driver's seat.

"Okay, okay, see you at eight," he mimics, rapping on my windshield in farewell before I drive away. As I pull out of the parking lot and onto the street, I allow myself a scream worthy of a roller-coaster ride before I find my reflection in the rearview mirror and grin at the girl looking back. I hardly recognize her.

* * *

El Mirador is trapped in some sort of time warp. In the sixteen years I've been alive, nothing has changed—not the red vinyl booths with the crooked tears in them or the twinkling Christmas lights hung in lazy loops over the bar. The same paintings of pueblo scenes—a dark-haired mother holding her chubby baby, a mustached rancher standing proudly next to his horse—hang on the bright orange walls, perpetually crooked. The smell of warm tortillas and salty chips and queso fills the air. Mami says it was all exactly the same way back in the sixties when she first moved to Mariposa Island with our father. El Mirador is pretty much the only restaurant on the island that Mami will go to, and one of the few places she goes to at all that's not some sort of obligation, like her job or church. When I was in grade school, I asked Mami if it's because our father used to take her here when they were young, and she got so mad she took all my Barbies and threw them away, but at least Joaquin fished out my favorite one when Mami wasn't looking.

"Hey, *mi amor*," says Carlos, the owner's son and Joaquin's boss, looking up from a table where he is standing and finishing some side work, rolling clean utensils in bright red cloth napkins. Carlos is a big man, old enough to be my father or at least my uncle—if I had either one of those things. He has kind, dark eyes and a black buzz cut, and Joaquin likes him because Carlos never acts like he's too important to do small stuff like filling up the salt and pepper shakers. "You here for your good-for-nothing brother?"

"Yeah, if he doesn't want to have to ride his bike home," I say over the strains of accordion skittering out of the stereo. El Mirador plays conjunto music every day, all day. Joaquin once told me he hears it in his dreams.

Carlos hollers back toward the kitchen that I'm here. The restaurant is mostly empty at this hour since it's after the lunch rush and before the dinner crowd. The groceries are melting in the back seat of the Honda, so I hope Joaquin will hurry up.

"Hey, Elena."

It's Miguel Fuentes in his white busboy uniform, clutching a gray plastic tub. He offers me a smile. I haven't seen him since that first beach party of the summer when he asked me out and embarrassed the both of us. I wonder if he came out of the kitchen just because he heard I was here. God, I hope not.

"Hey, Miguel," I say, slipping my hands in the pockets of my jeans. I try to smile and not be rude, but I'm hoping Joaquin picks up the pace.

"Everything going okay?" he says, lifting up his shoulders and letting them fall, all forced casualness.

"Yeah, everything's good," I answer. My mind flashes back to J.C. Back to the kisses by my car that made my entire body pulsate. Back to the thrill of knowing in a few hours I'll be sliding into his VW Bug and heading back to *his place*. It's not that Miguel's not a nice person. It's more that J.C. is basically a man and Miguel isn't. Miguel probably shares a bedroom with his little brother. And he probably still plays Dungeons and Dragons with those weird guys he hung out with in junior high.

"I saw *Labyrinth* the other day at the Cinemark," Miguel announces out of nowhere, confirming what I've just been thinking. He grips the gray tub with his hands and smiles.

"Really?" That movie looks weird as hell. "That looks like a pretty good movie," I say.

"Yeah, it is," he says. "David Bowie's in it."

"Oh. I guess I never thought of him as, like, an actor or anything. Not that I really listen to his music, either."

"You don't listen to Bowie?" Carlos interrupts from his side work. He frowns at me. "He's a musical genius." I shrug. At least now I don't have to talk to Miguel by myself.

Miguel rolls his eyes. "If you think Bowie's so great, why don't we listen to *Ziggy Stardust* instead of Flaco Jiménez every day?"

"*Ziggy Stardust* doesn't really go with fajitas," Carlos argues.

At last Joaquin comes out, untying his white waiter's apron from around his waist and tossing it at Miguel, where it lands expertly over his left shoulder.

"Two points!" my brother cries. "Hey, Miguel, would you throw that in the laundry for me?"

Miguel acts all put upon, but he laughs and so does Carlos, and I experience this weird moment where I see what my brother is like out in the real world. Easygoing. Relaxed. Maybe even a little bit goofy.

"You can put your own laundry away, man," argues Miguel, but you can tell he's joking. It's obvious Miguel looks up to Joaquin. I get it, because Joaquin's older, he's a waiter and not just a busboy, and Joaquin's had girlfriends before, secret ones that Mami never knew about, but girls who held his hand as he walked down the halls of LBJ High. Girls who waited for him at his locker, excited to see him. Miguel has never gone out with anyone in his life. He probably hasn't even kissed anyone. It's pitiful, really. But I'm so embarrassed for him that all I can do is smile at him.

"You ready?" Joaquin asks.

"Yeah, and we gotta hurry," I say. "There's ice cream in the Honda and it's probably melted into a chocolate puddle in the back seat by now."

We head around the corner to El Mirador's parking lot, and I start up the car while Joaquin goes to retrieve his ten-speed from the bike rack at the side of the building. As I fiddle with the air-conditioning vents to make sure they're open to full blast, I see a girl with a short, dark-haired pixie cut walk up behind Joaquin. He doesn't see her approaching, and he jumps when she leans in and pinches his waist. When he turns around, she starts laughing, a laugh loud enough I can hear it through the windows of the Honda and over the insistent hum of the AC. Joaquin smiles so widely I know this is *xoxoAmy* in the flesh.

Joaquin nods toward the car, probably alerting Amy that his little sister is steps away, spying on him. For this I'm glad, because the last thing I need is to witness my brother kissing some girl while I'm sitting in a car full of melting groceries. I could just look away, I guess, but I can't stop myself from peering through the window out of curiosity. This girl is unusual, that's for sure. I think I've seen her in the halls of LBJ, hanging out with some of the few punks that exist on Mariposa Island. She's usually decked out in big black boots covered in complicated metal clasps, dark red lipstick, heavy eye makeup, black T-shirts, and knee-length denim cutoffs tattooed in black Sharpie with words and symbols I can't understand. *xoxoAmy* is definitely not the kind of girl who listens to Madonna or Power 104, and she isn't the type of sweet-looking, clean-faced pep squad girl that Joaquin has gone out with before.

Through all the weirdness she's cute, though. It makes sense, because even though it's gross to think about for even a second, my brother isn't a bad-looking guy. I'm convinced he got more of the beautiful genes from Mami's side of the family than I did, but the way they're arranged on Joaquin's guy face makes him more handsome than pretty.

He's acting like he knows it, too, because right now he's leaning against the side of El Mirador like he's some modern James Dean and he's got all the time in the world. He shrugs and motions with his hands and Amy keeps leaning her head back and laughing her ass off. My brother might not be bad-looking, but he's not *that* funny. *Relax, Amy, jeez.* Then I wonder if that's how silly I seem in front of J.C. I sigh and keep watching—the silly shoves and light touches and exaggerated laughs. Flirting. I check my watch. Mami's going to want us home soon. I lean on the horn.

The two of them glance at me. Amy actually raises her hand up, like a wave, I guess? I wave back, not wanting to seem rude. Finally, Joaquin nods, says one more thing, Amy laughs like a maniac one last time, and then he walks to the car, wedging his bike into the hatchback. Amy heads inside El Mirador.

"So who's that?" I say as we pull out of the parking lot.

"Amy," Joaquin says. "You don't know her from school?"

I glance at him, a knowing look. "Does it look like we hang out in the same circles?"

Joaquin nods. "Yeah, I guess. She's really cool, though." He allows himself the tiniest smile, and I know he thinks she's more than just cool.

"What grade?"

"Going into her senior year."

"Okay."

We drive in silence. I chew on my bottom lip a bit, getting up the courage. "So, does this mean you're not moving away to California?"

Joaquin doesn't react at first. Just keeps staring straight ahead. It's quiet for so long I'm embarrassed I asked the question.

"Forget it," I say at last.

"No, Elena," Joaquin jumps in. "It's . . . I don't know. I actually don't know what I'm doing." He scratches the back of his neck, a nervous habit, then exhales loudly. "Fuck it. There it is. I don't know what I'm doing." I glance at him. His eyebrows furrow. There are five hundred things he's not telling me, I know it.

"So you still might leave?" I ask, my voice soft. Hopefully not annoying.

"I mean, I guess I'm still thinking about it. But, Elena, it's not like if I leave, you'll never see me again."

We pull up to a stoplight and I give him a look. "Come on, Joaquin. Don't bullshit me. You know it won't be the same. California isn't exactly down the street. It's not even Houston."

Joaquin jiggles his leg a bit, drums his fingers on his kneecap. "Let's just say I don't know. And if it makes you feel any better, right now, no, I have no immediate plans to move to California, okay?"

I take a deep breath, satisfied. "Okay. Good." I choose to ignore *right now* and *immediate* and just hold on to *no plans to move to California*.

We're getting close to home, but I guess Joaquin thinks he's allowed a question now, too, because he says, "So . . . what's up with you and Mr. Grateful Dead?"

"His name is J.C."

"As in Jesus Christ?" He laughs a little at that, but it hits me that I have no idea what those letters stand for and probably should. "It stands for John Christopher if you must know," I say, making my voice extra snotty. "And he's great. He's super nice. We're hanging out tonight."

"The Callahans need you?"

"No, they're out of town. I might just sneak out if you're going to be home? Or do you have plans with Amy?" We turn onto our street.

"Well, I didn't have plans for sure," Joaquin says, his voice the tiniest bit prickly. "I mean, she's working until close, so I guess not."

"I'll figure it out," I say.

"You know, maybe if you were hanging out with a guy like Miguel this wouldn't even be an issue," he says.

I pull into our driveway and park, glad I can give Joaquin all of my attention as I fire him the most incredulous look I can come up with.

"Miguel? From El Mirador?"

Joaquin throws his hands up like he shouldn't have said anything. "Relax, Elena. I'm just saying Mami might actually let you go out with a guy like Miguel, and then you wouldn't have to sneak around like you have to with Mr. Grateful Dead."

I cut the engine and slide the keys out of the ignition with force. "Could you please call him J.C.?" I say, my voice thick with frustration. "And could you please stop living in a fantasy world where Mami would let me go out with *any* guy, even a guy like Miguel Fuentes?"

"Maybe if you stood up to her once in a while, you might get lucky," Joaquin shoots back, giving me a pointed look. But I can tell he's regretting this already, like he always does the moment he tries to analyze Mami with me.

"Please stop talking about something you know nothing about," I say. In the thirty seconds we've been sitting here without air-conditioning, I've already started to sweat. I open the door, signaling to Joaquin that this conversation is over. I get out and Joaquin follows my lead.

"Look, Elena, all I'm saying is . . ." He pauses, looking up at the front porch before lowering his voice to a stage whisper, "Forget Mami. What I mean is that Miguel is a nice guy and I know he likes you . . . I mean, he's always talking about you. Asking about you. You deserve a nice guy is what I'm saying."

I peer at Joaquin over the rusting hood of the Honda, my anger softening by a few degrees. "Okay," I say. "Okay, fine. But J.C. is a nice guy, too, you know." I'm not sure how Joaquin defines nice, but hasn't J.C. been nice to me? Hasn't he kissed me dizzy and told me I'm pretty and smiled and laughed at the funny things I've said?

Suddenly, there's the whine of our screen door opening.

"What's taken you two so long?" Joaquin and I both jump. Her voice is thick with bad mood.

"Sorry, Mami," I say, hurrying to open the back passenger door and grab two paper bags.

"It was my fault," Joaquin says, coming around to my side and taking the bags out of my hands. "Carlos made me finish some side work before I could go." I give Joaquin a kind look, gratitude swelling inside my heart for my annoying big brother.

"Your shift ends when it ends," Mami says definitively from the porch, like she's some expert on restaurant management. Her blouse is untucked from her khakis, and she scowls and runs her fingers through her mussed-up hair, glancing around to see if anyone is out on the street. She'd hate to be spotted by neighbors looking less than her best, even if she never talks to any of them.

"I'm sorry I made Elena late," Joaquin says, heading toward the porch steps. I grab more groceries and follow him. Mami doesn't answer, just turns and heads inside, leaving the screen door to slam in our faces.

"That was helpful," Joaquin says, with such perfect comic timing I can't help but laugh, and Joaquin laughs, and we forget everything from before and allow ourselves this little moment together on the porch, straining under the weight of the groceries, like the only two survivors on a life raft who have no choice but to hold on together.

CARIDAD

1961

It all fell apart, both quickly and slowly, like a child's tower of blocks that teeters for what feels like an eternity before collapsing in one loud clatter.

How strange it was for Caridad to see Juanita counting out ration tickets for meat and sugar, returning from *el mercado* with her shopping bags more deflated than full. How awful it was to learn one morning that her school was no longer open, that she would be sent to a new school where she would be taught not by her beloved nuns but by bright-eyed, earnest young teachers who spoke of revolution and change and asked Caridad if her parents ever spoke ill of El Comandante. How odd it was to hear her own mother and father speak in slow, careful English—Caridad knew it was their way of keeping things from her—and how frustrating it was not to know what they were speaking about. It didn't matter that

Caridad spied on them regularly, hovering in hallways, listening from the other sides of doors. The foreign sounds were awkward as they climbed out of their mouths, like babies trying to take their first steps. Caridad could understand none of it.

And soon came the awful afternoon Caridad had to say goodbye to Juanita, who was dismissed after Caridad's parents discovered her listening to El Comandante's speeches on the kitchen radio, her duties shirked so she could follow his rousing, barking voice for what seemed like hours. How much Caridad's heart had ached when Juanita had held her close to her starched white dress and whispered, *"Nuestro mundo está cambiando por algo mejor, no lo olvides."* Her last words to Caridad had been nothing about their relationship, nothing about their years together—only about how much the world was changing and how that wasn't even a bad thing, at least not according to Juanita. Caridad had watched her walk down the street and not look back, not even once, until she disappeared around a corner. Caridad had burst into tears, standing there in the noonday heat.

There was a new maid the next week, a gruff, short woman named Marta, who flung herself around the kitchen like a bad storm. She frowned when she discovered Caridad sneaking food out of the kitchen before reminding her of the newly instituted government rationing. She didn't draw Caridad's bath or pull the tangles out of her hair or slip her extra dessert. There wasn't even dessert.

One Sunday when leaving Mass, Caridad and her parents

were surrounded by protestors on the street, jeering at them. God was dead and they were too stupid to know it. They were hanging on to the old way, not the new revolutionary way of being. Caridad made eye contact with one little boy, his fists clenched, his mouth open wide and pink. *"Estás perdida!"* he shrieked. Caridad thought the little boy might be right. Didn't she feel lost? It seemed, in a way, that God was dead. Everything that had ever mattered to Caridad, everything that she had come to know and claim as her own and believed had been given to her by God had slipped away, as if it had disappeared into the cool blue waters off Varadero Beach where *los barbudos* had long since taken over. Where they had laid claim to the homes of the really rich, who had been smart enough to leave early, sewing their jewelry into the hems of their skirts and hiding money in books with false bottoms.

But Caridad got out, too, eventually. Although when it started, she didn't realize she would be leaving, never to return. One morning her mother and father called her into the *salita* and explained that soon she would be leaving for the United States to practice English. She would be gone for thirty days.

"Will you come with me?" Caridad had asked, confused. She touched the soft velvet of the couch. She studied the silver seashell ashtray on the table in front of her. And she heard her mother say, "No, we already know English. But it's a good opportunity for you, and when you come back we can speak it with you." Her father got up, lit a cigarette, and stared out the window, saying nothing. Caridad wished not for the first time that Juanita was still there to make sense of it all, but as soon as she allowed that thought she reminded herself that Juanita had abandoned her, and the soft spaces of her heart that she'd kept for the woman who'd cared for her since birth continued to harden and shrink.

"Graciela's parents aren't making her leave and learn English," Caridad spat. "I think it's so mean of you." She crossed her arms and pouted, not capable of reading her mother's pained face. Not capable of registering the strained expression on her father's face when he turned away from the window to look at her with sad eyes. Her parents could deliver no good words to comfort Caridad, although they tried, clumsily. The truth was they had not raised their daughter to suffer. In many ways they had not really raised her at all.

And so it was that one morning, dressed in pink pumps and her sweetest pink dress with the white Peter Pan collar and clutching her duffle filled with her favorite clothes and an album of photographs, she got into a car with her parents and headed to the Havana airport, her heart thumping hard in her chest. Her mother waited in the car. Only one parent could go inside with her, they explained, but her mother got out and held Caridad close to her, no longer smelling of Arpège because Arpège could no longer be purchased on the island. Her beautiful mother only smelled of soap and talcum powder. Something about it made Caridad furious, like she was being denied a proper goodbye.

"I will see you in one month," her mother said, smiling, pulling back from Caridad. Her eyes were wet, but she was not really crying. Caridad was.

"I don't understand why this is happening to me," Caridad answered, hot tears streaming down her face.

"Please trust us, *mi vida*," her mother said, giving her one more squeeze before ducking back into the car.

The airport was stuffy and crowded. Families milled about, babies wailed. Caridad found herself standing dumbly by her father as he spoke to one of the authorities, a large military man with a thick beard, much like El Comandante's, a pistol strapped to his hip. Caridad's father handed the man several papers and the man studied them. The air smelled of cigarettes and cheap cleanser. Caridad resisted the urge to take her father's hand. She was too old for that now, and besides, part of her was still too angry at him.

Soon, however, she felt her father's arms around her, her ear full of his instructions. Be good. Be safe. Do as you're told. And then Caridad found herself in a holding room of sorts, surrounded by glass on all sides. Caridad's duffel was searched by a different soldier, a gruff, pockmarked man with red cheeks.

"Do your parents ever speak ill of El Comandante?" he asked, shoving his grubby hands through Caridad's clothes. Her lime-green sundress. Her flowered pajamas. Caridad noted the dirt under his uncut fingernails and resisted the urge to scowl as she told the man no. Then the man tilted her head forward without warning and picked through her hair like some sort of undomesticated wild animal searching for seeds in a field. Later on, Caridad would understand he had been searching for hidden jewelry woven through her thick dark locks.

At last that was finished, and Caridad eyed the crowd inside the fishbowl in which she was being kept. She noticed the room was only full of children, and at seventeen, she was one of the oldest. A girl several years younger than her gripped the hand of what was probably her little brother, their faces both white as paste. Another boy, maybe eleven or twelve, had managed to find a piece of paper and was writing messages and holding them up to the glass to be read by a woman on the other side, a woman whose tears had cut through her mascara, leaving coal-black rivulets running down her cheeks. Grade school–age children wandered around aimlessly. They sniffed and sobbed.

Caridad searched for her father and found him standing still on the other side of the fishbowl, staring at her. When Caridad was able, she moved to the glass and held her hand up, pressing it firmly toward her father in some sort of salute. Her father responded, his hand held straight up, a sad smile on his face, so handsome in his linen suit. And it was in that moment Caridad knew that her parents had lied to her.

This was not going to be a thirty-day visit to the United

States. Perhaps she was not even going to return. That her mother and father believed she was young enough to still fool made her burn with anger at the same time that her throat ached with sadness at their last attempt to spoil their only child.

Years later, Caridad would think back on this day, on how after hours of nervous waiting she was led onto the airplane, the black letters of PAN AMERICAN on its side. She would remember how she searched for her father's eyes one last time but was unable to catch them. She would recall the blond, slim-hipped stewardess not much older than Caridad herself, wearing a powder-blue suit and a big bright smile and speaking terrible, broken Spanish that made some of the younger children giggle. And she would remember the white squares of chewing gum—Chiclets—that the stewardess handed out, the first gum Caridad had chewed in so long. How sweet it was! How she had relished the crunchy peppermint taste in her mouth until it gave way to rubbery nothingness in a matter of minutes.

Years later in Texas, even after she began dreaming in English instead of Spanish, she would still be able to conjure up the rumble of the engine and the sudden lift of the plane off the ground. The sight of bright blue water below. She would remember all of this. And when she looked back on this day, on the day she was spirited out of her homeland, she would not know if what had happened to her was good or bad, lucky or unlucky. It would be a question she refused to consider.

To answer it would hurt too much, dig too much under the skin. If life was going to push her along like a wave, Caridad decided, it was best to let it do it, filling herself to the brim with a seething rage, pulling a tight perimeter around the little she could control.

ELENA

CHAPTER EIGHT

THE ONLY REASON I CAN WATCH THE FOURTH OF JULY fireworks each year is Mami knows I go with Joaquin, where the two of us find a spot on the beach and sit on one of our old ratty towels and maybe Michelle comes by to keep us company. Joaquin brings cans of Budweiser and he never lets me have one, and as soon as the red and blue and green starfishes and sunbursts cease exploding across the night sky over downtown, Joaquin stands up and says, "All right, let's get back to the car fast and beat the crowd."

The first summer we were allowed to go, I was eleven, and Joaquin and I rode down to the beach on our bikes, a smile plastered on my face. I was filled with the sheer, delicious delight of being let out of the house without Mami. Let out of the house to do something cool. I'm not sure how Joaquin convinced her to let me come along, but he did. How fun it was to spend the holiday with so many people, even if it was crowded and sometimes hard to find a seat.

I imagine the Callahans are spending this evening on the upper deck of their home in Point Isabel with a direct, private view of the fireworks. Matthew and Jennifer are probably dressed in crisp white shorts and red-and-white-striped T-shirts that cost more than my entire wardrobe. Maybe Mrs. Callahan has tied a big blue bow around Jennifer's light blond curls, which even at eight still hold the softness of baby hair, so soft the headbands and hairbands I try to place there often slip out and go missing. I can picture Mr. Callahan, laid out on a deck chair looking all super prep, the *Wall Street Journal* resting open in his lap. He admires Mrs. Callahan's tan, trim figure dressed in pink and green pastels as she makes cocktails. It's so bonkers that Mami would think Mr. Callahan is cheating on Mrs. Callahan. She's a bombshell, and so nice and sweet. Sure he's gone a lot, but it's so he can work hard providing for his family. In my heart, I know he and Mrs. Callahan will be together forever.

It may not be an upper deck in Point Isabel for us, but I hope Joaquin and I are getting to the beach early enough to get a good viewing spot for the fireworks. It's a Friday night, so everything feels like it could be just that much more exciting. Joaquin is supposed to meet up with Amy. I managed to sneak a phone call to J.C. during Mami's afternoon nap, and in between a long list of chores she wanted me to tackle, so I could meet up with him, too. I imagine kissing J.C. under the fireworks—far away from Joaquin and his girlfriend, of course. I imagine it will feel cinematic and thrilling. But first we have to pick up Amy, and I have to get into the back seat of our Honda like a passenger in a cab.

"Hey," Amy says, sliding into the front. She gives my brother a quick peck on the lips as I glance outside, embarrassed. "You're Elena, right?" she asks, peering over her shoulder at me. She's wearing black lipstick.

"Yeah, hey," I say.

"I've seen you in the halls at prison," she says, then laughs at herself. Joaquin laughs, too, maybe a little too loudly. I laugh a few beats too late, missing the joke. School might be a prison to Amy, but I'm pretty sure Amy's able to come and go from her house whenever she pleases, so she actually doesn't know what she's talking about.

The two of them disappear into their own whispered world, Amy digging through Joaquin's cassettes and commenting on them. I stare out the window, trying to glimpse my reflection, wanting to look pretty for J.C. I grab the hairbrush I brought with me and run it through my hair a few final times. At last Joaquin finds a parking spot, and we hike toward the beach, Joaquin and Amy in front of me. She reaches out and grasps his hand easily, naturally. Joaquin glances over at her and smiles, happy. Amy might be weird, but I want my brother to be happy. If he's happy, maybe he'll stay.

"Is it okay if we don't stick together?" I ask as we arrive at the beach. I scan near the lifeguard stand where I told J.C. I would meet him.

"As long as you meet me by the car right after," Joaquin says. "And don't do anything dumb."

Amy shoves Joaquin in the ribs with her elbow. "Stop being so protective. Your little sister is entitled to a boy-friend, you know." She sends me a wink in solidarity. I can't tell if I feel embarrassed or pleased she knows about J.C. and even called him my boyfriend. But I manage a glance of gratitude and I promise I'll meet them at the car right after. Then I slip my flip-flops off and head across the sand, looking for J.C.

I spot him where I'd told him to meet me, but he doesn't notice me approaching. He's leaning against the tipped-over lifeguard stand, talking to another guy in board shorts and a white tank top who looks about his age. People are milling about everywhere—families with kids, young couples, old people struggling with their folding chairs. Everyone is try-ing to stake out the best spot for watching the fireworks. But through the moving bodies, I spy J.C. palming something the other guy hands him before slipping something out of his own pocket—it looks like a rolled-up plastic bag—and sliding it to the other guy in one practiced movement. He glances around like a bad spy in an old movie. He still doesn't notice me even though by now I'm just a few yards away.

The other guy nods and disappears into the crowd, and I finally reach J.C. and touch him lightly on the shoulder. He jumps and turns to face me.

"Hey!" he says, too excited. He slides his arms around me

and kisses me on my neck, and I lose myself in the good feeling for a minute. But I can't blank out what I've just seen. "Hey," I answer. "Who was that guy you were talking to?"

J.C. shrugs. "Just some dude from the beach. He knows Michelle, too, I think." I blink, trying to refocus on the images in my mind. I know what I saw. But then I look at J.C. At his anxious, sloppy grin. His broad shoulders. His sweet, dark eyes. Maybe he sells pot, fine. The truth is, it's probably better for you than alcohol. J.C. never gets mean and nasty when he's high like Mami does when she's drunk. And if alcohol is legal, why isn't pot?

"Why don't we find a place to sit down?" I ask, grabbing his hand, an act that still feels exciting and new. As the sun starts to set and dusk settles over us, we hunt down our ideal spot and spread out the ratty blanket I've brought along.

"Is Michelle around?" I ask.

"Haven't seen her," says J.C. He's got a plastic bag with two Tall Boys, each wrapped in a small paper sack. He hands me one and I open it. I realize I didn't really make plans to find Michelle this year even though normally she watches the fireworks with me and Joaquin. Guilt seeps through me. I haven't been good at keeping up with Michelle these past few weeks, and I miss her. I know it's because of J.C. But Michelle will understand, I think, that I'm lucky to have a boyfriend at all. Besides, once school starts up again, J.C. could leave. I tell myself that Michelle will cut me some slack.

J.C. takes a sip from his can and leans back on his elbows.

I drink down half the can as fast as I can, trying to ignore the taste. A soft numbness starts to settle over me. The image of J.C. and the guy by the lifeguard stand gets hazier in my mind. J.C. is so good-looking. So funny. And he likes me.

"Hey," he says, knocking his knee into mine. "Where'd you get that scar?" He points to a faded white line on my chin, lets his finger graze alongside it until I shiver.

"Oh, that," I answer. "I got it wrestling with tigers at the Houston Zoo."

J.C. startles and looks at me, his brow furrowed. "What the hell?"

"Uh, I mean I got it parachuting out of a helicopter over a remote part of the Sahara Desert." I grin.

"Are you fucked-up?" J.C. asks with a snort. "What the hell are you talking about?"

"It's just a game," I say, taking a sip from my beer. "My brother and I used to play it. Sometimes we still do. We used to make up stories about our scars. I don't know how it started." I do, actually, but that's not a story for tonight. Or maybe ever.

"So you just came up with bullshit for fun?"

"Yeah," I say, and I tell J.C. how Joaquin and I played the game when we were younger, stuck in front of the television on Saturdays, bored out of our minds while Mami nursed a hangover or forced herself out of the house to do the grocery shopping. The scar from the time I burned my forearm on the oven became the time I defended myself from a rabid dog roaming the streets of our neighborhood. The patchy white circle on Joaquin's knee from the time he had a wart removed transformed into the bite of an anaconda that he wrestled with his own bare hands while on a solo safari. The slim, crooked gash on my calf that had healed into a rubbery mark was no longer from running into the coffee table but due to a street fight between me and whatever scary presence was on the television news—Richard Ramirez, Gaddafi, some nameless Communist.

"That story almost makes me wish I had a brother or sister," J.C. says when I finish talking. He drains his beer. "But really. How did you get the scar on your chin?"

I find my fingers resting there. The scar is so faded I can barely feel it. I tell J.C. that I don't remember how I got it, and he believes me.

When it's finally dark enough for the fireworks to start, J.C. and I cuddle up together. He kisses me and then, with a wink, he slowly reaches under my T-shirt and tucks his hand possessively around my left breast. His thumb worms its way inside my bra and he grazes my nipple once. Twice. My body grows warm and something pulses deep inside me.

"This okay?" he whispers into my ear. I nod because I can't speak.

"I wish we could get away from here," he says. His thumb moves again, gentle but sure.

"Me too," I manage.

"We can walk back to my apartment from here, you know," he says.

"Yeah," I say, my face buried in his chest. "I know."

Suddenly, I hear a burst in the sky and a collective gasp of happiness. A little girl's voice calls out, "Mommy, they're starting!"

J.C. doesn't wait for me to agree with him, really. He just stands up, and I find myself numbly following him through the crowd, stepping on other people's blankets, getting annoyed mutterings from strangers. I only know J.C. wants to take me to his place and I need to follow. He has my hand in his, tugging me along. Wordlessly, we walk the block to his apartment, the smell of cheap fast food and salt water consuming the air. Cracks split the sky behind me, followed by a chorus of *ooohs*, but I don't even look back as I make my way up the stairs and inside.

• • •

By the time I get back to the car, Joaquin is fuming and Amy is half a block up the street, I guess looking for me.

"Where the hell have you been?" my brother snaps. He hollers at Amy that I'm back before turning his full attention on me. A troop of teenage boys walk by—they look like tourists in their pressed Polos and Chinos—and they erupt into laughter at my expense. "Someone's in trooooooubbble," one of them singsongs.

"I'm sorry, Joaquin," I say, "the time just got away from us." And I am sorry. I really am. I thought I would be able to hear the fireworks end from J.C.'s apartment, and maybe I could have if I'd tried, but it was like I was lost in some fever dream once I got inside his place. We didn't go all the way or anything, but it was the closest we'd ever gotten. Just thinking about it makes my heart start to race, and I have to look down at my feet. It's too embarrassing to have those thoughts in the vicinity of my older brother.

"Jesus, I thought something happened to you," he says, his voice furious. Guilt rips through me. I check my watch. It's way past ten o'clock. I wonder if Mami is awake and wondering where we are. My heart still races but in a bad way now.

"When did the fireworks end?" I ask.

"Almost half an hour ago," Joaquin snaps as Amy catches up with us, her face glowing with sweat under the streetlight.

"Hey," she says, out of breath.

"Sorry you had to go looking for me," I say.

"No problem. Joaquin wanted to do it, but I told him to wait by the car and calm down. I thought if he found you he might really lose his shit." She knocks into my brother a bit and smiles. Under the glow of the streetlamps, her white teeth look even whiter against her black lipstick. "Come on, cut your baby sister some slack." She tugs him toward the car, effectively ending the conversation between Joaquin and me. I meekly slide into the back seat.

"I gotta drop Amy off first," Joaquin says in a gruff voice, and he drives toward her neighborhood. I peer out the window at mothers sitting on porch steps of bungalows and cottages, dressed in tank tops and denim cutoffs and smoking cigarettes. This area is working-class like ours. Little kids chase each other around in postage stamp–sized front yards, burnt sparklers clutched in their hands like magic wands. Joaquin parks in front of an old but tidy house and wordlessly gets out. Amy starts to follow but turns toward me first, smiling. "Hope you had fun with your boyfriend," she says.

"Thanks," I answer, hoping I don't sound like some dumb kid.

I realize once they've gotten out of the car that Joaquin has parked a house away from Amy's place. He doesn't want me to watch him walk her to her front door. A few minutes later, he's back. When he opens the driver's side door he says, "You can get in the front seat, you know."

"It's fine back here." I'm still embarrassed. Plus I know Joaquin is angry and I don't like it when he's angry at me. I frown. Any good feeling in my body leftover from J.C. has long since evaporated.

"So where'd you go anyway?" Joaquin starts, making eye contact with me in the rearview mirror. I look away. "And don't tell me you spent the entire time watching fireworks."

I sigh and cross my arms. "We just went back to his apartment for a while to hang out."

Joaquin snorts. "I'll bet," he says, shaking his head.

"Just stop. I said I was sorry."

"Fine."

We continue the rest of the drive in silence until we finally arrive home. I look at our house. The lights are off, and for that I'm grateful. Mami should be passed out at least.

Joaquin parks the car but he doesn't turn the engine off. He shifts into park, letting it idle.

"What?" I ask, bracing myself.

"I just wanted to know . . . why didn't he walk you to the car at least?"

"Huh?"

"Cut the crap, Elena. Why didn't J.C. walk you back to the car tonight?"

"I don't know," I answer. I reach for the door handle, trying to signal that this conversation is over.

"Look, it's fine if you don't want to answer," he says, finally cutting the engine and turning around so I can see his full face. "All I'm saying is he should have. That's all. A guy should walk the girl home. To the door, to the car. Whatever. Just know that, okay? That's what a guy should do."

I fume and roll my eyes. "Fine," I say. "It's not like he didn't want to. He did, and I told him not to worry about it." I open the door.

"Sure, Elena," he says, his voice withering.

"Joaquin, can we just go inside now?"

He glances up at the house. "Lights are off. Hopefully she's out cold."

"Yeah," I say, grateful for the change in subject.

"All right, let's go," he says, and we make our way out of the car, the sound of the gravel driveway crunching under our tennis shoes. As Joaquin unlocks the front door, it occurs to me I didn't see a single firework all night. I guess there's always next year.

CHAPTER NINE

MICHELLE HAS TO BE PISSED AT ME ABOUT NOT MEET-
ing her for fireworks. It's Sunday midmorning after the Fourth
of July, and I snuck a call to her house while Mami was nap-
ping after Mass, but her stepdad said she couldn't come to the
phone. I don't think Michelle has ever tried that excuse with
me, not even once.

I think about sneaking a call to J.C., too, but I don't want
to seem too desperate, not since the Fourth of July was just
two nights ago.

I have a babysitting job with the Callahans later because Mr.
and Mrs. Callahan are going out to dinner. I have it all set in
my mind. I'm going to take the kids to the chintzy boardwalk
and we'll get funnel cakes or soft serve or maybe both. Then
I'll let Matthew and Jennifer play some games at the arcade.
Afterward, I'll tuck them in and read them *Mrs. Piggle-Wiggle*

and do all the voices until they laugh so hard that Jennifer has to run to the bathroom before she wets the bed. They love Mrs. Piggle-Wiggle so much. I do, too, to be honest. I used to check those books out on the rare times Mami would take us to the library. The Callahan kids don't have to check them out—they own the full set.

I told Mr. Callahan he could pick me up at seven thirty, but I can tell Mami they need me after lunch. That way I can get away early, before my job, so I can go and try to see Michelle before heading back for Mr. Callahan.

And then I can see J.C., too.

I hold my breath at the thought and think back to the two of us in his apartment during the fireworks. His hands on my skin. The scent of him. I exhale. J.C. makes me feel hungry. It's the only word I can think of to describe it.

No, not hungry—starved.

Mami exits her bedroom and I hope I'm not blushing. She squeezes her eyes shut and then opens them wide. Then she sighs, like she's disappointed. We've lived in this crummy house since I was three years old, but I think Mami still believes that one day she'll wake up and it will be different.

"Where's your brother?" she asks, peering around.

"Work," I say.

Mami nods and walks toward the coffee table, straightening up a few coasters and some magazines.

"This place is a mess," she mutters.

"I'll help," I offer, and I refold the already-folded quilt that rests on the back of the couch and plump up the thrift-store throw pillows that forever need to be plumped.

"Have you cleaned out your closet recently like I told you to?" she asks, crossing the room toward the kitchen to make herself a drink.

"Yes," I lie. "Last week. I took the stuff over to the Callahans so they could give it to their cleaning lady for her daughter." Mami likes giving to charity. Joaquin says it makes her feel superior. The truth is, when we were small there were a few Christmases when some of our toys came from the church. I only knew because Joaquin told me. His friend Billy Goodwin's family had donated an Erector set and the Hungry Hungry Hippos game just for us, he said. I think Joaquin was embarrassed. At the time, I was too little to care, just mad that we had to play Hungry Hippos on the porch because Mami said it made too much noise.

Mami sits at the kitchen table and sips her drink, staring out at nothing. I tense, anticipating the worst.

"So what has your brother said to you about moving to California?" she asks at last. I walk to the kitchen to get the glass cleaner and a rag to start on the living room windows. My heart is in my throat.

"So what has he said?" she tries again.

"Well, I think maybe . . . he mentioned it?" I start, spraying Windex and closing my eyes so the mist doesn't accidentally burn them. Mami is always doing this—trying to get information from one of us about the other. Joaquin is better at playing dumb. Me, not so much. Mami knows this weakness of mine. She preys on it.

"What do you mean you *think* he mentioned it? I overheard you two talking about it the other day." She pauses to sip her drink. "You think I don't hear things through that door but I can." Ice rattles in the glass. Almost time for a refill. I don't know how she can drink that stuff so quickly.

"I meant that I think he mentioned it once, like, maybe visiting?"

"Visiting or moving there?"

"I'm not sure which one."

Long pause.

"Why would he do that?"

She knows. She knows and she wants me to say it. Silence looms over us. She's not going to give up until I answer.

"I think," I start, bracing myself, "I think that maybe he wants to track down our father."

Silence again. I scrub at the already sparkling window until it squeaks like a mouse.

"I don't know what he thinks he's going to find," Mami says. "The last address I have for the man is from 1974." It's more of an invitation to actual conversation than I'm used to with her.

"Yeah," I say, seeing an opening at last and turning to look at her. "I don't know why he would bother. I mean, I don't know why he's so excited to look for the man who abandoned us."

Mami offers me a rare smile. The brief moment of pleasing

141

her is a rush, like the first bite of dessert. She gets up for another drink.

"You're exactly right," she says, her back toward me now, her head in the freezer hunting for ice. "It's why I have my rules, Elena. It's why I want to protect you. I don't want the same thing to happen to you that happened to me. To have your life damaged by some man."

"I know, but Mami, don't say I said anything," I plead, while I have the chance. "I don't want Joaquin to be mad I told you."

"Not a word," Mami says, enjoying the conspiracy. She fills her drink and comes back to the table, then sits down again and swirls the drink with the tip of her pinkie.

"By the way, I have to leave in a bit for a babysitting job," I say, taking advantage of her good mood. "Mrs. Callahan wants me to take the kids to the beach before she and Mr. Callahan go out for dinner."

"That's fine," Mami says, filling me with relief. "How are they?" she asks. "The Callahans?"

"Well," I begin, "I think you're right about Mr. Callahan having an affair." This isn't true, of course. But Mami loves the gossip. Especially gossip that tarnishes the Callahans' charmed existence. And she's so happy with me right now it might be nice to give her one more reason to stay glad.

"Really?" she asks, arching an eyebrow.

"Yes," I say. "When I sat for them the last time, Mrs. Callahan came home almost crying, and it seemed like they were in the middle of a fight. And when Mr. Callahan drove me home, he smoked, like, three cigarettes and told me marriage was hard work."

Mami scowls. "Smoking is such a filthy habit."

"I know," I say, nodding vigorously.

"Do you think he smokes around the children?" she asks, concerned.

"Not sure, but the way things are going, maybe." I feel guilty, actually, throwing Mr. Callahan under the bus like this. He would never smoke a cigarette or tell me his marriage was anything but amazing. I can tell he thinks so from the way the Callahans always come home holding hands or the way he kisses Mrs. Callahan softly on the cheek before he drives me home after a babysitting job. I mean, who kisses his wife before doing some short little errand like taking the babysitter home? But Mr. Callahan does.

Still, this sort of gossip could give me permission to have this babysitting job for as long as I want. So I offer a silent apology to Mr. Callahan.

"Well, hopefully they'll work it out," Mami says. It's the right thing for her to say, she knows. But I know she hopes otherwise. For her, other people's disasters are something delicious. Suddenly, she jumps on a different angle.

"Do they ever ask about me?" she asks. "I mean, do they know I came from a good family in Cuba? *Una buena familia?*"

"Oh, of course," I say, and I can see Mami puffing up a bit. "I told Mrs. Callahan about your *quince* once when she mentioned Jennifer having her debut one day at their club in

Houston. She said it sounded so glamorous." This isn't true, of course. Why would I want to bore the Callahans with stories about my reclusive mother? But I know Mami thinking the Callahans believe she is high-class like them will score points.

"I can't imagine any debutante ball in this country could match my *quince*," Mami demurs, "but I'm sure they'll have a lovely party."

"I'm sure," I say, proud of myself for putting her in such a good mood. "But I've got to get ready to leave. Mr. Callahan will be picking me up soon."

"Fine," Mami says, draining her glass. "But leave the Windex out. I can see you missed a spot."

• • •

I take the city bus to Michelle's house. She's my best friend, and I should come over here more often. But Mami's restrictions make that too hard—especially during the school year.

"Elena, how lovely to see you," Michelle's mom says, opening the front door. Her brown curls streaked with gray are pulled back into a banana clip, and she has a baby on her hip— Michelle's niece Ashley. Ashley sucks at her fingers. She's covered in something green.

"We're trying peas for the first time," she says, stepping back to let me in. "It's not proving to be a favorite."

I offer up a soft laugh and walk into the entryway, feeling awkward. I catch a glimpse of the kitchen down the hall. The table is covered with newspapers and empty cups. The sink is full of dishes. Mami would spaz out. But Michelle's mom is relaxed. Mami says Michelle's mom lets her daughters get away with murder, which is why Michelle's older sister worked as a dancer and got pregnant with Ashley without being married. The thing is, I know Michelle's mom wasn't thrilled with the news. Michelle says their mother cried when her sister announced she was pregnant, before she insisted that Michelle's sister move back home so they could help her raise the baby.

I also know that Michelle can tell her mother anything, because Michelle has admitted as much to me, and I know that her mom is always kissing Michelle on the head and telling her what a great kid she is—even though whenever she does Michelle acts annoyed and tells her mom to stop acting weird.

"She's upstairs in her bedroom," Michelle's mom tells me, so I climb the steps, dodging piles of folded laundry and books and shoes waiting patiently for someone to give in and take them to their proper homes.

Anxious, I tap at the door covered with a huge poster of Journey. Joaquin once told me Journey was Satan's soundtrack in hell. But Michelle loves that band.

"Mom?" comes a muffled voice over music playing.

"No, it's Elena."

Long pause. I've missed Michelle. Even though I have J.C. now, I'd be lost without my oldest friend. The long pause grows longer. What if she doesn't let me in?

"Come on, Michelle. Please open up."

Finally, the door swings open. Michelle is dressed in a ratty T-shirt and jeans, her summertime tan a thing to envy. She raises an eyebrow at me, but I know the moment she looks at me she can't stay mad. Relief floods through me.

"You're lucky I'm letting you in," she says, motioning me through the doorway and flopping on her unmade bed. Michelle's room is a disaster, like the rest of the house. A half-full bowl of cereal sits on her cluttered dresser. Mountains of clothes are heaped onto the back of a ratty pink armchair she found deserted in an alley and talked her mother into letting her keep. The carpeted floor is filled with teetering stacks of cassettes and music magazines and chewing-gum wrappers.

I push aside some of the clothes and curl up on the armchair. Michelle leans over to lower the volume on the stereo next to her bed.

"Michelle, I'm sorry," I say, frowning.

"That's a start," she says, her legs dangling off her twin bed, her face turned toward the ceiling.

"I got sidetracked."

"You mean you got laid," she snaps.

I gasp and throw a dirty T-shirt at her. "Michelle, shut up. You know I'm still a virgin." The atmosphere warms. Michelle sits up, a smirk on her face. We're going to be okay.

"Like a *virgin*, virgin, or just, like, you know . . . a *technical* virgin?" Michelle asks, curling up in a ball and raising an eyebrow at me again. It's her signature move, one I've loved since we were kids in elementary school.

"Whatever," I say, shaking my head. "Don't be gross."

"Look, if you can't talk about doing it, then don't do it."

"So how is it you talk about doing it, like, all the time, and you've *never* done it!" I shout back, but I'm laughing and so is Michelle.

"I bet your brother's done it. With that girl Amy."

"Gross!" I shriek, squeezing my eyes shut. "Gross, gross, gross!" I don't want to think about my brother's sex life and whether or not it exists.

Michelle is laughing harder now. Her torturing me is part of the payback she's earned for me ditching her on Friday. Once we settle down, she throws me a stick of gum from the collection on her nightstand and takes one for herself. After a few chomps in silence, she grows serious.

"So I guess stuff with J.C. is . . . intense?" she asks.

I shrug. "I guess." Without stopping to think, I say, "I think he sells pot."

"Oh, I know he does," Michelle answers, not skipping a beat.

"Yeah?"

"Yeah. Lots of the kids down at the beach buy from him."

I curl my knees up to my chin. J.C. is risky. And exciting. It's like the pot stuff should bother me, but I just can't get myself to care that much.

"He's the best kisser ever," I say, ready to change the topic. "I mean, you wouldn't believe."

Michelle rolls her eyes. "Based on how much experience?"

"Enough," I say.

"Tara Morgan's cousin during spin the bottle? Not sure that counts."

"It wasn't nothing," I fire back. "He put his tongue in my mouth."

Michelle mocks gagging and falls over. I throw another T-shirt her way, and then we sit in silence again, chewing our gum. I hear the shrieks of the little neighbor kids next door running up and down the alley behind Michelle's house. *"Olly olly oxen free!"*

"So how'd you get out of the fortress anyway?" Michelle asks. "You haven't been to my house since spring break."

"I told Mami I have a babysitting gig."

"A babysitting gig."

"Yeah," I say. "Hey, turn it up. I like this song."

Michelle complies, and we lie there, chewing our gum and listening to music over the sounds of the kids outside. When the song is over, Michelle sits up and rewinds the cassette so we can listen to it again. When it's done, she leans over and ejects the tape.

"Elena, when it comes to J.C. . . . you'll be . . . careful, right?" she asks, her eyebrows furrowing slightly. Her voice is soft. Uncertain.

I stare at the girl who gets why I can never sleep over at

her house or go to parties during the school year or talk on the phone whenever I want. At the girl who puts up with me despite all of that and who doesn't make fun of me. Who still somehow thinks I'm cool and funny. Who still wants to hang out with me. My best and oldest friend.

"Yes, Michelle," I answer. "I'll be careful." But I'm not sure what she means. Careful not to get my heart broken? Careful because J.C. deals drugs? Careful not to get pregnant? Just the thought of that last question fills me with a strange mix of anxiety and excitement that makes my body remember J.C.'s apartment on the Fourth of July.

"So do you have time to eat before you have to leave?" Michelle asks, bringing me out of my J.C. daze. "We could heat up a frozen pizza or something."

I check my watch. I have time. "Sure," I say.

"I could curl your hair all pretty, too," she offers, smiling. "Before you go."

"I'll be the prettiest babysitter on Mariposa Island," I say, grinning back.

"You'll be the prettiest something," she says, her smile turning into a smirk as she slides off the bed and heads for the door. I catch up to her and bump her hip as we clamber down the stairs to the kitchen.

"Hey, maybe we can do a full makeover," I suggest. "That could be fun. And I never get to do that stuff." Michelle has access to all her sister's makeup—eyeliner and mascara and stuff I'm never allowed to buy.

We head to the kitchen, past the family room where Michelle's mom is watching television and playing blocks with Ashley. "Sure, we can do a makeover," answers Michelle. "But what would your mother say?"

"I'll wash it off before I get home," I tell her. "You know my motto. What she doesn't know won't hurt her."

"Now *that*," Michelle says, pulling open the freezer to hunt down our pizza, "is the understatement of the year."

CARIDAD

UNITED STATES

1961

What struck Caridad was how quickly a person could get used to something if she had to, if she absolutely must. And how strange time was. How one moment she could be sleeping in her own soft bed with soft cotton sheets washed daily and the ocean waters of the Atlantic only yards away, and how the next moment she could find herself still near that ocean water, only now in a featureless building in South Florida, sleeping on the top of a bunk bed with a mattress so uncomfortable Caridad had to learn how to curl herself up just to avoid the pokes of the springs. She learned how to block out the murmurs and snores of the girl who slept underneath her, too, and the way the security light on the side of the building shone in from dusk until dawn.

What she could not learn was how to enjoy the milk in

paper cartons that was served for breakfast, lunch, and dinner. It smelled used and foul to Caridad, who still remembered the thick, creamy taste of the fresh milk Juanita would pour for her after it was delivered to the back steps each morning by a man in a white uniform. In the dining room at the camp, Caridad would sit with other girls and rub her fingers along the blue-and-white cartons, moist on the outside from being stored in tubs of ice to stay cold. She would give her milk to one of the other girls, and she didn't even ask for a trade. There was a girl named Blanca who guzzled the milk happily and seemed to be one of the few girls putting on weight, while Caridad and the others struggled to keep meat on their bones, picking through the unfamiliar food with their forks, sliding the tines over the plates slowly as if something more delicious could be dug up underneath.

Blanca was enthusiastic about learning English, unlike Caridad. Blanca was younger, and that made a difference. Her mouth mastered words and didn't trip on the *B*s and the *V*s or the *on*s and the *in*s. Blanca's eyes smiled as she perfectly executed words like *Florida* and *popcorn* and *shampoo*. She was a star pupil during lessons, and Caridad stoked the resentment inside of her and remembered the academic medals the Ursuline nuns had given her back in Cuba, pinned onto a sash she could drape over her uniform. She'd had to leave those medals behind along with almost everything else.

The camp was only temporary, Caridad learned. Longer

than the thirty days her parents had promised her, but still only a few months. Soon, she was told, she would get to leave the place with the bunk beds and the security light and the foul milk and Little Miss Perfect Blanca, and she would move to a new place. Texas. One of the guardians who worked at the camp unfolded a paper map of the United States and put one finger on Miami and another on a dot halfway across the country.

"There, that is where you are going," the woman said, her voice slow and loud. "You are going to a town called Healy." Caridad wished she could find a way to tell this woman that speaking more loudly didn't help her understand English.

The guardians who looked after them at the camp soon took her shopping for new clothes. Really they were used clothes, purchased at a thrift store. Images of her closet in Cuba filled with smart dresses and outfits tailored to fit only her crept into her mind, but Caridad pressed her lips together and nodded at every item the guardian pulled out. The white blouse with the yellowing collar. The circle skirt that had faded from forest-green to lime. The sad little socks. Caridad simply nodded—what else could she do?

Inside she fumed.

There were sporadic phone calls with her parents. They were few and far between and could only last a few minutes, and she had to strain to hear her parents' voices, tinny through the static. Caridad tried to connect the sounds she heard with the physical objects she knew her parents were close to when they spoke with her. The silver ashtray shaped like a seashell. The large picture window that faced the street. The ceiling fan circling slowly above like a curious vulture. Picturing these things made her parents' voices seem more real. Actual.

¿Cómo estás, preciosa?

Estoy bien.

¿Estás comiendo bien?

Sí, muy bien.

Their conversations felt rehearsed and strange, with topics limited to the superficial and mundane. The new maid's cooking. The weather in Havana. A neighbor falling ill with the flu. Only by picturing objects she remembered from her home back in Cuba could Caridad convince herself the phone calls were even real. A silver ashtray shaped like a seashell. A picture window. A ceiling fan. Her mother's voice.

The day she left for Healy, Texas, Caridad packed her duffle with her thrift-store clothes and stared out the airplane window while the girl next to her—another girl from the camp who was headed to another town in Texas—silently wiped tears from her eyes and twisted her fingers together and sniffed. Caridad ignored her. What was happening to her was what was happening to her, and there was nothing that could be done about it. She was going to a place called Healy, and this could not be changed. Better to let life's wave push her forward and not fight it. Better to survive.

The girl on the plane next to her sniffed and sniffled, but

Caridad shifted in her seat and turned her back to the girl, ignoring her. Even though she knew the girl's cries signaled she needed someone to talk to, Caridad wondered how she could block out the noise for the entire flight. Because honestly, what could she possibly say?

· · ·

The room was off the kitchen. That was what really bothered her. It was not even a proper bedroom but some storage room that had been put together into a fake bedroom, and haphazardly, too. Heinous yellow paint had been slapped on the walls—she supposed they thought it made the space look cheerful. Worn-out sheets and a tired quilt rested on the twin bed, and two windows overlooked the backyard, which was a patch of dirt with a rusty swing set where the little children in the family played.

There were five children in the Finney family, most of them younger than her and full of scraped knees and snotty noses, and Caridad was immediately overwhelmed by the voices and the movement and the faces and the too-eager toothy smiles and the loud English sentences spoken over and over again.

How nice to meet you!

We are glad you are here!

What can we do for you?

If you need anything, just let us know!

She was supposed to be grateful. This Caridad knew. She

was supposed to be grateful for the fact that she had a roof over her head and a space of her own, when she knew that some of her campmates were being sent to orphanages. To places where there were no private bedrooms, not even off the kitchen.

So Caridad did her best to smile and nod, and when Frank, the oldest Finney boy, helped her with her duffel she smiled widely at him, and she tried to be grateful that his face was not too bad-looking at all but pleasant enough with big brown eyes and good teeth. She nodded eagerly at the dinner table and took bites of the thing they called meat loaf, and when she was asked to help clear the table and do the dishes, she did not balk, not even when she had to be taught how to scrape the chewed on, saliva-covered meat loaf leftovers into a Tupperware dish for safekeeping before carefully soaping up, rinsing, and drying each dish. Not even when her mind was flooded with thoughts of Juanita serving her family dinner in her starched white uniform. Not even then.

What happens when your language is stripped away from you? You learn a new language, and soon Caridad found herself speaking in English and even thinking in English sometimes, skipping the exhausting step of translating in her head. She enrolled in Healy High and navigated classes, and after school the sweet Mrs. Morelli next door helped tutor her even though she was a newlywed just a few years older than Caridad herself. After school Caridad would walk over to the Morelli house and enjoy the quiet and comfort of being in a space with only one other person, and she would linger in Mrs. Morelli's neat and spacious kitchen with the yellow gingham curtains and she would practice conjugating verbs and reciting sentences.

I go.

I went.

I have gone.

English was a ridiculous language, Caridad decided, but somehow, with Mrs. Morelli's help and the constant, never-ending chatter of the Finney children, she began to absorb it. When Frank asked her to go on a walk one evening after dinner a few months after her arrival, she said "Yes" in English without even stopping to think about it. It was simply the word that came out. Its appearance startled her. *Yes.*

They walked the streets of Healy, the spring heat spilling over them. It was a stickier, more consuming heat than the heat Caridad had known in Cuba, without any ocean breezes nearby providing any sort of relief, and she hated it. She walked with her hands folded behind her, her head held high.

"I'm glad you are here with us, Caridad," Frank said, choosing his words with care. Caridad could sense she made him nervous. She couldn't explain why, exactly, but she liked that she did.

"Call me Carrie," said Caridad. It was what the teachers at Healy High called her. It was easier than Caridad, more

161

American. And Caridad liked how it split her in two, saving her better name for her better Cuban self, which existed somehow, somewhere, in the recesses of American Carrie's mind.

"Okay, Carrie, if you're sure," said Frank.

They bumbled along, filling the air between them with stupid patter and silly comments, and when Frank tugged her hand and pulled her behind an oak tree and kissed her, his dry, overeager lips moving awkwardly against her own, Caridad couldn't help but let her mind wander to images of Ricardo back in Cuba. Handsome and self-assured. Smart and good-looking. And from such a good family, too. Caridad knew if she'd been given the chance to kiss him, it wouldn't have been like this—rushed, clumsy, and stupid. But Ricardo was dead and she was here, so she leaned back against the tree and had her first kiss with an American boy named Frank. She still could not believe this was her real life. But it was.

•　•　•

The phone calls with her parents became fewer and further between. There were letters, but they dwindled. The sentences her mother crafted in dark black script seemed forced and formulaic, all about how much they missed her and how the weather was on the island. Caridad spent hours sorting through the old photographs she'd been able to bring with her, her eyes lingering on those taken the afternoon of her *quince* by a professional photographer her parents had hired to come to their home.

She spent nights sitting up in her fake bedroom, staring out at the yard, imagining she could hear the ocean. Hoping one day she would return even though she knew, somehow, in every cell of her body that she would never see Cuba again. Sometimes, late at night and gripped by insomnia, Caridad would dig out a bottle of glass cleaner and a rag from under the kitchen sink and scrub down the eight square panes of glass in the windows that looked out to the yard, remembering how Juanita would clean the kitchen windows without leaving behind a single streak. Caridad would clean the windows in her bedroom once and then clean them again. The quiet, easy motions and the simplicity of the act soothed her.

She went to classes at Healy High. She studied with Mrs. Morelli next door. She had no real friends because she made no space for them. It grew harder to fake niceness. She loathed every moment she had to spend washing the dirty, spit-covered dishes of the little Finney children. She despised every time Mrs. Finney cheerfully asked her to "pitch in" and carry out the garbage or feed the toothless old mutt the Finneys treasured as if he were an actual member of the family when all he was to Caridad was a stinky, dirty dog. None of her daily routine provided the solace that cleaning her own windows over and over again offered.

She allowed anger and resentment to fester inside her and never scab over.

On weekends Frank would take her on walks and to the diner downtown, and in the car he would paw at her while music played on the radio, but he never pushed it. He seemed in awe of her. Overly eager. Caridad enjoyed the power she felt when she was with him even if she didn't enjoy him as a person very much.

"You're a lot of fun to be around," Frank would tell her before he shoved his tongue in her mouth. In these moments Caridad would sometimes recall the warnings of her grandmother back in Cuba, who, before she passed away, liked to warn Caridad that a young woman should stay pure like a fine piece of Baccarat crystal until her wedding day. But like so many memories of Cuba, her grandmother's words were becoming hazy, slipping from her memory no matter how hard she tried to hang on to them.

One weekend a little over a year after her arrival in the United States, Caridad was called into the den by Mr. and Mrs. Finney. When Caridad walked in, she was surprised to see Father O'Dell from the parish sitting on the sad little green couch with the weird stain on the arm that Mrs. Finney tried to cover with ugly, homemade doilies. Mrs. Finney was sitting next to him, her eyes watery and lined in pink. Mr. Finney was seated in the armchair and his mouth was set in a firm line. He had his hands clasped in his lap, but it was like he couldn't find a comfortable position. He kept clasping and unclasping, and then he coughed.

Caridad's body went numb.

"Carrie, why don't you sit down?" Mrs. Finney said, patting the couch cushion the same way she did when she wanted the toothless, stinky mutt to join her. Caridad went and sat down, crossing her legs at the ankles. She recalled the little *salita* back home and Juanita and pink lemonade and the silver ashtray shaped like a seashell. She willed herself to be there again.

And then the priest was speaking and Mrs. Finney was crying and Mr. Finney was moving his hands over and over again and coughing. God, why couldn't he at least stop coughing?

There's been some confusion coming from out of Cuba.

They spoke of her homeland like it was some strange spot on a map—not a real place.

Carrie, we have to tell you something that is going to be difficult to hear.

Her mother's Pall Malls and the sweet smell of Arpège.

The latest reports seem to indicate that something has happened to your parents.

Dancing with her handsome father at the *quince* before it was all over. The strained expression on his face as she stared at him through the fishbowl before getting on the plane.

We have received confirmation that they are no longer alive.

Not dead, Caridad noted. Simply no longer alive. How clever language could be. Even a stupid language like English.

There were more words about the pro-Batista movement and being turned in and neighbors reporting on neighbors, but it all slid past Caridad. She could not absorb it.

Mrs. Finney reached out to touch her, but Caridad flinched and Mrs. Finney drew back.

"When did this happen?" Caridad asked. She wished for tears so she could feel something, but there were none.

"Well, we've heard reports for a few months now, but we didn't know for certain until very recently," the priest said.

Caridad blinked hard at the priest. She took a breath.

"You knew?" Caridad said, finally feeling something at last. Anger. "You knew there was a chance they might be dead and you didn't say anything to me?"

"Carrie, we wanted to be sure, and the reports are not always reliable," Mrs. Finney said.

"But you knew there was a chance of trouble? That something was going on?" she demanded. How good it felt to have someone to direct her anger toward. She clenched her fists and pounded them into the couch. How dare they. How dare these stupid people let her walk around for weeks—for *months*—allowing Frank Finney to maul her in his car, making her do their filthy dishes, letting her stare out the window into the backyard and dream of her homeland, and all the time they knew the truth about her mother and father.

"You should have told me!" she shouted. Caridad never shouted. Her loud voice sounded strange, even to her.

"We wanted to keep you happy for as long as we could," Mrs. Finney said, her pale, pancake face offering up a weak, dumb smile.

Caridad stared at her. Happy. Mrs. Finney thought she was happy.

Mr. Finney coughed again. Why was he even in the room, Caridad wondered? He was the most useless one of them all.

Mrs. Finney was leaning back now, away from Caridad. Caridad could read her distance as displeasure. She was supposed to be grateful to Mrs. Finney. This she knew. She was supposed to be grateful and show emotions and sob into Mrs. Finney's arms because Mrs. Finney had shown her Christian kindness. But Caridad would not give her the satisfaction.

"Perhaps we should pray," said Father O'Dell, and only because she knew her mother would have wanted her to, Caridad bowed her head and tuned out while the priest spoke of loss and God's wisdom and who knows what else.

When he was finished, Caridad gathered herself and stood.

"I need to be by myself," she told them. "Leave me alone."

And with that she walked back toward the kitchen into her sad little bedroom and shut the door. She lay facedown on the quilt that served as her bedspread, the smell of cheap detergent impossible to ignore. Her mind was flooded with images of Juanita. Of clean sheets. Of *agua de violetas*. Of the island life that was due to her—that had been her birthright—and that had been stripped away from her.

And only then did she allow herself to cry.

ELENA

CHAPTER TEN

MAMI'S FACE SCREWED UP WITH DOUBT WHEN I FIRST brought it up about a week after the Fourth of July, so tonight I wait until at least her second rum and cola before I ask her about Mr. and Mrs. Callahan wanting me to spend the night on Saturday so they can attend a fundraising dinner in Houston and have a little getaway, just the two of them. I claim they are probably trying to work on their marriage.

"You alone with the kids in the house? What if something happens?"

"Mami, what's going to happen on Point Isabel?" I say. "It's a gated community and there's a guard there all night. They're going to pay me extra."

Mami scowls and my heart sinks. *Please please please let her say yes. I'll never want anything else in this life if she just says yes.*

"I don't know about this," Mami says. She stands up to head toward the kitchen, probably to refresh her drink.

"I'll do it," I say, reaching for her glass. She swats me away, and I stand awkward and hopeful in the no-man's-land between the den and the kitchen, facing her back as she mixes another cocktail.

"You know, my parents were very well-off, but they always spent time with me," she says to the rum bottle. *Glug glug clink clink.* "I never wanted for anything, but they didn't dump me with the help all the time. *Qué barbaridad.*"

I hold my breath. There's no right response when she brings up Cuba. I know she's going to say no, and I realize how reckless I've become when I start thinking there might be a way to sneak out all night. But then she slams the refrigerator and turns around, sliding her pinkie into the drink and giving it a quick swirl before taking a swallow. Then she looks at me again, her eyes hard.

"Fine, you can go. I suppose if you don't do it those poor little children will have no one."

I resist the urge to shoot my eyebrows up in shock, agreeing with her that I'm the kids' only hope and promising to call her after they're in bed.

"Okay," she says. "You'd better."

The next day when Joaquin gets home from work, I'm packing my overnight bag and Mami is in her cocoon of a room, drink on the nightstand, romance novel in hand.

"I've got a babysitting job overnight," I tell him, zipping

open my school backpack and dumping out crumpled left-over papers that are trapped at the bottom. I wish I had a duffel bag or something normal to pack my stuff in, but I don't.

"Overnight?" Joaquin says, shifting his weight against the doorframe. I look at him and he's eyeing me carefully. I can't tell if he's mad or anxious or just surprised, and I have an urge to try to reassure him about the whole thing. But I don't. It's my life, I tell myself, looking down at my bag. And my heart is thrumming with possibilities.

"Yeah, the Callahans are going to Houston for a fundraising dinner and . . ." I start.

"Elena, Mami's not even here to hear you," he interrupts.

I ignore him and open my top dresser drawer where I keep my underwear and pajamas. This would be easier without Joaquin standing three feet behind me.

"Can you just let me pack?" I say, not turning around. My fingers pause on my favorite bra. A soft pink one that clasps at the front. My cheeks warm.

"I'm home tonight if you need anything," he says. "Just, you know . . . call."

"I told her I'd call after the kids are in bed," I answer. My thumb grazes the bra's clasp and my head gets swimmy with images that make my cheeks get even hotter. I really want Joaquin to leave.

"Okay," says Joaquin.

"Can you shut the door?" I ask, hoping he gets the hint.

I finally manage to look over my shoulder. Joaquin is chewing on his thumbnail, an old habit that Mami tried to break when he was little by making him soak his fingers in vinegar so they'd taste too nasty to chew on. It didn't work, but I never knew if it was because Joaquin didn't mind the vinegar or if he kept biting them anyway just to spite her.

"Fine, I'll shut the door, your highness," Joaquin says, taking his thumb out of his mouth and giving me a half bow. I sneer at him, but I don't really care what he says if he leaves me alone so I can focus on packing.

Twenty minutes later and five minutes before Mr. Callahan is supposed to pick me up, I hover outside Mami's door, my backpack slung over one shoulder. Saying goodbye might not be such a safe idea. What if she changes her mind at the last second? Still, I know she's awake, because I can't hear her usual soft snores.

"Mami?" I say, rapping lightly on the door.

"You leaving, *mija?*" she asks. "Come in for a moment."

I swallow hard, my mouth suddenly dry, and I turn the knob, peeking my head in. She's on her stomach in her nightgown, her novel tossed to the side. A half-empty tumbler sits on the nightstand. On the pillow in front of her are a few old black-and-white snapshots from Cuba that she likes to paw through every once in a while, usually after her third or fourth cocktail. Her favorite pictures are of her in her *quince* dress, which she wore on the night of her fifteenth birthday party. She always talks about that magical evening as one of the best nights of her life.

"Mr. Callahan should be here any minute," I say, hesitating.

"Did I ever show you this photo of your *abuela*?" Mami asks, ignoring me. She always refers to her mother as my *abuela*, like we had some personal connection. Like we spent Saturdays baking cookies and doing other things grandmothers do. Or that I think grandmothers do—not having any grandparents I really wouldn't know. Anyway, I wish she would just refer to her mother as her mother. It's creepy otherwise.

Mami rolls over onto her side and hands me an 8 x 12 photograph of a stunning woman seated on a couch with her legs crossed at the ankles. I've seen it before, and every time I look at it, I selfishly hope there's a trace of this strange person's high cheekbones and big eyes in my own face.

"She was so beautiful," I say. It's what Mami likes to hear, but it's actually true.

"Mm-hmm," Mami says, nodding. "And she never got old, so she never got ugly, either. Not like me." She runs her fingers through her dark, dyed hair.

"You're not ugly, Mami." I glance at my watch. I'm supposed to get picked up in two minutes.

"Please. You have to say that," she spits, snatching her mother's photograph from my hands.

"No, I don't," I say, straining to sound sincere. Mami was beautiful once. But she's turned into something hard and sharp, her complexion full of tiny broken blood vessels and scowls.

She pats the photograph gently and looks at it for a moment, then glances back at me. She leans over and grabs her drink, takes a swallow or two.

I've got one more minute to get out of here.

"Your *abuela* was beautiful, but she was a lady," she says, setting her glass down, taking her time. "Always a lady. She used to tell me that a lady keeps herself like a fine piece of Baccarat crystal until her wedding day."

"Yes," I say. "I remember you telling me that."

"You do?" she says, suspicious. "You remember me telling you that?"

Of course I do. She's mentioned it hundreds of times.

"Yes, you've told me before, Mami. Listen, I'd better . . ."

"Well if you remember it, then you'd better live it, *mija*," she says, cutting me off. "Nobody likes a whore."

My eyes widen. Mami never uses words like that. She seems to realize it, too, because she smirks at me like she's a little kid caught doing something naughty.

"I'll call you," I say. I don't kiss her or hug her goodbye. It's not what we do. Instead, I turn and hurry out, heading toward the front door. Joaquin is on the couch drinking a beer and watching television.

"You'll call?" he says, not looking up.

"Yeah," I say. "Don't worry."

And I get the hell out of there.

• • •

J.C. is grinning when I slide into the car at the corner of Esperanza and Fifteenth. He leans in and kisses me, ignoring the fact that he's blocking traffic. A car honks but he doesn't stop until he wants to.

"Don't say hey or anything," I tell him, tossing my backpack into the microscopic back seat of the VW. But I'm grinning as I say it.

"Hey," he says with a wink, and I melt inside. He's so good-looking I still can't believe he likes me. He pulls into traffic and checks his watch. "I just gotta make one pit stop and then I'm yours all night." The words *all night* make my stomach flip, but I'm ready for whatever happens next. It's time to grow up a little.

I wish we didn't have to do the pit stop though. I know it's to sell pot. Part of me wishes he would just tell me, but maybe he thinks it would mess up the romantic vibe if he did. When he climbs the steps of the Surf's Up apartments two at a time and leaves me sitting in the car, windows down so I don't get too hot, I find myself counting to a hundred over and over again to busy my brain until he reappears.

All night. I'm yours all night.

After he comes bounding down the steps, that irresistible grin on his face, we swing by Tony's Pizza to get a pie. The sun is just beginning to settle when we get to his apartment and head upstairs.

"Where's your roommate?" I ask as we walk inside.

"Went to Austin for the weekend to visit his parents," J.C. says, sliding the pizza on the counter and turning around and kissing me in one swift motion. His hands slide down to my hips and he pulls me close. He's kissing me like he can't get enough. My entire body softens.

"I'm really glad you're here," he whispers when we finally stop to catch our breath.

"Me too," I say. And then I can't help it. I lean in and kiss him right back. I kiss him like I might never get the chance to kiss him again, fiercely and full of desperation. My fingers travel to the hem of his black T-shirt. I sneak my hands underneath and slide them all the way up his chest. His skin is smooth and warm.

"Whoa," J.C. says, pulling back but just barely. "This is nice."

I don't have the words or the witty banter. I only have this night. This chance. I pull him toward me and suddenly he's sliding his shirt off over his head in one swift motion, dropping it into a puddle at his feet. I'm hungry for him, kissing his neck, his shoulders, tasting sunscreen and salt.

"Elena," he says, and his voice has changed from playful to something husky. Needy. "Are you . . . sure?"

I answer by pulling him back toward the bedroom. He follows wordlessly, and soon we are on his unmade bed with the mismatched sheets next to the nightstand covered in empty beer cans and rolling papers, surrounded by mostly plain white walls—the only decoration a painting of a beach at sunset that looks far prettier than any actual beach on Mariposa Island.

"I'm sure," I say, and I look him right in the eyes so he knows I mean it.

"We can go as slow as you want," J.C. says, his voice so soft and sweet and dreamy, and I think how good it is that this is happening with him, with this older boy, a boy who has experience, a boy who has his own apartment, a boy who seems to like me a whole lot.

"Okay" is all I can manage to say in barely a whisper. *This is really happening*, I think to myself. *This is really happening*. And the next thing I know, clothes are sliding off and losing themselves in the sheets and hands are searching, reaching—mine hesitantly, his much more confidently. I try to take in every moment, every sound—even the sound of the air conditioner cycling on and off and the honks of distant traffic on Esperanza Boulevard. I need to document this in my mind. To know it's real.

And soon, much sooner than I expected, I'm on my back, crossing into unknowable territory from which there is no return.

So I close my eyes and give in.

•   •   •

Afterward, J.C. gets the pizza from the kitchen and it's still pretty warm, and we sit in the middle of the bed naked and eat pizza and drink beer and I giggle a little when J.C. gives me knowing looks. We don't talk much, but it's okay. It's not as weird as I thought it might be. I mean, it's a little weird. But mostly good. Then I go to the bathroom and stare at myself in the spittle-covered medicine cabinet mirror.

"You just had sex," I whisper to my reflection. Then I start laughing at myself, so loud I have to clamp a hand down to shut myself up before J.C. overhears and thinks I've lost it completely. I crinkle up my nose at the dirty toilet and wipe it down with some wadded-up toilet paper. It hurts a little to pee and there's the smallest bit of blood. I hope that's normal. I can't wait to dissect all of this with Michelle, but at the same time I don't know what she's going to think about this happening with J.C. in the first place. Maybe I just won't tell her.

I crawl back into bed and J.C. stops eating to give me a kiss.

"You're so pretty, Elena," he says, and I smile and fantasize about running away from home and holing up in this crummy apartment forever, cleaning it up and living on minimum wage because we don't need much anyway if we have each other. Of course that's probably ridiculous, but I still think it.

After we finish eating, I check my wristwatch—it's so weird that I'm totally naked except for my watch.

"I should probably call home," I say, even though I really don't want to. I pull the bedroom extension onto the bed, take a deep breath, and punch in my home number. I twist the cord in my fingers as I listen to the tinny ring.

"Hello?" It's Joaquin.

"Hey," I answer. I close my eyes, hoping it will make the conversation feel less weird, like a baby who closes her eyes and thinks she's invisible.

"Hey," he says. "You okay?"

"Yeah, fine." I can hear J.C. lighting a cigarette next to me. I wonder if the click of the lighter and his sharp inhale are loud enough to make it through to the other end of the line.

"Is Mami there?" I ask.

"Yeah, hang on," he says. There's a pause and then her voice. The same voice that always calls to check and make sure I'm wiping down the baseboards or ironing the shirts or cleaning out the refrigerator. *Well, not this time, mother.*

"What's going on over there?" she asks. I imagine her standing in the kitchen, drink in hand.

And I imagine myself in the Callahans' fancy Point Isabel mansion, talking on the living room extension while seated in the middle of the white leather couch, sipping brand-name soda.

"The kids are asleep," I say. "They were so heartbroken their parents were gone. It's really sad, just like you said." She likes hearing she's right.

"I told you," Mami answers, and now we're conspirators, so it'll be okay.

"They're supposed to be back tomorrow around lunchtime," I tell her. I hear J.C. take another drag and I shift away from him just in case. "I can call you first thing tomorrow morning."

"All right, yes, do that."

"Well, I should go check on them," I say.

"They were very upset, weren't they?" she asks. She's enjoying this.

"Oh, they cried and cried when Mr. and Mrs. Callahan left. It was sort of a scene."

Mami *cluck clucks*. It's enough to satisfy her, and at last I can hang up the phone and hand it back to J.C., who is sitting next to me, eyeing me with a bemused grin.

"Drama at the Callahans?" he asks, stubbing out his cigarette in the ashtray by his nightstand before slipping his arm around my waist. He is all the right parts of warm and heavy and soft and strong. His fingertips graze my navel.

"Oh, totally," I answer, collapsing into his arms as he curls up around me. He kisses the back of my neck and I shiver.

"Do you think she'll ever figure it out?" he asks.

I tense up, not expecting that question. "Sometimes . . ." I manage, "sometimes I wonder if she already knows."

"You mean that they don't even exist?"

I startle. J.C. has just spoken a truth so rarely acknowledged by the two other people who know it—Joaquin and Michelle—that hearing it out loud unsettles me. I'm glad J.C. can't see my face. I'm sure my eyes are wider than a lost child's. Finally, I come up with an answer. "Sometimes I think she *has* to know," I say. "But I also think she likes believing they're real."

J.C. laughs softly into my neck and it irritates me. It's not something I can laugh at.

I've worked so hard to create the Callahans. I know Jennifer's and Matthew's birthdays and allergies. I know the layout of their Point Isabel home and even sketched it out once in a journal I keep hidden in my closet. I know exactly how they look, too—they're the spitting image of Michelle's cousin's

179

kids who visited from Corpus Christi last summer—the ones I took a Polaroid of to show Mami.

I know which pediatrician's office they use when they're on the island and what sorority Mrs. Callahan was in at UT, and I know that Mr. Callahan proposed to Mrs. Callahan in his parents' living room in Houston, just the two of them under the Christmas tree, Mrs. Callahan's pretty eyes twinkling like the tiny white lights that encircled the Virginia pine.

I know all of this because I invented them, and I invented them so I could have all of this—a boy's arms around me and his lips near my neck. A few hours out in the world every summer.

A normal girl's life.

"I'm lost," J.C. says, not letting go of the question. He pulls back and props himself up on his shoulder, and I roll over onto my back so we can look at each other if we want. But I don't look at him yet. J.C. keeps talking. "If you think your mom has caught on that you've been lying all this time, why would she want to believe the Callahans are real?"

My gaze traces the crooked, light brown circles in the ceiling—water marks from old leaks. I chew on J.C.'s question before finally answering.

"Because I think the Callahans being real is, like, proof to her that she's actually a really good mother," I say. "She can tell herself she wouldn't do anything like leave her kids with a sitter all day long and ignore them during what's supposed to be family vacation time. And she can tell herself that just because the Callahans are rich, that doesn't mean they're better than her." I pause. "I actually think she kind of likes that they're rich. She grew up rich, in Cuba. Maybe she hopes somehow it will rub off on me." I train my eyes on the water marks. I've never said these things out loud, not even to Joaquin.

"That's kind of fucked-up," J.C. says, and blink like I had forgotten he was there. Like I thought I was alone.

I finally glance over and make eye contact. "Yeah, I guess it is."

J.C. ponders this for a moment, then he sits up. "I'm gonna make a drink," he says. "Want one?"

"Sure," I say. He slides off the bed. I would have liked a quick kiss goodbye, but of course he's just going to the kitchen. Soon I hear the familiar sounds of making cocktails—*plink plunks* of ice, *glug glugs* of alcohol, *fizz pops* of soda cans. I picture Mami in our kitchen back home, making her own drink, mixing it with her pinkie, taking that first sip. I picture Joaquin holed up in his bedroom listening to one of his moody bands, staring at a map of California. Dreaming of leaving us as soon as he can, even if he won't admit it's what he wants.

And I even picture Mr. and Mrs. Callahan, the two of them more beautiful than beautiful, kinder than kind. I imagine them tucked together on their white leather couch, their own drinks in hand, smiling as they talk about Matthew and Jennifer and what silly and wonderful things they did on the beach that day. Mrs. Callahan sips white wine. Mr. Callahan kisses her neck just like J.C. kisses mine. Maybe he's even a better kisser than J.C. After all, he's older, so he's had more experience.

I realize I'm smiling as I think of them, of the Callahans, of the family I invented so carefully. So tenderly. I think of them so safe in their house on Point Isabel, tucked away like dolls in a dollhouse, always there for me whenever I need them, always ready to help me spread my wings and be free.

JOAQUIN FINNEY

MARIPOSA ISLAND, TEXAS

1986

CHAPTER ELEVEN

AMY MITCHELL TASTES LIKE PEPPERMINT AND PARLIA-ments, smells like Aqua Net and vanilla, and—even during her busiest shifts at El Mirador—she walks as slow as Christmas, her ass shifting left–right with every casual drag of her feet.

When Carlos hired her at El Mirador in May, I couldn't help but grab a peek every once in a while, and then I'd immediately feel like a creep for doing it. I'm not some sort of eunuch or whatever, but I sure as hell don't like to think of myself as a creep.

I kind of trained myself to stop it, but one time she walked past me while I was doing some side work at the bar and she spun around at the worst possible moment, like she just knew she would catch me in the act. I shifted my gaze back to the utensils I was wrapping up in bright red cloth napkins, but I was too late.

"Looking is free but touching will cost you," she said in a singsong voice, and loudly, too, so loud that even Miguel the busboy overheard and cracked up. I didn't say anything—I just blushed. But I played that line over a few hundred times in my head, that's for sure. *Looking is free but touching will cost you.* Just hearing it in my head turned me on.

It wasn't long after that when I got a mixtape slipped into my locker in the break room. Written on the spine was *xoxoAmy*, and it was filled with songs by Social Distortion and Black Flag and Really Red.

Amy Mitchell is so fucking cool.

The first time I kissed her was a week or so after she gave me the mixtape, when she invited me to her house after our afternoon shift. Her parents were at work, she said, and her little brother was at a friend's house.

I thought she'd be all aggressive and punk rock or whatever, but when we got to her place, we made scrambled eggs together and she was quieter than I expected. I actually thought she might be nervous from the way she kept twisting up her mouth and running her fingers through her short black hair. It didn't seem possible that I was the one who was making her nervous, but maybe I was, and when I realized that all of a sudden, I became relaxed. Something about seeing her in her own house with the crappy, cracked linoleum floor and the avocado-green refrigerator covered in finger-paint pictures by her little brother made her less intimidating. And she wasn't that good of a cook, either, as it turned out, so I had to help her.

"Is it weird we're making sad scrambled eggs when we could have had a Tex-Mex lunch for free?" she asked, sliding my eggs onto a plate from the frying pan.

"I guess we're rebels," I said, my voice deadpan. "We live and die by our own rules." And Amy had laughed so hard she'd snorted. That's the other thing about Amy Mitchell. She thinks I'm funny. Maybe I am when I'm with her.

It wasn't long after the eggs that Amy asked me if I wanted to listen to music in her room. We sat cross-legged on her blue shag carpet and we played some Minor Threat and the Circle Jerks, and I started writing her a playlist of songs so I could make her a mixtape, and at one point during a 7 Seconds song we looked at each other and sort of leaned in and my hand slid up around the back of her neck and we were kissing and then we were on the carpet and then we were making out.

The shag rug left red marks on our backs, but I didn't care. Being with Amy Mitchell felt so fucking good.

It still does, too, weeks later. On days like today, the two of us in Amy's bedroom, in Amy's bed, I'm still sort of in awe that it's real, even though I know every detail of the space by now—the band posters tacked up above us and the rows of black nail polish on her nightstand and the stacks of paperback novels and spiral notebooks and cassette tapes taking up every inch of free space.

"I have to get home," I say eventually, and I roll over onto my back and slide on my jeans. I've dumped Mami on Elena all morning, making up some lie that I needed to help Carlos with something. Guilt saddles me. With a sigh, Amy sits up, her cheeks red. She pulls on her T-shirt. With supreme effort I sit up, too. If I don't, I'll never leave.

"Wanna hang out after our shift tonight?" she asks, blinking hard, like she needs to remember exactly where she is.

"Yeah, sure," I say, running my fingers through my hair, my body on fire. Just then I hear a sound coming from the other side of Amy's shut bedroom door, and Amy and I make eye contact. Her blue eyes are wide in panic.

"Shit, my mom is home early," she whispers.

"The closet?" I manage, my heart thrumming hard.

"The window!" she answers and shoves me in that general direction.

"Amy!" comes a muffled woman's voice from down the hall. *Fuck fuck fuck.*

Struggling, Amy and I manage to jam open the beat-up aluminum frame, and I toss myself out, landing on my back into some bushes. Amy sticks her head out, her eyes still wide, but this time her bright red mouth open and laughing. She tosses my shoes out one at a time, and I dodge so they don't hit my head. Then I grin back widely from the bushes, stand up, and dust myself off. Amy shuts the window above me. I take a deep, shaky breath. We pulled it off.

I slip on my shoes and haul my bike from its hiding spot at the side of Amy's house and head home, my mind full of Amy. Amy's lips. Amy's breasts. Amy's body. The way Amy smells and laughs and how she knows the best bands and the weirdest books and how being with her makes me so happy. Happier than I've been maybe in my whole life.

Not that the bar's super high or anything. I'm not in such an Amy haze that I can't objectively see that.

"Watch it, asshole!" comes a voice behind me. I swerve to miss an old Dodge with a loose understanding of what it means to share the road with bicycles. I like the way the wind cuts through my hair and makes me feel wide-awake when I bike, but I sure as hell wouldn't mind owning my own car. Even an old Dodge. It would get me out of this shitty Texas heat, for one thing.

Elena is sitting on the porch steps when I roll into our driveway. She's picking at her fingernails.

"Don't go inside," she warns me, her face a scowl.

"Why?" I say even though I can guess the answer. I look at my kid sister more carefully. She isn't wearing any shoes and is dressed in a ratty red-and-white T-shirt that used to belong to me back when I was on the track team at LBJ. I hope that means she isn't planning on going out with that idiot douchebag anytime soon.

"Mami is being a bitch," Elena mutters, leaning over to pick at a mosquito bite on her ankle.

It must be bad for Elena to say that. She's better at deflecting. Or ignoring. Or pretending, if you want to describe it most accurately.

I lay my bike on its side right there in our joke of a front yard and sit down next to her. "What happened?" I peek over my shoulder to make sure we're not being spied on. You never know. Mami's so tiny she can creep up on you without a sound—even when she's loaded. I slide a thumb into my mouth and chew on my thumbnail absentmindedly.

"She's super drunk, and I didn't clean the baseboards right," Elena says glumly, staring at the street in front of us. "She cursed me out in Spanish and made me scrub the same spot for, like, five minutes."

"What are baseboards?" I ask. I wish I had a beer right now. Maybe I could grab one from the fridge really fast without being noticed. I imagine a slippery cold can in my hand and how good it would taste while we're trapped outside in this ninety-something-degree weather.

"What are baseboards?" Elena answers, her voice incredulous. She turns her dark eyes toward me like missiles. "See, that's what I'm talking about. You think I would be able to do whatever I want if I spoke my mind, but you're not stuck cleaning baseboards, because she doesn't think that's a boy's job! You're off boning your girlfriend or whatever."

"Jesus, Elena, please," I say. "Enough." I don't want to discuss Amy with my sister. I want to keep all that separate. Just mine. But Elena rolls her eyes and exhales. "Tell me I'm wrong, then," she mutters. "Tell me you're not boning your girlfriend."

"Elena."

"Fine," she says, giving in and dropping her chin into her

hands. "But you're still not here cleaning baseboards." The thin white scar just under her mouth is visible through her splayed fingers. I push down the fear and guilt that percolates whenever I get a good look at it.

"You're right," I pause. Elena doesn't look at me, but I can see her shoulders soften a little with my apology, so I continue. "You have it harder than I do. I'm sorry."

"We just have to wait a while for her to pass out," she says. "Then I'm off babysitting anyway."

I lean back against our porch steps. I have to be careful not to push things, given her mood. But I also can't say nothing because I worry about her. She's my baby sister.

"Where is he taking you?" I ask.

Elena shrugs. "I don't know. Just out somewhere. Probably the movies."

"Okay," I say, even though I know she's lying. Even though I know this guy probably considers a six-pack and the couch in his crummy apartment a date. Even though I use my hard-earned El Mirador money to take Amy out to the movies or to Putt-Putt once in a while because it's what you do if you're a fucking halfway decent guy. I wish I could say all this to Elena, but she's on edge and anyway, she's not going to listen.

The two of us sit out there for a while, not talking. Just sitting. When it feels like it's been long enough, I climb the steps to the screened-in porch and slide my head inside the house to survey the den and kitchen. The lights are dimmed. It's sticky inside because the air isn't working well—it never does during the peak of the summer. The kitchen clock plods on, the ticktock the only sound to be heard over the hum of the fridge.

My breathing tightens. My senses sharpen. But there's no dark lump on the couch. There's no scowling face staring out from the recliner. I spot Elena's beat-up pink flip-flops in the corner and snatch them up quickly, like a kid on an Easter egg hunt.

"She must be passed out in her room," I say, turning back and heading out toward the land of the living. I toss the flip-flops in Elena's direction.

"Well then, it's our lucky day," she tells me, standing up and stretching her arms out wide. Her answer is laughable and we both know it, but the truth is that when it comes to luck, we take it where we can get it.

"Let's go for a walk," I say, motioning toward the flip-flops.

Elena gives me a look. "Okay, but no heavy-duty conversations, okay? I'm not in the mood."

"We'll just talk about the weather, I swear."

We head off down the sidewalk, past other clapboard homes in varying stages of disrepair. When we were tiny kids in grade school and Mami got irritated with us and made us leave the house so she wouldn't have to look at us, Elena and I would take walks around the block, estimating how many rotations we would need to make before we could safely venture back inside. Once we guessed too early and were greeted with a shoe flying at our heads. After that, we always added on one more round, just to be safe.

"No heavy-duty conversations like I promised," I start, "but do you need money for tonight?"

Elena scowls a little, embarrassed. She wants to say yes but is ashamed to. I should have just slipped her the money like I normally do.

"Only if you have some to spare," she says at last, quietly.

"Okay," I say.

I'd have more money earning interest at the credit union if I wasn't bankrolling my sister all summer, but there's no other way for her to have spending money, so it doesn't bug me too much. I once overheard Elena casually explaining to Mami that Mr. Callahan was investing most of her babysitting money in a special fund to pay for nursing school. This impressed Mami and stopped her from asking too many questions. I don't think it's occurred to Elena that this lie will catch up with her eventually. Or, if it has, she's chosen to ignore it along with so much else.

After a few circles around in silence, we reach our front door again. Elena steps back, lets me go in first like when we were kids.

"She's still out cold," I report back, like a soldier on reconnaissance.

Elena nods and follows me inside. As we step into the kitchen, I remember the money and I slip her a five-dollar bill. She folds it carefully and shoves it in her back pocket, then shoots me a grateful smile.

"If I don't need it, I'll give it back," she promises.

"Keep it," I tell her. "You might need it later on."

• • •

Elena may have made up her job, but I have a real one to go to. Mami is still dead to the world when I head out for my shift. Elena is in the bathroom putting on makeup to hang out with J.C. The faucet is dripping again, and I make a mental note to take a look at it before Mami gets on me about it.

I hate thinking of Elena spending time with that idiot douchebag from the beach. It was easier when she was just using the Callahans to spend time with that ditz Michelle and go to lame keggers. Just normal teenage girl stuff that she's never allowed to do. But now it's this J.C. creep. I know I've never really met him, but I just don't like the guy.

On the bike ride to work, I think about Elena and J.C. and Mami and the baseboards and Amy and California and the hazy, unknown future ahead of me.

I pedal harder down Esperanza Boulevard. I can't wait to get to work to take my mind off shit. I should ask Carlos for some extra shifts.

But that means leaving Elena home alone more often with Mami.

But if I move to California, then Elena will be home alone with Mami all the time.

And if I leave for California, I won't see Amy anymore, either.

Fuck fuck fuck.

By the time I make it to the restaurant I could really use a beer, but when I walk in, the smell of queso and enchiladas verdes and warm tortillas takes over my senses, and I calm down a little. The tiny white Christmas lights hanging low over the bar twinkle at me as if saying hello. Antonio Aguilar is playing on the stereo, his voice trembling over the swell of trumpets.

"Hey, man," says Carlos from the bar, where he's mixing a drink for one of our regulars. "Good to see you."

"Good to see you, too," I say, heading toward the employee break room for my apron.

"Hey!" shouts a familiar voice behind me. Amy.

"Hey," I say, smiling before I even turn around to find her coming out of the kitchen, wiping her hands on her apron. She leans in and gives me a peck on the cheek. "I still can't believe we didn't get caught this afternoon," she whispers into my ear. Her warm breath tickles. I feel an ache in my chest.

"I know," I say. "My stealth moves saved the day."

She pulls back and her face cracks wide open into a beautiful smile, and we're standing there staring at each other like idiots until Carlos coughs a little too loudly and says, "Okay, you two, break it up over there, there's work to be done."

"Okay, *Dad*," Amy answers, sneering for good measure. Carlos laughs at that and so does the regular at the bar and so does Amy and so do I, and even after I've made my way into the staff room and I'm all alone and sliding on my apron, I realize I'm still grinning so hard my face hurts.

CHAPTER TWELVE

WE STILL GO TO MASS. I DON'T THINK OF MAMI AS PAR-
ticularly religious or anything. Sometimes we pray before
meals but only when she feels like it. She has a small picture
of the Virgin Mary that Elena bought her at a church bazaar
hanging in her room, but that's it in terms of religious stuff
around the house. She doesn't correct us if we say "Oh my
God!" but she'll be all over us for any other curse, unless she's
the one who decides to curse, of course.

I asked her once when we were kids why we went to
church at all.

"I went to Mass when I was a little girl in Cuba, and I'll go
to Mass now," she told me. That didn't really explain to me
why Elena and I had to go, but that's how Mami is. It's her
world. We're just living in it.

So we still go to Mass almost every Sunday, and when we

were little Elena and I had to go to CCD classes before Mass in the classrooms at the Catholic school. We would sit with the other public-school kids and try to mess around with the stuff in the Catholic school-kids' desks while volunteer mothers from the parish with eager smiles and rosy cheeks trained us in making our First Confessions and First Communions. I still remember the itchy, used, blue polyester suit I wore the first time I received the Eucharist and the way I kept rubbing my sweaty palms on my pants as I made my way up the aisle to receive the wafer or—as the priest and the overeager volunteer mothers would say—the body of Jesus Christ himself.

"You look very handsome," Mami had told me as she snapped my picture on the front porch that morning. Mami's compliments are as rare as Texas snowstorms, so that one is stuck in my brain. I don't know what happened to the card from the drugstore with the five dollars inside that she gave me after Mass was over and we went to El Mirador for a rare restaurant lunch. I don't think I saved it.

Maybe the morning I made my First Communion I was seated here, in this very pew, midway down the aisle from the altar. Elena would have been a kindergartner back then, and now she's almost seventeen, sitting next to me, flipping through the hymnal as Father Harrison drones on through the homily. A serious look on her face, Elena tips the open, red leather-covered book toward me slyly and points to a page so I can catch the title—"How Great Thou Art." Only some kid at some point in the past had penciled in an *F* before the *Art*.

Elena and I make eye contact and I offer her a grin and a roll of the eyes, and Elena has to slip a hand over her mouth so she doesn't let loose with a laugh.

From next to Elena, Mami coughs pointedly, and Elena shuts the hymnal and sets it down. Father Harrison goes on about something, gesticulates with his old-man hands, pauses dramatically, and looks out at us with his rheumy eyes.

I can't believe that guy has never been and never will get laid. I mean, most likely. That's been my number-one thought about priests since I was in junior high—that they'll never have sex—and I feel kind of shitty that's my first thought because some of them seem like nice enough guys, but it's where my head always goes. I don't even think they're allowed to jerk off, which seems totally inhumane. My brain starts to wander to Amy Mitchell and her slow, ass-shifting walk, and I squeeze my eyes shut and give my head a little shake. I can't think about jerking off in church, and I definitely can't think about having sex with Amy Mitchell. Shit.

I probably shouldn't be cursing, either. Not even in my head.

Finally, Father Harrison is finished with the homily, and we stand and we kneel and we sit and we sing and Elena shows me "How Great Thou Fart" one more time just before the final blessing to try to make me laugh, and finally we head outside, pausing to dip our fingertips in room-temperature holy water and cross ourselves. Then Mami digs into her purse and hands me the keys to the Honda.

"You drive," she says. She might be hungover. Or maybe she just doesn't want to drive. Sometimes it's hard to tell.

"Okay," I answer.

I'm not even out of the parking lot before she starts in. "Did you see what that woman in front of us was wearing?" Mami asks. "So tacky." I try zoning out like I do with Father Harrison. You would think church would have some sort of positive impact on her. Then again, I'd be a hypocrite if I said it had any impact on me whatsoever.

"What did she have on?" Elena answers, humoring her. Probably to keep me quiet. I decide not to fight it and I blank out as Mami prattles on about a woman's short skirt not being appropriate for church. But just as I'm turning down Thirteenth Street, Mami says, "So, Joaquin, I hear you might be going to California?"

I squeeze the steering wheel and try to stay calm. Don't let her see you sweat. That's rule number one—even though I always break it eventually.

"What?" I ask, like I didn't hear her. That always pisses her off, but it's one of my signature moves—force her to repeat herself just to piss her off. I peer into the rearview mirror. Elena is staring out the back window, but her face is tight.

"I said that I heard you're going to California," Mami repeats.

I stop at a red light. The car next to me has the window rolled down and some shitty heavy metal is pouring out, so loud I can hear it inside the Honda. I don't say anything. Maybe she'll drop it.

Who am I kidding? That's Elena-level wishful thinking.

"I just thought that you would tell your mother something like that," she says. "Or were you just planning on leaving your sister and me like a thief in the night?" She's calm. Collected. She has the upper hand and she knows it.

She got it out of Elena. I know she did. Elena's so good at lying about herself, you'd think she could lie well enough to protect me. But sometimes Mami knows just how to find the soft spot and go for the kill.

"I've got no plans to go to California," I say, stepping on the accelerator as the light turns green, grateful at least to have driving to focus on.

Mami examines a fingernail and pauses, letting the tension build. "Well, that's good. Because I think if you're going to look for your father who abandoned you and your sister, that's a really stupid idea. I mean, I know you weren't an A student, but I didn't think you were that dumb."

God damn it, Elena.

I say nothing even though I want to yell *everything*. How Mami's the one who's kept information about our dad from us and how it pisses me off. How all we know is that he took off when we were tiny kids—I can barely remember anything about him, not his smell or his voice or anything—and she didn't even try to track him down. How the few pictures of him are somewhere in her bedroom, guarded protectively. It's been years since I've seen the fading square-shaped snapshots.

"Well, wouldn't you agree it's a stupid idea?" she presses,

her voice even. Calm. We're almost home. I glance in the rearview mirror again. Elena's face looks pained.

"I'm not sure what I'm doing at the end of the summer," I say. "It's just the middle of July."

"You should do what I suggested and start classes at MICC," she says. "They have a good program for radiology techs."

Mami wants me to be a radiology tech and she wants Elena to be a nurse. She's obsessed with it. She thinks they're reputable jobs, I guess, and they make good money. She's been pushing them on us since forever. When I was in fifth grade and had to do a project for career day at school, I made a big, dumb poster about being a radiology tech because I wanted to make her happy. When I got to school everyone else had put down stuff like professional football player or archaeologist or zookeeper, and I had to stand up and talk like taking X-rays was my dream.

We pull into our driveway, the tires crunching over the gravel. I can't hold it in anymore. I turn to Mami. "What's a stupid idea is thinking that I should already know what I want to do with my life. I'm eighteen. I don't know what the hell I want to be."

Mami shrugs, still in control but close to erupting. "You should go find your father," she says, picking the words that will hurt the most. "You're a lot like him. A total disappointment." She puts her hand out and I give her the keys, and she gets out of the Honda with a slam of the car door before walking inside.

"Oh shit," Elena mutters.

"Oh shit is right!" I spit, turning around toward the back seat. I know I'm a dick for yelling at Elena—it's not like I hold up under Mami interrogations any better—but Mami's not here, and I have to yell at someone.

"Why'd you tell her?" I shout. "Why'd you say anything about California?"

Elena crosses her arms tight across her chest. "I don't want to fight with you, Joaquin."

"You never want to fight," I say. "You never want to acknowledge reality, either."

"That's not fair," she says. Little splotches of red are breaking out on her face and her chest. "That's not fucking fair."

I roll my eyes. "Oh, but telling Mami I want to leave for California at the end of the summer without telling me you're going to *is* fair?"

Elena snaps and jumps forward like an angry cat. "She *heard* us talking about it one night through her bedroom door. I just confirmed it." Then she slumps back, and I can see her eyes are wet. She does hate fighting with me and Mami—she hates all conflict, really. In the end, her life is probably easier because of it. But something tells me she's going to be living in our house with Mami when she's twenty-five years old, Mami trying to control her every move, and this kills me so much I can't let myself think about it.

The Texas heat is already starting to turn the Honda into a sauna. I open the front door and Elena opens her back door.

A mosquito ventures in, curious, and circles above me. I swat at it, annoyed.

"She really overheard?" I ask, embarrassed for snapping.

"Yes," she insists, looking down at her lap. Her voice drops. "I did say that you maybe were going to look for our dad though. Don't be mad, okay?"

Her face reminds me of a little kid's, with pudgy cheeks and anxious glances. She brings a finger up to the slim, rubbery scar on her chin and picks at it. It's subconscious, I know, but my stomach knots up anyway.

"I'm not sure I could find him, you know," I tell her.

Elena nods. It's hot as Hades in here. I think of the AC pumping inside our house, but inside is where Mami is, either mixing a drink or sitting and stewing and preparing for the next round of our fight's predictable course—lots of screaming and shouting and slammed doors by both me and her. It's exhausting to think about it.

"So do you actually think he's in California?" I ask, trying to direct the conversation away from Mami, away from *us*. Elena shrugs.

"Maybe," she answers. "Not that it matters."

I draw a thumbnail to my mouth to chew on. I guess she's right. It shouldn't matter. So I don't know why I wonder about him—this man who's responsible for my physical existence. This man who dumped us before Elena could even walk or before I was speaking full sentences.

"Listen, I haven't made any decisions about leaving," I say, and at this she looks up and makes eye contact. She nods, grateful.

"I hope you stay," she says. "Even if it is for Amy and not me."

I scowl, embarrassed. "If I stay, I stay on my own terms, okay?" I haul myself out of the Honda. I need to stretch my legs, get some air.

"Fine," Elena adds, joining me outside and slamming the back-passenger door. "I'm sorry I mentioned Dad to Mami."

The casual way she says it—Dad, like he's somehow deserving of this title—makes me prickly. But I don't push it.

"I don't want to go inside," Elena says, peering toward our front screen door.

"I could use a beer," I answer.

"Joaquin, it's, like, lunchtime."

"Can't I have a beer at lunch?" I ask, and Elena laughs a light, little girl laugh, and I think maybe it's okay between us.

"Walk with me to the Stop-N-Go?" I ask. "I could get a soda at least."

"Okay," she says, glancing toward the clapboard house slumping there like it's disappointed in itself. In us. Then we start the short walk toward the Stop-N-Go, wordless. Not even walking next to each other, really, but me slightly ahead of Elena, my arms swinging at my side, my feet automatically stepping over cracks in the sidewalk.

Step on a crack, break your mother's back.

"Will you buy me a Snickers?" Elena asks.

"You don't have any babysitting money?" I tease, not turning to look at her.

"Come on, Joaquin," she says, annoyed. But I feel a push on my shoulders, gentle enough to know she thinks my joke is funny.

"I think I have enough to get you a candy bar, *hermanita*," I say, using the nickname she hates.

"Just one Snickers is all I ask," she says, making a break for it, dodging me on the sidewalk until she is ahead of me, falling into a skip, a bounce. Her dark ponytail swings, her steps are light like nothing could bother her.

Like nobody, not even once, has ever let her down.

"Come on, Joaquin," she says, annoyed. But I feel a push on my shoulders, gentle enough to know she thinks my joke is funny.

"I think I have enough to get you a candy bar, *hermanita*," I say, using the nickname she hates.

"Just one Snickers is all I ask," she says, making a break for it, dodging me on the sidewalk until she is ahead of me, falling into a skip, a bounce. Her dark ponytail swings, her steps are light like nothing could bother her.

Like nobody, not even once, has ever let her down.

CARRIE

TEXAS

1967

She said she would marry him only if he took her away from Healy. If he moved them somewhere where Carrie could smell the air coming off the ocean waters—even if it was the dingy, tired waters of the Gulf of Mexico, it would have to be better than staring at dumpy downtown Healy and the fields of nothingness that surrounded it. So the Christmas after Kennedy was killed and everything in her strange new homeland felt stranger and more off-kilter than ever, she was almost grateful when Frank dropped to one knee in the middle of Healy Park and dug clumsily into the pocket of his pants and pulled out a ring. It was the next wave that would push her forward, would give her life shape, but this time—by demanding the move, demanding Frank take her somewhere in exchange for her *yes*—Carrie felt she had some control over the wave.

She had graduated from high school and was working as a teller at the bank downtown, still sleeping in her yellow bedroom off the kitchen and waiting for Frank to come home from the University of Houston on the weekends, where he was studying nothing that seemed of any use or interest to either one of them. The Finneys charged her rent now, which she paid begrudgingly even though she knew it wasn't unfair to be asked. She was waiting for something to happen to her. And when Frank asked her to be his wife, finally, it did.

"Let's get married right away," Frank had said. "I'll take you anywhere you want to go." He was charmed by her, Carrie knew, to the point of idiocy. Charmed the way boys are by beautiful girls. So charmed he could not grasp the fact that Carrie still found him awkward and gawky, all skinny limbs and unkempt hair. His face was not so bad, though, she acknowledged, and over the years he had improved his kissing skills to the point that his kisses could sometimes even be enjoyable.

"So when can we leave Healy?" Carrie had asked, keenly aware of the weight of the new ring on her finger. Of all it could gain for her. "I want to live by the ocean."

Frank had nodded, insistent he could make it happen. And, to his word, he did. But first, there had been the matter of the wedding. Frank's parents had painted on tight smiles during the ceremony at St. Martin's with only Father O'Dell and family present. They had long since become aware of the fact that their little Cuban refugee thought she was far too good for them or their family, and what a mistake it had been to take her in in the first place. And to make everything worse, here she was, taking their son away from them. Filling his head with ridiculous ideas like dropping out of college and leaving Healy and moving to Mariposa Island, where their lovestruck, stupid oldest child promptly filled his new apartment with fancy furniture he couldn't afford.

But Carrie didn't care that Frank bought the furniture on credit or what the Finneys thought. She was happy. As happy as she could be and probably as happy as she had been since leaving Cuba. And Frank had made her so, taking her away from Healy and giving her a space she could call her own, at last. Everything felt new and possible. In the mornings Frank went to his job as a salesman at a mattress store and Carrie played house, scrubbing their little apartment until it gleamed, folding and refolding their laundry into perfect squares. Arranging cans and frozen dinners into sweet little rows. That she was no longer Caridad de la Guardia but Carrie Finney—that she'd had to trade in a name full of rococo flourishes for one that was all hard edges and sharp syllables—had seemed like a fair exchange at first, especially when she took a city bus to the beach and walked on the sand and dipped her feet in the ocean. In the beginning, it had been easier to ignore the obvious inferiority of the Mariposa Island beaches to the beaches of her homeland. Carrie even liked to imagine that the water she was touching was the exact same water she had once splashed in as a little girl in Miramar, holding hands with her *abuelita*.

For a brief time, all had been glorious.

But there was the problem of boredom. Other young wives in their apartment complex would get together in the courtyard during the afternoons and smoke cigarettes and gossip while their husbands were at work. But Caridad found them unseemly, somehow, and ignored them. A few were newlyweds, but already they had allowed themselves to grow soft and blowsy. They gained weight in their middles and under their chins. They didn't keep their hair or clothing fresh. Carrie avoided them because she didn't want to turn into some trashy housewife, but that left long stretches of time to fill even after she had cleaned the apartment from top to bottom and prepared dinner for when Frank got home. And if she let her mind wander too much, it had a tendency to travel back to Cuba. To images—increasingly fuzzy—of her parents. Of Juanita. Of the night of her doomed *quince*. She didn't like those images in her mind.

The Finneys back in Healy had allowed her to drink a glass of wine with dinner on holidays, and Carrie had enjoyed the soft warmness it had always offered her, so soon she took to purchasing bottles of cheap Merlot at the grocery store and pouring out several swallows into a juice glass while she watched the black-and-white television set they still did not own outright. She liked the buzzy, swimmy feeling the wine gave her, the way it made the passing of time more interesting, or at least more bearable. When Frank came home from work and wanted to take her directly into the bedroom, a wolfish grin on his face, she found that if she'd had a glass or two of wine beforehand, she sometimes even enjoyed it.

She didn't get pregnant right away. She worried out loud to Frank that something was wrong, but secretly, Carrie wasn't in a rush to be a mother. Not like Frank, who talked often about having a son and calling him Frank Jr.

"Maybe once we have kids and they're a little older, we can move back to Healy. Be close to my parents again, go to St. Martin's with them on Sundays. Raise the kids near their cousins." He'd said this in bed one evening after they'd slept together and he was full of possibility.

"Maybe," Carrie had answered, staring at the ceiling and wondering—worrying—what could be happening inside of her body at that very moment.

As the years began to pass, it made less and less sense to have a baby. First of all, Carrie and Frank were not compatible at all. Once the newness of married life had worn off, they realized they had little in common. Frank liked to read the newspaper, watch the evening news. He wanted to know Carrie's opinion on the situation in Vietnam. Carrie hated to talk about the news—it only depressed her. Plus, they didn't find the same things funny. They didn't like the same movies or books. Frank's awkwardness and nervousness around Carrie disappeared, taking away one of the few things about him that she had found charming. She no longer felt she had any sort of real power over him.

On top of that, they really couldn't afford a baby. They

owed money. To the furniture store. To the grocery store. To the landlord. Frank took to snapping at Carrie for spending too much on clothing and knickknacks for the house. Carrie would defend herself—she was only trying to make their home a happy one for him—but that was a lie, really. She wanted to make it happy for her, or at least bearable. The apartment was closing in on her. The landlord's cheap paint job was starting to show its wear. The women in the courtyard had babies who grew into toddlers, and soon the women would spend their afternoons outside smoking and yelling at their children, whose shrieks and whines would travel up to the dingy, impossible-to-clean windows of Carrie's second-story apartment. Carrie traded in the red wine for rum, partly because rum reminded her of Cuba, partly because it didn't stain her teeth.

And then during the summer of love, when so many young people Frank's and Carrie's ages were dropping out, running away, rejecting all the norms that Frank and Carrie were clinging to, however poorly, Carrie missed her period for the second time and she knew. She knew before the doctor confirmed it with a big wide grin on his doughy face. The entire ride back to the apartment she stared out the cloudy window of the city bus and thought about what her parents would have thought. About what Juanita would say. They all had only known her as a teenager, of course. They would be properly scandalized until Carrie explained that she was a married woman now. A married American woman with TV dinners in the freezer and not a single bottle of *agua de viole-tas* in the house.

Carrie tried to make it celebratory. She cooked Frank a nice chicken dinner to announce the news, and when she told him, blushing even as she did, he jumped up from the tiny table in the kitchenette and embraced her so tightly she almost felt guilty for being so ambivalent about all of it. And that night after Frank was in bed, she crept out into the living room and then out the front door and onto the balcony that overlooked the ratty courtyard. Suddenly, panic threatened to overtake her. Her heart started to race and her throat was closing up.

Carrie took a deep breath. She thought if she inhaled deeply enough she might be able to smell the ocean, and this might calm her even though what she would smell wouldn't be the real ocean anyway, but a poor and lacking substitute. She blinked into the dark night and clutched the balcony railing until the anxiety passed, though she couldn't breathe away the sadness that came with it. Somewhere out there in the world was her real life, the one she should be living, but the waves that had pushed her along had pushed her out too far now, and Carrie knew that she was drowning.

JOAQUIN

CHAPTER THIRTEEN

AMY OPENS THE DOOR SMILING BROADLY AND HOLDING A can of Milwaukee's Best.

"Hey," she says, and we kiss right there on the front stoop. Her lip balm tastes like cherries. When we finally pull apart, she leads me into the kitchen.

"My dad just bought a case," she says, handing me a can of beer from the fridge. "He won't notice if a few are missing."

"Thanks," I say, popping open the can. Amy leans against the kitchen counter and takes a swig, wiping her chin when some beer accidentally dribbles out of her mouth and down the front of her black T-shirt.

"I have a drinking problem, I guess," she says, then laughs out loud at her own dumb joke.

"So you're sure we have the place to ourselves?" I ask, half expecting Amy's mom to walk in, sending me running for the window again.

"Yeah, they took my little brother to visit my grandparents in Houston, and they're staying overnight," she says. "I told them I wasn't feeling well. Am I, like, the worst granddaughter in the world?"

"Yes," I say, "but you're the best girlfriend in the world."

I immediately cringe at my own words. I've never called Amy my girlfriend out loud before.

"Just come over here, you big dork," she says with a grin, and after another kiss she leads me into the den where we collapse onto the couch that has seen better days and make out for a little while. After, we drink a few more beers and Amy turns on MTV. Some big-haired band is on.

"This music is shit," Amy announces.

"I know," I say as the lead singer swivels his Spandex-covered hips and snarls. "How much do you think these guys are worth?"

"Millions, I'll bet," Amy says, rolling her eyes.

"We should drive up to Houston sometime," I say. "Try to see a show." Bands don't come to Mariposa Island very much, and there aren't that many local punk bands to speak of. I entertain the image of driving up I-45 with Amy in the passenger seat, playing whatever we want to on the tape deck.

"That would be cool," Amy says, her eyes on the television, her nose wrinkled. "We should try before the summer's over. Once school starts, I'm on fucking lockdown."

"Yeah, school," I say, my stomach knotting up. I don't like thinking about late August, when LBJ High will be back in session and my future will be laid out like some puzzle I'm supposed to solve.

"What's it matter to you?" Amy says, knocking her knees into mine and then sliding in a little closer. "You don't have to go back."

"Yeah," I acknowledge. "But if I had to go back, at least I wouldn't have to decide what the hell I was supposed to be doing next."

Amy nuzzles in even closer, and one of her hands creeps across my ribcage, tucking in tight as she rests her head on my chest. Even this basic contact with her feels good, and a crop of goose bumps breaks out on my arms. I glance at the television. The group of big-haired dudes has been replaced by a different group of big-haired dudes.

"So . . . you're still thinking California?" Amy asks the screen, her voice hesitant.

"Maybe," I say. I lean in and kiss Amy on the top of her head. "I don't want to think about it." I want Amy—and Amy's house—to be a refuge from Mami and Elena and everything that isn't Right Now With Amy. Only Amy won't let me. She tilts her face up to look at me.

"Just stick around for, like, one more year and then we can move to Austin together after I graduate," she says. "We can go to UT."

"Yeah, maybe I will," I say. I'm not sure if I'm humoring her or if I believe it's a good idea.

Amy wants to go to the University of Texas and major in

English, and after that, move to New York City and become a writer. She has it all planned out, and I bet she'll do it, too. I try to picture myself hanging around Mariposa Island for one more year, working at El Mirador, waiting for Amy to graduate, then following her to Austin. It could work. I try to imagine telling Mami this is what I'm doing. Or Elena. Would they think it's better than my leaving for California? Elena would probably just be happy that I was sticking around for one more year. *One more year*. One more year in that house with Mami skulking around, looking for a fight and me giving it to her—unless, of course, she's passed out in her bedroom. And Elena. How the hell is she going to keep seeing this J.C. guy once summer ends and her imaginary babysitting family leaves town?

I take a big swallow of my Milwaukee's Best and empty it. Immediately, I want another one, but the music video ends and Amy pushes herself up.

"Wanna go to my room?" she asks.

"Yeah," I answer.

• • •

When I think back to how Amy made me so nervous at the start of the summer, to that first afternoon when she asked me to come over and we made scrambled eggs, it almost seems laughable to me. I mean, I still get excited just being around her because she's hot and funny and smart, but the truth is, at some point over the past few weeks, hanging out with her has become pretty comfortable. Even easy. We talk a lot about music and movies. Sometimes novels. A few times I've let things slide out about my family and Mami, even though I've kept the worst of it private. I don't know why. Maybe it's just too embarrassing. The last time we hung out, I did swear her to secrecy and told her about the Callahans. She seemed sort of impressed by Elena's ability to get around Mami's rules, but I could tell she also thought it was weird—she described it as "semi-tragic." At least she didn't think my family was so strange we shouldn't keep hanging out.

Tonight, seated close to each other on her bedroom carpet, we avoid the big stuff. "What about this one?" she asks, tossing me a cassette. Amy keeps all her cassettes arranged alphabetically in shoe boxes. Her stereo is on a little stand just a few inches off the ground, so it makes sense we always end up sitting in front of it like it's our own version of a fireplace.

"That's a good one," I offer, and she pops it in. We paw through her cassettes, trading opinions and offering theories about what certain bands will do next and which ones might come through Houston. When I find the soundtrack to *Grease*, I hold it up and give her an accusing look.

"I don't care what you say," she responds in mock anger. "John Travolta is cute in that movie. And anyway, I was in junior high when I bought that."

I dramatically roll my eyes. "Please," I say. "Travolta is a poor substitute for a real man like myself."

Amy laughs out loud and shoves me gently, and I fall on my

back and pull her down with me. It's what all of this banter back and forth has been working toward, and we both know it. My body starts to buzz with anticipation.

"Hey, baby, kiss me like Danny Zuko," Amy says in a husky voice, like some vamp from an old movie.

"I'll kiss you better than Danny Zuko," I say, and she falls back down onto the carpet again. I slide on top of her, pushing away the worry that maybe I can't kiss as well as her junior high dreams of Danny. Soon we're a tangle on the shag rug, her soft mouth searching mine, her hips twitching underneath mine, making me crazy. Eventually she tugs me toward her twin bed.

Wordlessly, we slide underneath the covers. It's like a warm cocoon. Amy reaches over and tugs the blinds on her window extra tight, shutting out the last sliver of daylight. I can hear the occasional sound of a car driving by, but soon my ears become deaf to anything but our breathing and the shifting mattress underneath our bodies. It's not long before our shirts come off, and Amy's bra, and our pants, somehow. Giggling, we kick our jeans to the bottom of the bed and mine slide to the floor.

The first time Amy and I had sex a few weeks ago, I'd somehow managed the courage to whisper into her ear, "I've never done this before." She had—she dated Nico Ricci all of last school year. But she never acted like I didn't know what the hell I was doing, even though I didn't. She'd just said, "That's okay," and proceeded to help me figure it out until I forgot all about being embarrassed and nervous and instead was just thankful as hell that I was having sex with Amy Mitchell.

I kiss Amy again. My heart is hammering. My body is aching for her. I know I'm not, like, some sex expert now, but I hope, not for the first time, that I'm at least better at this than Nico Ricci.

"You want to?" I whisper, kissing her under her ear.

"I want to," Amy says. "Do you?"

Hell, yes.

"Hell, yes," I say.

Amy laughs and so do I. I close my eyes, breathe her in.

"Hey," she says, "wait a sec." I open my eyes as she tumbles out of bed in just her pale pink lace underwear. It doesn't really seem like the type she'd wear but who cares because her ass looks amazing in it, and she runs across the room and finds a cassette and pops it in. Then she bullets back to the bed and slides in next to me. The first few familiar notes start playing.

"Is this *Psychocandy*?" I ask. It's the first album from the Jesus and Mary Chain. One of my favorites. And Amy knows it.

"Yeah," Amy says, pulling back to see my reaction. "I thought it would make it extra nice."

A wide grin breaks out on my face, and Amy's grin soon matches it.

"Definitely," I say.

This girl.

The first track really kicks in—that melty one about honey. Jim Reid's voice drones on in that cool way it always does, like he doesn't give a shit but at the same time he *does*. I kiss Amy, wanting her so much.

And afterward, when we're lying there catching our breath and glancing at each other and cracking up and smiling and kissing again, I wonder how in the hell I could even consider moving to California.

· · ·

We doze for a while, relaxed in the knowledge that no one will catch us. When we come to, Amy sits up, rubs her face a little, and yawns.

"Do you have to leave soon? Please say no."

I think back to my house that evening, before I'd left for Amy's. Mami has been ignoring me since our blowup after church about a week ago. After several drinks over an early and nearly silent dinner, she'd escaped to her bedroom and was still in there, stewing, when I'd written her a note on the kitchen counter letting her know I was picking up a shift at El Mirador and would be home late. Elena had made some crack about not being the only one with a fake job. She had plans to hang out with J.C. tonight. I'd slipped her another five and told her to be careful at least three times before driving the Honda to Amy's house.

"I can stick around a little while longer," I say, glancing at her clock radio. It's almost ten o'clock. I wonder, briefly, if I could just stay at Amy's all night. Her parents aren't coming back, after all. Elena pulled it off that one weekend, telling

Mami she had an overnight babysitting gig. Hell, if I got home early enough tomorrow morning, Mami might not even realize I never came home at all.

"I'll get us more beer," Amy tells me, sliding out of bed and tugging on her underwear and T-shirt. I watch her leave and lie back, my arms folded behind my head, fantasizing about staying here with her until the sun comes up.

A few moments later, I hear the telephone ring and Amy answering it in the kitchen. I can't make out most of what she's saying, but I assume it's her parents checking in from Houston. Until she yells my name.

"Joaquin, come out here. Hurry!"

My first thought is that somehow Mami has figured out I'm here, naked in a girl's bed, but how could she? Even if Elena somehow divulged Amy's existence—and I don't think she would ever unveil a secret like that—she doesn't know Amy's last name or phone number. But then who is calling?

I slide on my underwear and jeans and race to the kitchen shirtless. Amy is holding the phone out to me, her face pained.

"Who is it?" I ask, not pausing to listen to Amy's answer. I just put the receiver to my ear and say, "Yeah, hello?"

"Joaquin, it's Miguel. From work?" Miguel the busboy. Introducing himself to me like he must be utterly forgettable and I haven't worked with him for two years. That's the kind of nice, dorky kid he is.

"Yeah, Miguel, what's up?" I notice background noise again, like Miguel is calling from outside. Cars on pavement, horns honking. Loud shouts.

226

"Um, so this is sort of weird and a little bit awkward," he starts. There's a pause. More noises. I start to feel sick in the pit of my stomach. My heart is picking up speed.

"Where are you calling from?" I ask, raising my voice so he'll be sure to hear me. Amy stands feet away, her brow furrowed. *What's wrong?* she mouths. I shrug back. *I don't know.*

"I'm calling from a pay phone near Thirty-Fourth Street," Miguel says slowly. He's choosing his words carefully, I can tell. "I tried your house but no one answered, so I thought I'd try over there. I called the restaurant and Carlos gave me the number."

"Miguel, what's up?" I interrupt, half irritated and all worried.

"So there's a party at the beach and your sister . . ."

I grip the receiver and turn my back on Amy, going as far across the kitchen as the phone cord will let me, which isn't much.

"Miguel, is she okay?"

"Yeah," says Miguel, "I mean . . . I think. She's not hurt or anything. She's just . . . she's with that guy? I'm just sort of worried about her. It's hard to explain, but . . . there's a lot of booze here? And some other . . . shit?"

I want details but I also don't want to waste time.

"I'm leaving now," I say. "Keep an eye on her, okay? I mean, if you can."

"Yeah, of course," says Miguel, and I hang up on him without saying goodbye. Keep an eye on her. The idea is ludicrous, but I had to say it. I race down the hall to Amy's bedroom, filling her in as she follows and I start hunting around for my shirt and shoes. I glance at the bed with its messed-up, faded sheets and sunken-in pillows, hardly able to register that just a little while ago Amy and I had been in our own world there, unbothered and happy and safe.

Now Elena needs me.

"I'll come with you," Amy says, searching for her own clothes. I want to tell her no, to keep her away from my fucked-up family. Shame courses through me at that thought, but it's the truth.

"You don't have to," I say half-heartedly, because even though I sort of don't want her there, I think I might need her.

"I want to come," Amy says, not pausing to discuss it as she throws on some sandals. "Let's go."

And with that we race toward her front door, the keys to the Honda already clutched tight in my hand. Outside is muggy and dark, but I barely have time to register it before we are speeding down Esperanza Boulevard toward my kid sister and God knows what else.

CHAPTER FOURTEEN

AFTER I FIND A PARKING SPACE, AMY AND I RUN TO-
ward the beach. I catch a glimpse of the party by one of the
rock jetties that juts out into the bay. There must be at least
a hundred high school kids down here, playing music out of
boom boxes, guzzling beer, and being obnoxious. It's a wonder the cops haven't come, but we aren't near the more prime
beach vacation real estate. This is strictly townie territory.

"It's the jock and douchebag crowd," Amy mutters as
we get closer and survey the scene. The sweet smell of pot
lingers in the air, mingling with cigarette smoke. The fluo-
rescent lights hovering over the nearby parking lot cast an
unnatural brightness. On the perimeter of the crowd I see
a shirtless surfer type crushing an empty beer can into his
forehead, followed by the maniacal cheers of the apes sur-
rounding him.

"Do you see Miguel?" I ask, scanning the crowd. "Or my sister?" There are so many people it's hard to tell.

"Look," Amy says, pointing. Out of the mob runs Miguel, looking young and out of place. He jogs up to us.

"She's over by the jetty," Miguel says, nodding toward the black rocks that jut out into the still water. "She's with that guy." His expression turns sour.

"Her friend Michelle isn't around?" I ask.

"I think she's out of town," says Miguel. "Anyway, she's not here."

It's too crowded for me to get a good look, and I can't spot Elena yet. Amy slides her sandals off so she can move faster on the sand, but I just charge ahead, not wanting to slow down even to take off my shoes. I push past big-hair girls and pimply underclassmen I vaguely recognize from the halls of LBJ. I used to go to stupid keggers like this as recently as the spring. Now they just seem like juvenile bullshit.

Finally I spot Elena. Balancing on the jetty, she's dressed in blue denim cutoffs and a bright pink bikini top. Where the hell did she get a bikini top? A cigarette is in her fingers and a beer is in the other hand. She perches barefoot at the edge of a rock, staring out at the water. A few kids are seated on the rocks near her, nursing beers and sharing smokes.

"Elena?" I say, approaching her, Amy and Miguel at my heels. "Elena?"

Elena turns and looks at me, blinks once and then twice.

"Brother!" she shouts. *"Hermano!"* A wild grin spreads over her face, so big, her pale pink gums peek out.

"Hey," I say, uncertain.

"*Hermano*, have you ever really looked at the ocean?" Elena asks, tossing the cigarette away and setting the can of beer down by her feet. She stands up again and folds her hands under her chin like she's praying. She stares at the Gulf of Mexico like it's an apparition. A miracle. Then she speaks to me again, each word rolling in her mouth like a marble. "I mean, have you ever really, really looked at this water? This amazing water?" She flashes her eyes at me and smiles broadly again.

"Yeah, I've looked at it," I answer. "Why don't you get down from there?" I scan the crowd for that dickhead J.C., but I don't know exactly what he looks like. All the guys here seem like the fuck-up type that dates underage girls. So he could be anyone.

"I can't get down," Elena says, each word moving lazily. "I'm one with the ocean tonight." Then she squats down and touches the black rocks of the jetty. "I'm one with these rocks, too." Her hand caresses one rock carefully, as if it's the most interesting object on planet Earth. A couple of the kids seated around her laugh quietly to themselves. One guy rolls his eyes.

"She's tripping," Amy says to me, her voice soft. "I'd bet my college savings she's on acid."

At this, Elena turns and looks at Amy and me. "Hey," Elena asks, her voice cut with giddiness, "are you xoxoAmy? Oh my god, yes, it's you! It's xoxoAmy! Hi, xoxoAmy!" She smiles broadly at Amy and reaches out for her, only her footing isn't strong and she slips.

"Elena, be careful!" I shout, reaching for her. My little sister grabs my hands, giggling uncontrollably as she tries to regain her footing on the jetty. "Why don't you come down from there?" I insist. My mind is racing. I can't leave her here like this. I can't walk away. But I imagine trying to bring her home like this. What if Mami sees her? She'll lose her shit. Elena will be done for.

"What's wrong with her?" Miguel asks, anxious. I'd almost forgotten he was there.

"It'll wear off by tomorrow morning," Amy says. "But she's not sleeping tonight."

Fuck fuck fuck.

Elena has wrestled her hands away from my grip and is back on her perch, watching the dark water. Party chatter and shitty music surround us. As I'm trying to figure out what to do, a figure cuts through the darkness, and immediately I know it's him. Faded board shorts, no shoes, and a Grateful Dead T-shirt. I hate him already, if I didn't before.

"Hey, Elena," J.C. says, wandering over to the jetty from wherever the hell he's been. He's fucked-up, too, obviously. "Elena, what do you see?"

Seething with rage, I watch as J.C. attempts to climb up on the jetty, fails, and tries again, laughing the entire time. Finally he is balancing next to her, slipping his arm around her waist. I want to puke.

"Hey, I think I need to take Elena home," I hear myself saying. J.C. looks down, blinks a few times.

"Who are you?" he asks. He smiles at me like he knows a secret. Enough with the goddamn smiling already!

"I'm Elena's brother," I say. "I'm here to take her home." I picture Mami waking up, leaving her bedroom, and finding Elena studying the refrigerator magnets for two hours. My stomach twists.

"Dude, hey, chill," J.C. says, smiling again. "It's so cool. It's awesome you're here. It's . . ." he searches, "it's serendipitous."

Amy snorts, but I don't see anything humorous about this situation. All I want—besides getting Elena somewhere safe—is to be back in Amy's bedroom, just the two of us, alone.

"Hey, Elena," Amy says. "Can you come down and look at my nail polish? It's so pretty. I think you'll like it." She reaches out her hand, confident. Elena drags her eyes away from the ocean and considers Amy's fingers.

"It is pretty, xoxoAmy," Elena says, and she reaches for Amy's outstretched hand.

"Come on," Amy coaxes her. "Come down here with us."

J.C. observes this exchange and then says, "Elena, I thought we were gonna go swimming. Swimming in this beautiful, beautiful nighttime ocean."

Miguel sucks in his breath but says nothing. I give J.C. a dirty look as Elena pulls her hand back from Amy, unsure of her next move.

"Oh," Elena announces, "that's right. We were going to take

acid and go swimming. That's the best way to swim, you know. On acid." She laughs like this is the funniest thing anyone on the planet has ever said.

"Elena, don't do that," Miguel warns. "It's dangerous."

"Stay cool," Amy says in a low voice to Miguel. She reaches her hand out again. "Elena, you can swim in a minute, but please come down and look at my nail polish first. It would make me so happy if you did."

Elena frowns, confused. J.C. stands next to her, unsteady on his feet, staring out at the water, ignoring Elena. It's taking everything in me not to haul him off the rocks and punch him in the face.

"Well, okay, but just for a minute," Elena relents, and she takes Amy's hand and steps down carefully, before collapsing into Amy's arms with a tidal wave of giggles. I breathe a little more easily once Elena's feet are on the sand, and I watch as she takes Amy's hand in hers to study her chipped black polish.

"So pretty," Elena announces. "Not as pretty as the ocean, but pretty." She lifts her face up and stares at Amy. "You're so pretty, too," Elena says. "I'm so glad, because that means you're going to help my brother stay here and not go away to California."

Amy shifts uncomfortably and humiliation courses through me. I don't know what to do, so I turn to J.C.

"Hey, fuckhead," I yell, not caring who hears. A few of the kids on the rocks exchange glances and drift over to get a better view of an impending fight. I haven't been in a fight since junior high——I have no idea what I'm doing. But anger is coursing through me, hot and insistent.

"What's up, dude?" J.C. responds from the rocks. "Why so fucking hostile?"

"You got my sister all fucked-up and you were going to take her swimming?" I ask, incredulous, my voice rising. I sense Amy trying to entice Elena to move farther down the shoreline, but Elena's focused on us.

"Joaquin, no," Elena begins, breaking away. "Joaquin, J.C. is a really great person. I want the two of you to be friends. I want you to be best friends!" She cracks a grin again, only it's lopsided and uncertain.

"Well, that's never going to happen," I spit, angry. At this, Amy places a hand on my arm. "Joaquin, let's go for a walk. You, me, and Elena." I feel bad for Miguel——his crush on my sister has always been so obvious. But Amy is right. It would be best if he stayed behind. Hopefully, J.C. will, too.

And, of course, J.C. does. He's not interested in keeping an eye on my sister. He's only interested in getting fucked-up and fucking around.

I thank Miguel for his help and promise to update him later. Then Amy and I lead Elena down the shoreline, pausing every few seconds as Elena stops to examine a shell or a piece of seaweed washed up on the beach. At least she's still in a good mood. She runs ahead of us for a moment. Amy slips her hand into mine.

"I'm sorry," I manage, embarrassed.

"For what?" Amy asks. "Your sister isn't the first person to drop acid."

"Have you?" I ask, curious.

"No, that's not my thing," Amy says, shaking her head. "But I was with Nico a few times when he was tripping." I nod, trying to be cool at the mention of her old boyfriend. I wonder if Nico ever forced Amy to chase after his little sister on a night that was meant to be just for the two of them.

"I can't take her home," I say, "but I'm worried my mom is going to wake up and find out she's gone. I can't decide which is worse." I watch Elena trotting ahead of us, every so often turning to smile like a demented kindergartner on a scavenger hunt. I want to be angry at her. But she's so vulnerable, all I can do is protect her.

"We could bring her back to my house," Amy says, her voice uncertain. "I mean, like I said, if she took it recently, she's going to be wired for the next couple of hours at least."

I shake my head no. "I can't ask you to do that."

"Yeah," says Amy, "but what if you take her home? Your mom . . . what would she do if she found out?"

My mind flashes on Elena's scar on her chin. My heart starts pounding.

"It wouldn't be good," I say. I can't bring myself to say anything else.

"Would your mom flip?" she asks.

"Yeah," I answer. "She would definitely flip."

We walk in silence for a little while longer. I glance back over my shoulder, looking to see if J.C. is coming after us, if he's at all worried about Elena. But he's never there. Finally, after about half an hour of our walk up and down the shoreline, dodging drunk partiers and couples making out way too aggressively in public, Amy starts guiding Elena back toward my car.

"Hey," Amy says to Elena, "you want to go back to my place and get something to eat?"

Elena stops, screws up her face, and stares at Amy. "Can J.C. come?"

Amy and I exchange glances.

"J.C. had to go home," I say. "He had something important he had to do." Why the hell am I covering for the asshole?

"Well," Elena says, screwing up her face again, thinking hard. "I guess we can go to your place. It might be fun to see your bedroom, xoxoAmy." She smiles like she's having some sort of religious experience.

"Okay," Amy says, and Elena follows us without a struggle, sliding into the back seat of the Honda, giggling the whole time. I drive us back to Amy's place, not saying anything. Elena keeps up a steady stream of patter from the back, commenting on how amazing the stoplights are at night and how incredible it is that we live by the ocean. Amy and I just nod in response.

"We're here," Amy says, as I pull into the driveway.

"Amy, I can't ask you to do this," I say.

She shrugs, and I think I see a flicker of irritation cross her face. *Oh god, she's going to dump me tomorrow.*

And suddenly my uncertainty shifts to rage. I'm so fucking pissed off. At Mami. At J.C. And at Elena, too. Maybe her most of all.

"Let's go in," Amy says, and soon Elena is in Amy's den, watching the test pattern on the television like it's Saturday morning cartoons. It's well past midnight. I think about Mami back at the apartment and immediately start chewing on my thumbnail.

"I should go home just to make sure my mom isn't wondering where the hell we are," I say, praying she's still asleep or passed out in her room. Then something occurs to me. "Shit, tomorrow's Sunday."

"So?" Amy asks.

I flush. "Usually we have to go to Mass."

"Oh," says Amy, surprised.

"Listen," I tell her, trying to formulate a plan, "I'll go home, check on my mom, and then, like, at dawn I'll come back and pick up Elena. By then do you think she'll be . . . normal?"

Amy nods. "She probably won't be a hundred percent, but she shouldn't be that spaced out." At this she motions toward Elena, who is still staring at the bright blocks of color frozen on the screen, grinning like a clown.

"Okay," I say. And then I get brave and reach for Amy's hands, smaller than mine but not too small. Amy isn't a tiny girl, which I like. You don't feel like you're going to crush her every time you hug her.

And I want to hug Amy right now. Feel safe with her. Disappear with her.

"I don't know how to thank you," I manage. "I can't fucking believe our night turned into this."

Amy leans over and presses her lips to mine, sure and steady. My chest swells. She pulls back. "Don't worry about it," she whispers. "Just go."

• • •

Back home, I creep into the living room, certain that Mami is going to be stewing on the couch, that she's going to start yelling about how she's called the police and the hospitals. Instead the house is still. Dark. I rip up the note I left saying I was going in for an unexpected shift at the restaurant and bury it at the bottom of the trash can. Then I make sure Elena's bedroom door is closed tight and press an ear against Mami's until I detect light snoring. She's been asleep this whole time, certain that I'm in my bedroom and Elena came straight home after her babysitting job at the Callahans'.

The goddamn Callahans. I remember when Elena and I first dreamed them up, picked out the kids' names. I was young and gross and horny, and I used to imagine Mrs. Callahan as some foxy blonde with all the right curves. Early on, I even fantasized about subbing in for Elena on a night when she couldn't make her babysitting job, only I would imagine biking over to their fancy house on Point Isabel and it would just be Mrs. Callahan who answered the door in her lace bra and underpants. It's embarrassing to remember that, but that's all the Callahans are for me. Just some stupid memory from our childhood.

For Elena, the family is still very much alive.

I brush my teeth and change into a clean T-shirt and boxers and lie down on my bed, my mind running over everything that happened tonight—from being with Amy to rescuing my sister to that J.C. asshole. It's my job to protect Elena, but I haven't been able to keep her from Grateful Dead fuckups. I've been preoccupied with Amy.

Guilt surges through me, and I toss and turn in my bed. If this is what happens to Elena when I'm at a house across town, what could happen to her if I'm in a different city, a different state?

Then, not more than an hour after I start to drift off, I hear Mami's bedroom door open with a creak. I sit up.

"Elena?" croaks a voice. "Elena, are you home?"

I freeze for a moment before racing out into the hallway, panic filling my body.

"Mami, Elena's sleeping," I say, my voice low. "She came home from the Callahans' with a headache, so she took some Tylenol and went to sleep."

Mami frowns at me, her face ghostly and strange from the porchlight streaming in through the front windows. She's a full head shorter than me but still manages to give the impression that she's looming over me. Her face looks stripped and naked without her ever-present makeup, and her dyed hair is in loose scraggles around her face. She scowls and peers around as if I'm lying. Which I am.

"You've been home all night?" she asks, looking at me.

Maybe she got up while we were gone and saw my note about working at the restaurant, so now she's trying to trip me up. I take a chance. "Yeah, I've been home."

She says nothing, just stumbles toward Elena's door. "She's asleep?" she asks. "Maybe I should check on her."

I seize up. Of all the nights for Mami to wake up before the sun to check on us. I can't remember the last time it happened.

"Maybe you should just let her sleep," I say. Please God, don't let her go in there. *Please, please, God.*

"What's with you?" Mami whispers, frowning. "Why are you even awake?"

Why are you? I want to ask. Maybe I can provoke her with my fresh mouth, distract her from my absent sister.

"I had insomnia," I answer instead. "I watched a scary movie on television." I sound like an elementary school idiot. Elena is so much faster than me at making up off-the-cuff lies, but of course she's had more practice at it.

Mami shrugs, already bored by my answer. She stares past me at Elena's door again, then finally, fortunately, she heads back to her room. At the door, she turns and announces, "We're going to eight o'clock Mass, so you'd both better be up and ready."

Shit. "Why not the later service?"

She turns, and I realize this is the most she's spoken to me since The Incident after church last Sunday. Staring at me coldly, she waits a beat before responding. "We're going to eight o'clock Mass because I want to go to eight o'clock Mass."

Then she walks into her room and shuts the door.

I spend the next few hours staring at various spaces in my bedroom, my stomach in knots, wondering how Amy and Elena are faring. Finally, a little before six o'clock in the morning while it's still dark out, I creep out of the house to the Honda and drive to Amy's place, stopping to get a dozen donuts at Shipley Do-Nuts. (*Thanks for taking care of my fucked-up sister, Amy, here are some donuts. Please don't break up with me.*)

I knock on Amy's front door and she greets me with a yawn, dressed in her ratty pajamas.

"I brought you donuts," I manage, holding forth the red-and-white box like an asshole.

"You didn't have to," she says, yawning again, then raising an eyebrow. "Okay, wait. I guess you did." She takes the box from me.

Inside, Elena is sleeping on the same couch she was on when I left, only now she's wearing one of Amy's old Black Flag T-shirts. For a moment, the situation strikes me as hilarious—my sister in my girlfriend's T-shirt promoting a band she has almost certainly never heard of, much less listened to, me standing with my hands limply at my sides while Amy holds a box of donuts.

"She passed out, like, thirty minutes ago," Amy whispers,

setting the donuts on the kitchen counter. "Did you know the bathroom tiles in my house are super-fucking fascinating? We spent about an hour in there discussing them."

I rub at my face, exhausted and embarrassed. "I'm so sorry, Amy."

"It's cool," she says, "but I really need to sleep."

I attempt to rouse Elena for two or three minutes before she finally sits up, blinks a few times, and then looks at me. The wild, manic expression is gone, replaced by tired, confused eyes.

"Hey," she croaks. "We're at your girlfriend's, yeah?"

And now I'm pissed. The situation isn't funny. And I don't need to feel bad for Elena. I need to be waking up with Amy or at the very least waking up alone in my own bed after a decent night's sleep.

"We gotta go. Mami wants us to go to eight o'clock Mass."

Elena rubs her eyes. "Fuck," she exhales, shaking her head. "Wait, you went home?"

"I'll explain it in the car," I say, hoping she's picking up on the curtness in my voice. Hoping she's feeling at least a little bit guilty. "Let's go. I'm serious."

Elena frowns at me, but she must be clearheaded enough by now to know she shouldn't push it. She glances down at Amy's shirt, confused.

"I'll bring your shirt to work," I say to Amy, who is eating a chocolate-glazed donut and watching us from the kitchen.

"No rush," Amy says, and I can't tell if her voice is tight

like she's ready to dump me, or tired like she just needs some sleep.

"I'm really sorry," Elena says to Amy as we head for the front door. At least she apologizes.

"Don't worry about it," Amy says. But I can tell she's ready for us to leave.

"I'll call you?" I ask, my eyebrows popping up along with the uncertainty of my voice.

Amy nods, offers a half smile. "But not for the next, like, five to seven hours. I'm about to pass out. Thank God I'm not working today."

"Yeah," I answer, and I leave without kissing her or touching her at all, which sort of crushes me.

On the drive home I fill Elena in on what she needs to know (Mami thinks you were sleeping the whole time, she woke up in the middle of the night, yes, I covered for you), and then silence consumes us. When we pull into the driveway, the sun is just starting to pink up the sky. Finally, Elena opens her mouth to speak.

"Joaquin—"

"Not now," I say, holding my hand up. "I can't right now."

"Okay," Elena responds, wounded, shrinking back into her seat.

"I just want to know one thing," I say, unable to stop myself. "Do you understand that J.C. just let you go last night? Just abandoned you while you were on acid, and he didn't even make sure you got home okay?" My face is flushed with rage.

Elena crumbles a little, her eyes immediately glossing over with tears. She doesn't say anything, just looks at me like a scared toddler.

"You could have been really hurt," I spit, all my resentment from the past few hours forcing its way out. "And I suppose you won't care because he's not fucking *cool* or whatever, but it was Miguel who called Amy and me to come get you." I think this would make for a good dramatic moment to get out of the car, slam the door, and stride into the house, but we have to be quiet, so I don't. I just sit there, fuming, and Elena says nothing for the longest time until finally, at last, she whispers, "I'm sorry." Then she puts her face in her hands and cries. She cries so hard her shoulders shake in her borrowed Black Flag T-shirt.

Shit.

"Hey," I say, still pissed but now guilty, too. *Shit shit shit.*

"I'm so sorry," she says into her hands, her voice muffled. "I didn't even know what acid would be like. J.C. just said it would be fun. I'm sorry."

Tentatively, I rest my hand on her back, trying not to imagine the scuzzy apartment where J.C. plied my kid sister to drop acid, trying not to hear whatever surfer-dude-hippie-dippie-Grateful-Dead-bullshit-language he used to convince her. And I just wait there with her until she finally stops crying and stares at the house. She sniffs and takes a deep breath and wipes her tears from her cheeks with her fingertips.

After a few beats she turns to look at me, game face on, her expression neutral and her mouth set in a firm line. It's wild to me how quickly she can transform when she needs to.

"She seriously said eight o'clock Mass?" she asks. "That early?"

I nod, and soon I'm checking the front room as usual, reporting back that all is safe. We each take a quick hot shower, get dressed for church, and tiptoe around the place nervously waiting for Mami to exit her bedroom. At seven thirty we debate waking her but decide against it. I make us scrambled eggs and toast, and we sit on the couch eating and watching a boring Sunday morning news programs since there's nothing else on.

Eventually, at around quarter to nine, Mami finally emerges, yawning. She walks into the den and studies us closely.

"How are you feeling, Elena?"

Damn. I never told Elena that I'd lied about her head hurting.

Without skipping a beat or taking her eyes off the television, Elena says, "I'm fine. I took some Tylenol."

I exhale, hoping Mami can't read the relief on my face. I'm not sure if she does or not because her only response is "What are you doing all dressed up?"

"You told me we were going to eight o'clock Mass," I say, turning to look at her, confused.

Mami stares at me as if I'm stupid, then rolls her eyes. "When in my life have I ever made us go to church that early? We'll go at nine thirty as usual. Now I'm going to take a shower."

Elena and I turn and give each other looks—the kind of looks only siblings can give, when not a sentence needs to be spoken.

Not even a word.

CHAPTER FIFTEEN

ELENA IS GOING TO BREAK THE DAMN PHONE STRETCH-
ing the cord like she does.

"Hey," I say, rapping my knuckles on her bedroom door as hard as I can. "I told you to stop pulling the phone in there so tight. And there are other people in this house who need to use it, in case you forgot."

Elena bangs three times in response to let me know she's heard me, but she doesn't hang up. Mami's at work, so she's talking to J.C., I'm sure of it. I sigh. Last week's debacle hasn't changed anything. Two days after I found her manic on the beach, she left me a homemade apology card on my pillow (*You're the very best brother a dumb girl like me could ever ask for!*), but I haven't had the heart or the energy to bring up that night. She's still playing it fast and loose, sneaking out after Mami is asleep or passed out, coming home reeking of smoke of all kinds, and dreaming up increasingly lazy reasons why she needs to babysit for the Callahans at the last minute. The other afternoon she insisted that Mrs. Callahan had a last-minute tennis lesson. Who the hell has a last-minute tennis lesson? But Mami fell for it, I guess, scowling at Elena over her tumbler of rum and Coke and then saying something about those poor, lonely children and their rich, absent mother.

I wait one more minute.

"Elena, come on!"

Finally, exasperated, my little sister pulls open the door with a saucy look on her face. She hands me the receiver.

"Here you go, your majesty."

But then she smiles so big her cheeks dimple. She's happy because I'm staying. I broke the news to her and Mami the night before during dinner. Poking around Mami's sad excuse for meat loaf, I'd managed to mutter that my plan was to stick around the island for a year, taking classes at MICC and then maybe applying to UT.

"Well, we don't have the money for UT," Mami had said definitively, taking a bird-sized bite of her meat loaf and a sailor-sized swig of her drink. "But I suppose you can save up over the next year. And MICC isn't that expensive. It's the right decision to make. And it shows you have some character, at least. Unlike your father." This was the most validation Mami had given me since telling me I looked nice the morning of my First Communion.

Elena had just clapped like a kid, grinning widely.

"I knew you'd decide to stick around," she'd said, giddy. "I knew it!"

"Fine, fine, let's not make a big thing of it," I'd told her, clearing the plates while Mami retired to the den to watch television and Elena went and got ready for a "babysitting job." I acted annoyed, but really I wanted to hold my breath and crystallize the weird moment when everything in my family seemed almost normal. Almost nice.

Almost.

I'm glad Elena's happy, but it was actually Amy who prompted my decision to stay. I thought she might not want to see me again after I'd dumped Elena on her, so I was shocked when she'd walked up and bumped me with her hip and said hello at our next shift at El Mirador.

"You aren't . . . pissed?" I'd asked, half grateful and half confused.

Amy had shrugged. "Well, I wasn't wild about what happened, but jeez, Joaquin, it's not like it was your fault." My face must have looked really stricken because she reached out and lightly touched my cheek. "You need to have a little more faith in people."

Right.

That afternoon after our shift we'd slept together while her parents were at work and her little brother was at Vacation Bible School. In the groggy, post-sex haze, I said out loud, "I think I'm going to stick around for a while." Amy propped herself up on her elbow and smiled at me, but I could tell she was trying to stay cool.

"Good," she'd said, her grin wide. "I like you. Stay. Stay one more year and then come with me to UT."

"What would I even study?" I asked. "Actually, I don't even think I could get into UT."

Amy shrugged. "I bet you could, but does it matter? Just come with me and we'll figure it out. In the meantime, just take, like, English Comp at MICC or something to keep yourself occupied and your mother off your back."

And that was that.

So here I am, dialing the admissions office at MICC to find out how I can register for intro classes. A woman with a tight twang informs me that I'll need my birth certificate and my high school transcript. I scribble that down on a piece of paper before I hang up.

"What are you doing?" Elena asks as she slides into the kitchen and starts hunting around the refrigerator for something to eat. She finally settles on a piece of cheese, shutting the fridge with her foot and leaning up against the counter.

"Just finding out what I need to enroll at MICC," I tell her, shoving the paper into my back jeans pocket. I'm not sure where Mami would keep things like my birth certificate. The high school transcript I can get from LBJ High.

"Any idea where Mami keeps our birth certificates?" I ask Elena, as she finishes her cheese and starts unloading the dish drainer, making sure to wipe each dish extra dry with the red-and-white dish towel hanging from the oven handle.

Elena pauses to think, carefully handling a pale peach cereal bowl. "No," she decides. "You could check her room." She shoots me an uncertain look, her eyebrows raised. Mami's room is an unknown world that smells of Arpège and budget detergent. Of mid-shelf rum sweated out through pores caked in mid-shelf makeup, carefully applied. Elena goes into Mami's room more often than I do. The straightening of her bed sheets and the folding of her clothes feels too intimate for a guy— and better suited for the child that Mami likes best. Or at least tolerates more.

"Where in her room?" I ask, glancing at the clock. It's at least two hours until Mami comes home from work.

Elena shrugs. "Her closet? Or why don't you just wait until she gets home and ask her."

"I like to keep my conversations with her to a minimum," I say. "You know that."

Elena rolls her eyes and puts the last dish away. "Yes, Mr. Drama. I know. Go ahead and look, then. I'm going to watch television."

"No babysitting job?" I ask.

"Maybe later," Elena answers, her back to me. I can't tell if I've ticked her off with that question.

I turn the doorknob to Mami's bedroom, half expecting her to jump out from behind the door. She's never told us not to go in there without permission. It's just that I've never wanted to do it.

I hear Elena turn on the television to some dumb game show. Over the din of cheering and bells ringing and forced applause I make my way to Mami's closet, my eyes passing over her bed, the bedspread drawn up tight, the books on her nightstand in a little pyramid. On the wall opposite the door hang black-and-white photographs of her parents from Cuba, looking like Hollywood starlets in cocktail attire. Other than the photos and the image of the Virgin Mary that Elena gave her, the walls are bare.

It's almost like I'm in someone else's house, I'm in here so rarely. My heart starts to pump faster even though I know there's no chance of Mami coming home early. In all her years of working for Dr. Sanders she's left early exactly once, when she came down with the flu. I tug open the sliding closet door, wiggly in its tracks. Mami's clothes are organized by color and spaced out evenly on plastic hangers. Her shoes are lined up neatly like they're about to go off marching in formation. My eyes alight on the shelf above. There are a few photo albums and three shoeboxes stacked one on top of the other.

I don't know why but my throat tightens up. Elena and Mami and I have lived in this house since before I can even remember, and every corner of it is known to me—the musty smell of my own closet, the stain on the Formica counter, the wonky showerhead in the bathroom. But this could be the closet of some stranger in Dallas or San Antonio.

I reach for the top box—it's the easiest. I don't dare sit on Mami's bed and wrinkle the blankets, so I kneel on the worn carpet. Cautiously, I lift the lid. I take out old checkbook registers and canceled checks with Mami's loopy, over-the-top signature, careful to leave everything just as I found it.

I set this shoebox aside—making a mental note that it was resting on top—and I tease the next box off the pile. It's old tax returns plus Mami's naturalization papers. I know she became a citizen just before she married our father. In the black-and-white photograph attached to her paperwork she is staring out at nothing, unsmiling, her face unlined, her expression even. I stare and stare at it, trying to find evidence of the mother I live with now, but the picture is one of a stranger. *Caridad Serafina de la Guardia.* What a roller coaster of syllables. I whisper it to myself before I place everything back in just as I found it. I hear an explosion of applause from the other side of the wall. The phone rings. I pause, listening as the television volume is lowered and the muffled sounds of Elena talking start up. No doubt it's Mami calling to check on her, making sure she's home where she's supposed to be. Soon the television noise is louder again, and I open the third box.

It's my old report cards, and Elena's, too, in order going all the way back to kindergarten. I feel a brief fondness for Mami, for the fact that she saved anything belonging to us. Unlike Amy's house, ours has never been a place where nursery-school finger-paint creations stay pinned proudly to the refrigerator for years.

I flip over my eighth-grade report card, the year I had Ms. Gardner. She was my favorite because she always had us do fun stuff, like analyze Beatles' songs instead of boring old poetry. In the space for end-of-the-year comments, Ms. Gardner's careful, dark black script reads: *Joaquin has a clever mind for one so young. He asks good questions, which will no doubt take him far in life.* I read and reread Ms. Gardner's words, even bringing the report card up to my nose to breathe in the old paper smell. I vaguely remember eighth grade, back when I still raised my hand in class. By the end of senior year I was strictly a second-from-the-back-row guy, never talking, always turning in my work on time, and pulling a steady B average without trying too hard.

I sift carefully through the box until I reach the bottom. Only report cards—no birth certificate and no social security card. I resign myself to the fact that I'll have to ask Mami where she put them as I place the shoeboxes back in the right order, then lift the stack back onto the closet shelf.

That's when I spot it, shoved all the way back in the shadowed corner of the top shelf behind the shoeboxes. A flat box like the type dress shirts come in at Foley's. I peer at it carefully, like I need to be totally sure I'm seeing it. I lift the three shoeboxes back out onto the carpet, and then, checking over my shoulder for some reason, I reach up and back as far as I can. Despite being a few inches over six feet tall I can only touch the box with my fingertips. I pull the box forward, centimeter by centimeter, and finally grasp it, dragging it out and leaving fingerprints in the fine coating of dust on the lid.

What the hell is in here?

The noise of the television continues to blare. I picture myself carrying the box out to Elena, the two of us pawing through it on the couch. But I don't.

I place the box down carefully on the floor and gently wiggle off the lid, trying not to disturb the dust even more in case Mami checks on it from time to time. I realize I'm holding my breath.

Inside there are a few square color snapshots, faded into paler versions of their once-vibrant selves. I recognize me as a baby, propped up on the couch clutching a plastic rattle, and one of Elena and me as little kids—our pudgy faces, our stained T-shirts. And there's one with a man holding me above his head like he's won me as some prize at a fair. It's my dad. I recognize him from other photos I've seen, but I've never seen this particular photo. He's tall and lanky, with a wide, toothy grin. I don't recognize the background. This must have been back when we lived closer to where Amy's family lives, in one of those little garden apartment complexes that always looks like it could blow over in a big storm.

I dig through the box carefully, taking note of how everything is arranged. There are more pictures, including a few of Mami and my father back when she lived in Healy with my dad's family, the family that cut Mami and Elena and me off after their son married Mami because they didn't want him marrying someone who wasn't born in the United States. There's Mami sitting primly on the edge of the couch with a fake smile. There's another one of Mami and my father on what must be their wedding day, something I've never seen actual proof of. They don't look much older than me, and that's because they weren't. Standing on the steps of what I guess must be a church, they stare out at the camera. Mami looks genuinely happy, the smile even reaching her eyes. I stare at it for a long time because it's such a rare sight to see.

Then, underneath the photos, I find a slim stack of yellow papers, like the type you'd tear from a legal pad. The stack is held together by a rubber band so thin and old I'm afraid it might break if I pull it off. But I can find another rubber band, right? And how often can Mami go in this box if it's as dusty as it is?

I listen. The game show has ended. Elena has moved on to a soap opera. I slide the rubber band off slowly, then unfold the papers. A piece of newspaper slides out, but it's the letter that catches my eye.

> *Dearest Carrie,*
>
> *I'm writing this letter in the house where we first met, in the place where I first saw you and knew we were destined to be together forever. I don't even know what to say to you. I left because I need some time and I know you need it too, but now you're not even taking my phone calls, and the last time I called I could hear little Laney Bird crying and crying in the background. Please don't shut me out.*
>
> *We can work this out, at least for the kids' sake.*
>
> *Frank*

My heart is thumping. Hard. This doesn't make any sense. Our dad left us—he didn't want to work it out. A shiver travels up my spine and my mouth goes dry. I should stop right now. Something deep down tells me that if I keep reading, keep unfolding, keep looking, I'm heading toward a place I can't come back from.

But I don't stop. I never, not for even a second, consider stopping.

> *Carrie,*
>
> *I hope you're reading this since you won't answer my calls. My folks won't say it but I know they're hoping you come back here. I know you don't want that but for right now it could be the best option. You know they'd never support divorce and I know you wouldn't, either. If you come back here, maybe you can stay here in the house with them and they can help with the kids and I can start back at U of H again and get a better job and that will help our money problems. That would be one stress taken care of anyway. The only kid left in the house is Deirdre so there's a lot more room than you remember. Either way, something has to change. It's been too long since we've seen each other and since I've seen the kids and I miss the kids and yeah, I really do miss you.*
>
> *Love,*
> *Frank*

Mami told us she woke up one morning the summer before Elena turned two, and the car was gone and the money was gone, and a week later she got one letter from him that was postmarked Los Angeles.

And he never sent us any money.

And he never gave a shit about us.

This is what she's always told us, what she tells us now, and what I have always believed to be true without questioning it. Always.

But before I even finish reading the rest of the letters I know—*I know*—that all of that was a lie.

My heart is racing now. Blood is rushing in my ears. The noise of Elena's soap opera is seeping through the walls, which sets me even more on edge. There's the sound of sweeping orchestral music that indicates that some cliffhanger moment, some crazy plot twist, is playing out on the screen.

I peel back the remaining pages. There are four letters in all, but none have dates on them. They all offer a different version of the same thing. Frank, my father, writing to my mother from Healy, Texas, where he's staying with his parents—my grandparents—begging my mother to communicate with him. To let him see us. The letters don't say why he's in Healy instead of Mariposa Island except for vague references to "needing time." Not just for him but for Mami, too, apparently. His multiple mentions of "Laney Bird" must be Elena even though I've never heard Mami use that nickname for her. I feel a weird pang of jealousy when Frank refers to me in his letters as Joaquin, no clever nickname.

I stare at the blue, inky scrawl that is my father's handwriting. He touched this paper, I think. He wrote this note. He smeared a word here. He accidentally tore the paper there. My father touched these letters. *These.*

My hands are shaking. How can I tell Elena? Suddenly, I imagine all the letters laid out on Mami's bed, facing up, waiting for her when she gets home from work.

It would be a shit show.

And she'd deserve it.

I hastily gather up the letters—one, two, three, four—and I'm about to get to my feet when I see the folded piece of newspaper. I set the letters aside. I pick it up. I unfold it.

It takes me less than five seconds to process what I'm seeing. Carefully clipped, not a snag or a tear to be seen in the newsprint, is my father's obituary. It's dated November 2, 1971. The picture chosen of my father is a formal one of him taken in a studio, wearing a suit, and in the photo he's staring right at me through years of lies and resentment. As if he's been wondering just when the hell he might be found.

The clipping is as light as a feather in my hand, the cheap pulp not even that yellowed after spending year after year tucked away in a box in the darkest part of the darkest closet in the house. I hold it tenderly, like a relic.

The rest of the room, the rest of the house, has fallen away, dropped off somewhere. I don't hear the television or anything at all. A wave of nausea rolls over me. I stare at the obituary.

Francis "Frank" Patrick Finney is not living in Los Angeles, California, and probably never even went there, because he died at the age of twenty-nine from reasons left unsaid. According to the *Healy Register*, he leaves behind a mother, a father, four siblings, and several nieces and nephews, all of Healy. Their rich, rolling Irish names are listed one after another, like floats on parade. As for Elena and me, there's no mention of us. It's as if we don't even exist. Like we're the tragic ending that's been edited out of an old fable to keep from scaring little kids.

We're just two children abandoned on an island with no one to look after us but the scary witch.

CARRIE

1971

The lesson that a baby will not magically turn a bad marriage good is a lesson that is almost always learned too late, and in this way, Frank and Carrie Finney were very typical students.

The day Joaquin had been born it was good. It was not perfect. Frank's parents came down from Healy. Carrie didn't want them in the hospital. Frank pleaded. Carrie held firm. She wanted control over this one thing. Frank's parents drove back to Healy, steaming mad and sure that their son had ruined his life by marrying this girl they had so stupidly tried to help.

There had been some ideas from Frank about what to name the baby, but Carrie had held firm on this one thing, too. The nurse at the hospital had pronounced it "Joe-a-kwin," and Frank had rolled his eyes because he knew this would be his firstborn's burden all his life, but Carrie didn't care. Her little boy's name was the weakest tether to the homeland she would never see again. And she liked how Frank couldn't really pronounce it, but she could.

The baby was a perfect pink gumdrop, and as sweet as one, too. He rarely cried, and if he did, it was easy to solve—gas, sleepiness, hunger for a bottle. Later, when her infant daughter Elena wailed with colic, Carrie thought to herself that Elena would not have even been born had Joaquin acted so horribly. Not that Elena had been planned, exactly.

But no matter how good an infant Joaquin was, everything was harder for Frank and Carrie now. Money was tighter. Free time was rarer. Carrie was moodier, angrier. Frank tried to placate her with little gifts—cheap boxes of chocolates from the drugstore. A small bottle of top-shelf rum. But nothing worked. Everything Frank did set Carrie on edge. The way he blew his nose. The sounds of his chewing. The sigh he expressed every damn time he sat down on the couch, like a train pulling into a station.

Each day was the same for Carrie. It was the same for Frank, too, but Carrie didn't see that. All she knew was that she was the one trapped at home with the baby, tending to the baby, trying to go grocery shopping on a very tight budget with the baby. At least Frank got to leave the crowded apartment each day to go to work.

At dinnertime, over frozen television dinners or sad spaghetti or cold sandwiches, Frank would try.

"How was your day?" he'd ask.

"Fine," Carrie would answer with a shrug, Joaquin in her lap.

Frank would wait for Carrie to reciprocate. And wait.

"My day was good," he would finally offer. "I made two sales."

"That's good," Carrie would answer. "We need the commission."

After dinner Frank would settle in on the couch to watch television and Carrie would escape to her bedroom with Joaquin, whom she cuddled with a fierce protectiveness. Here was a living little creature that seemed to hang on every coo and every smile Carrie offered. Here was someone who really loved her, maybe for the first time since Juanita. Carrie would find herself finally relaxing a bit when she curled up with him, softly singing him the words of the songs she remembered Juanita singing to her when she was a little girl.

Duérmete mi niña
Duérmete mi amor
Duérmete pedazo
De mi corazón.

Sometimes Frank would wander into the bedroom and find Carrie and Joaquin asleep on the bed, and he would shrug and sigh and relegate himself to the couch in the living room.

When Joaquin was around a year old, a night of too much

rum made Carrie give in too quickly and soon she was pregnant again. Elena arrived and quickly was wailing at all hours of the night and day, and the walls of the apartment closed in on Carrie, inch by inch. Joaquin's little wooden blocks seemed to breed overnight, spreading everywhere. Elena's small pink mouth would open wide, wider than Carrie thought possible, and she would not shut it for hours at a time, driving Carrie to stuff her ears with cotton balls and drink cocktails at lunch. She could never keep the apartment totally organized, totally clean. She thought perhaps she should take the children out to the courtyard, but the idea of speaking with any of the other mothers made Carrie panicky, so she'd spend days inside the apartment with the babies, the television on at all hours, counting the minutes until Frank came home just to give her something else to look at.

Frank would give Carrie "breaks," as he called them, by driving Joaquin—and later Joaquin and Elena—up to Healy to visit with his parents. Carrie would spend those childless Saturdays on the couch, sipping rum from a juice glass, watching terrible television, and then bursting into tears over missing her babies, the only real things she felt were hers. When Frank would come home, Carrie would lash out.

"I suppose your parents think I'm a terrible mother," she would say, her arms crossed, her face in a pout.

With a strained expression, Frank would simply answer,

"No, Carrie, they don't. They want us to move back to Healy."

Carrie would think of the yellow bedroom. The dumpy couch with the cheap doilies. The landlocked small town of busybodies and nobodies. Her lying in-laws who hated her. The idea of returning made her skin crawl. The idea that by not returning she would anger Frank's parents made her feel vindicated.

"I'm never going back there," she'd announce with finality, and Frank knew she was serious. And he looked at the cluttered apartment, at the mounting bills, at this woman who had been his childhood crush and was now transformed into someone he didn't know at all, maybe had never known. And he began to panic.

One Saturday morning after a nasty fight about the late rent, Carrie woke up to a note and one hundred and fifty dollars on the kitchen counter.

> *Carrie,*
> *I went up to see my folks. I want to work this out but I need some time to think things through. I pawned my watch so you have some cash. I'll be in touch.*
>
> *Frank*

Carrie had stood there in the middle of the kitchenette, staring at the letter, reading it over and over again. Anger boiled so deep inside of her that she thought she might be capable of punching a hole right through the wall. In fact, she made a fist. She caught a glimpse of a smudge on the kitchen wall, probably made by Joaquin toddling around. All she could see was everything that was wrong. The rust on the refrigerator door handle. The chip in the coffee pot. The grime caked all over the stove.

When she was a little girl she had been waited on hand and foot.

She'd had the most beautiful *quince* dress in history.

She'd been a princess on a beautiful island. A real island, not some sad little substitute.

When the babies woke up, she dumped Cheerios in bowls (from the secondhand store!) and read Frank's letter over and over again, waiting for tears and finding none. She spent the next few days in the apartment, Elena fussing, Joaquin standing at the front door banging it and begging to go out. Carrie just watched him from the couch, unable to move. She somehow managed to feed the children: Cheerios, water, milk, and slices of orange over and over. For three days straight.

When the letters and the calls started—asking her to talk, begging her to move to Healy, urging her to pick up the phone—Carrie didn't respond. In fact, since Frank was the only one who ever called her, she stopped answering the phone completely once she knew it would only be him on the line. Not answering the phone was easier than having to answer it and then hang it back up again, although it was a bit less satisfying.

Carrie folded the letters that came through the mail slot and put them in her nightstand drawer. At night when the children were asleep, she opened them and read them, and she felt a small glimmer of that power she'd once held over Frank years ago when they were teenagers.

If he wanted to talk to me so much, he shouldn't have left, then, should he?

The power she felt emboldened her to leave the apartment at last. To take the children and make their way to the corner store and the liquor store. When they walked hand in hand, she smiled as Joaquin closed his eyes and relished the breeze finally blowing on his sweet, chubby toddler cheeks.

Then one Saturday afternoon there was a knock at the door. Carrie worried it was the landlord, asking for the later-than-usually-late rent. She slowly opened the door to find two Mariposa Island police officers. One younger, one older, both with crew cuts and ruddy faces. Carrie wondered if the younger one thought she was pretty. She pushed wisps of her hair back off her face. She had to start paying better attention to her appearance.

She invited the officers in, offered them glasses of water. She took a sip of her rum and cola. She wondered if they could smell it on her breath, but it was already almost four o'clock, and who could blame a mother of two small children for having a drink.

The officers settled in awkwardly next to her on the

couch, glancing at Joaquin and Elena, who were scribbling on old newspapers with nubby crayons that had seen better days.

"Now what's this about?" It was so rare that she spoke with anyone, so unusual for her to interact beyond the basic need to buy something at the store, that she wondered if they could pick up on her accent. If they would ask her where she was from. She loved when that happened, on the rare occasion it did. So many people knew nothing of Cuba. Or they only knew sad things.

Before everything happened, it was the most beautiful place on earth. This is what Carrie always told people. She hoped it made people jealous to know that she had once lived in the most beautiful place on earth.

"Ma'am, are you the wife of Francis Finney, originally of Healy?" the young officer asked.

"I am," Carrie said, nodding. How she hated Frank's given name.

"Ma'am, I'm sorry, but there's been an accident."

Carrie nodded again. She said nothing. She stared and blinked as the officers explained what they had been told by the Healy Police Department. That the night before Frank had been coming home (*but this is his home*) from downtown Healy and had run off the road into a tree. He'd died on impact.

"Ma'am, is there a relative or friend we can call for you?" the older officer asked.

"I'm afraid not," said Carrie.

Joaquin and Elena scribbled away on the newspaper, unaware. Carrie tried to make sense of their drawings. Messy black clouds. Big red explosions.

"It's possible he'd had a few drinks before getting behind the wheel," the younger officer said, shaking his head with proper remorse. The older officer grimaced. Carrie got the sense the younger officer wasn't supposed to have said that.

"Ma'am," the older officer said again, "are you *sure* there's no one we can call?"

Carrie shook her head no, but the officers didn't want to leave her alone. To Carrie's horror they knocked on a few doors in the complex, and soon a troop of the courtyard ladies showed up at her door in fussy rayon pantsuits and Dacron dresses to express their remorse. They eventually returned with covered dishes and faces full of concern, hungry with curiosity to get a glimpse of their reclusive neighbor, the one they referred to often and casually as "that strange Spanish girl."

And as Carrie allowed her apartment to be taken over, allowed her children to be bathed and changed by strangers (*"I don't know if she's given them a bath in over a week, the poor dears"*), she sat on the couch and allowed the bustling women to bring her a plate with heaps of casserole and cocktail after cocktail—the rum was medicinal, the ladies told each other. Carrie didn't care how fast they saw her drink them. Sitting there on the couch—as dumpy as the couch at Frank's parents, if she was being honest, although she didn't deserve such a dumpy couch—she was reminded of being in the *salita* back in Cuba, of being told by her beautiful mother and handsome father that soon she would be going on a journey to learn English. And as she sat there watching the women move about, she was reminded of sitting on the Finneys' couch back in Healy when she was told that her parents were dead. So much of her life seemed to unfold on couches while she sat helpless. So much bad news was delivered while she was seated and surrounded by well-meaning people who thought they were doing right by her.

Her parents had thought they'd been doing the right thing to send her to America. The Finneys had thought they'd been doing the right thing by bringing her to their house to live with them. And these strange ladies thought they were doing the right thing by invading her home and fluttering about performing their charity. And once again Carrie felt the waves pushing her along, wherever they wanted. She couldn't fight them. Sitting there on the couch she conjured up an image of Frank when he was very young, of him smiling shyly at her in the kitchen of the Finney home, his dumb grin taking up so much space. She pictured his well-worn, short-sleeved Oxford button-downs in Easter egg pastels. The soft curve of his Adam's apple. The warmth in his voice when he promised he would take her to live by the sea. She must have felt something at last, because warm tears slid down her cheeks, and as she shut her eyes she heard one of the neighbor women exclaim in a jumpy voice—a voice that was almost proud for having been the first one to spot it— "Oh, good grief, look, the poor thing's crying. I think everything's just hit her all at once."

JOAQUIN

CHAPTER SIXTEEN

I OWE CARLOS A MILLION FOR LOANING ME THIS CAR
even if it is a Chevette that can't get over fifty miles per hour
with my foot all the way down on the gas pedal.

Thirty more miles to Healy.

I didn't tell Elena. I walked out of Mami's room, numb
and foggy, like that one time I'd smoked pot at Kevin Anderson's house, and I headed into my bedroom where I'd gotten a
piece of paper and a pen and scribbled down the names of the
Healy relatives that appeared in the obituary. I'd looked at the
picture of my dad in the newspaper, his youthful face totally
unaware that it was smiling happily at me above his own death
notice. Robotically, I put everything back just as I'd found it.
I shut the closet door. I aimed a middle finger in the general
direction of my mother's bed, and then I walked out of the
house.

"Where are you going?" Elena asked from the couch, her eyes not leaving the television.

Our mom lied to us all these years.

"Out."

Our dad is dead.

"Well, bye to you, too!" That's what she'd yelled through the door as I walked through the screened-in porch and down the porch steps, patting my pocket to make sure I had my wallet.

Carlos will help you, I'd told myself. *Carlos has a car.*

So I'd hauled my bike out from behind the house and raced toward El Mirador. My legs burned as I pumped the pedals past the Whataburger and the DQ.

I opened the door to El Mirador. The smell of warm tortillas. The sound of conjunto. Carlos was at the bar, drying some glasses. He looked up at me, surprised.

"Are you on the schedule?" He smiled. He fucking smiled. My father will never smile at me again. But my boss does.

"No, I'm not on the schedule," I said. My voice cracked. So embarrassing. I tried to slide my hands into my pockets but I couldn't because they were clenched into tight fists. I looked around nervously for Amy.

"Joaquin, you okay?" Carlos asked, stepping out from behind the bar. In a booth nearby, a family with three towheaded boys still in bathing suits dipped their French fries in the queso and looked up at me, curious.

"Yeah," I said, and all of a sudden there's Amy, popping up

from around the corner where we do our side work, like a magic trick. My heart exploded. The rage released from my shoulders and fists.

"Hey," I managed.

"Hey," she said, all soft and surprised.

"Joaquin, are you sure you're okay?" Carlos asked again. "You look pale."

I walked back toward the bar, and the three of us ended up in the small hallway that leads to the staff break room. I stammered out a story to Carlos and Amy—something about finding my dad and needing to go to Healy. I don't know if I made any sense. Carlos frowned. Amy's eyes widened.

"You need to go to Healy?" she asked. "But where is that?" She took my hand in her hand. Her grip was warm. Gentle.

"Near Houston," I said. "Like an hour or so west of it."

Carlos and Amy exchanged glances.

"You want me to come?" Amy asked.

And I did. Damn, I did. But somewhere in me I knew I needed to face this all by myself. And anyway, I felt like I might cry. And I didn't want to cry in front of Amy.

"I need to go alone," I answered.

Amy just nodded, her face uncertain. Then she hugged me and kissed my neck, not even shy to do it in front of Carlos. Carlos just dug into his pocket and drew out a set of keys. "Take the Chevette," he said.

I took them and nodded. I think Carlos knew that if I said thank you, I might have started to cry. At any rate, he just nodded back.

And so here I am. Twenty miles to Healy.

Every ten miles or so, I wipe the tears from my eyes.

• • •

As I arrive in town, I scope out the main drag. A couple of fast-food places. A hair salon called The Curl Up and Dye. A drugstore and a movie house. I've driven balls to the wall without even stopping to go to the bathroom since I left El Mirador, but I don't have a clue where I'm heading. The only thing I've got going for me is that this seems like the kind of town where it would be super easy to find someone. Healy makes Mariposa Island look like a real metropolis.

Mami had mentioned growing up here with a foster family and that our dad was her foster family's oldest son. They'd treated her awful, she'd told us. Made her sleep in the garage. Made her do more chores than the other kids. The few times she'd talked about them—usually after one too many drinks—she scowled, her face as twisted as a pretzel. She only married our dad to get out of Healy, she'd told us. Only he was a good-for-nothing who took off when we were small. And that's it. That was the whole story, chapter and verse.

I spot a pay phone outside a gas station, and, pulling the wrinkled paper from my back pocket, I get out of Carlos's Chevette and finally stretch, my back cracking like popcorn. I open the battered phone book and flip through the pages. There are three listings for Finney. I'm tempted to just rip the page out, but I don't want to be a dick, so I have to go into the gas station and borrow a pencil from the guy behind the counter so I can copy down all three addresses. I decide to hit up the one for Francis Finney first. That must be Francis Finney Senior.

He must be my . . . grandfather? I can't stop to process that right now. I can only keep moving forward. When I return the gas station guy's pencil, I ask for directions, and soon I'm on my way, my stomach in knots. Eventually I pull up in front of a large, rambling two-story house with a wide porch. It's big but the flower beds have seen better days. The roof, too. An American flag sags in the summer heat, not a single sign of a breeze to make it move.

Am I really doing this?

I glance in the rearview mirror to make sure I don't look like a serial killer or a weirdo. Then I take a deep breath. I wish I had a beer to take the edge off. But I don't, so the next thing I know I'm walking up the cracked driveway and toward the front door.

When it swings open, I'm greeted by a girl. A woman? She's older than me, but probably not by much. Red hair pulled back into a ponytail. Black T-shirt. Bare feet.

"Yeah?" she says. Not unkindly or anything.

"Uh . . ." I start, and I realize that maybe I could have spent the long drive up here rehearsing what I was supposed to say. "I'm looking for Francis Finney? Frank?"

She frowns. Maybe the address is old. Maybe my secret grandfather has moved to Cleveland or something.

"Um, I'm his daughter. What's this about?" I see her brace

herself in the doorway just a little more firmly, so I step back on the porch so I won't make her nervous.

"This is really weird, but I think I could be his grandson?"

The red-haired woman's eyes open wide, followed by her mouth.

"Wait . . ." she says. She stares at me. Examines me like I'm a specimen in a science experiment. "You're . . . no. Wait, you're Frank's son? Joaquin?"

She knows who I am.

"Yes," I say, at a loss for how to say more.

"Well, hell," the red-haired woman says, and her use of the word *hell* makes me relax just a little. "I'm Deirdre Finney. I think . . . shit. I think I'm your *aunt*."

· · ·

A few hours ago, I didn't know I had a long-lost grandfather, and if you'd asked me to picture meeting one, I wouldn't have thought it would go much like how this is going. Me, standing awkwardly in the family room off the kitchen with this woman—this Aunt Deirdre—staring at a lump of a man in a recliner wearing a thin white T-shirt, brown slacks, white athletic socks, black sandals, and a vacant expression on his face.

"This is Dad," Deirdre says, placing her hand on his shoulder. She speaks loudly, in the direction of his ear, which is covered with wisps of graying hair that someone—I guess Deirdre—has carefully combed. "Dad, this is Joaquin. Do you want to say hello?"

I crouch down, stick my hand out. Francis Finney Senior sticks his hand out without making eye contact. Pumps my hand once. Twice.

"Hello, sir," I say. But all I'm thinking is that his blood runs through my veins. And I never even knew he existed.

Frank Senior drops my hand and shifts his own to his lap.

"Puppy?" he asks Deirdre. His voice sounds softer and more feminine than I would have imagined. Deirdre heads out of the room and comes back with a small brown stuffed dog, its ears worn thin. My grandfather takes it into his hands and smiles widely, revealing a few blank spaces where teeth used to be.

"Do you want to sit down?" Deirdre says, motioning to the couch. "Do you want a glass of water?"

What I really want is a beer, but I can't ask for that.

"I'm okay," I say.

Deirdre settles in on a chair next to the recliner. She gazes at her father for a moment, then switches her focus to me.

"It's dementia," she says. "I guess Alzheimer's. It started a few years ago, after my mom died of breast cancer. Honestly, I'm glad she didn't have to see him like this. It would have broken her heart."

I nod, and Deirdre grimaces. "Damn, I'm sorry. I just told you your grandmother is dead. This is just . . ." She shakes her head, smiles ruefully. "This is a lot to take in."

"I know. I'm sorry for springing it on you like this." I watch as Frank Senior pets his puppy and smiles to himself. At least someone in the room is relaxed.

"It's okay," Deirdre answers. She tucks her feet underneath her and really looks at me, studying my face. "I haven't seen you since you were a toddler. And my memories are pretty vague. I was just a kid then myself."

I shift a bit in my seat. I'm not sure how to respond.

"I wish I remembered more," I say. "But I just found out about you a few hours ago."

Deirdre listens as I tell her about finding my father's obituary, about living with my sister and mother on Mariposa Island, and about how I've always been told my father abandoned us by moving to California. At this Deirdre rolls her eyes.

"California? I don't think my brother ever left Texas." She looks at my grandfather, who has closed his eyes and drifted off into sleep. "Not to be weird, but . . . you wouldn't want a beer, would you?"

"Please," I say, and soon Deirdre and I are sharing cold cans of Lone Star. Bit by bit, a story unfolds.

"Like I said, I was little then, just a kid when my brother moved out and married your mom. I remember a few times when your dad brought you here for the day. We ate hot dogs, watched television. Right here in this room." She motions to the neat, orderly living room with its worn-out furniture and stacks of *National Geographic* and battered paperbacks on the shelves. "Wait, let me get something." She jumps up from her chair and scans the nearby bookshelves until she finds what she's looking for—a thick photo album.

"Here," she says, the cellophane pages crackling a bit as

she flips through them. She points out people in snapshots—another aunt, my grandmother, Deirdre herself when she was little, a few cousins. Everyone peers out from the pages with big grins. The men stand near charcoal grills, proud of both their beer bellies and their burgers. The women have been captured mid-laugh at Christmas parties, their mouths wide open and their eyes shut.

"That's you!" Deirdre shouts, stabbing at one picture with excitement. "And your sister." And it is us, playing in someone's backyard—maybe this one—sitting in a sandbox, Elena chewing on a red plastic bucket. Me diligently working on a castle. I blink once. Again. All these years of living with Mami, this little artifact, this proof that, however briefly, we belonged to another family has been here in this photo album. There's nothing to say. I just stare at it. Deirdre leaves it open on the coffee table.

"So from what I've been told, and from what I remember," she says, sitting back, glancing at her father, who is still sleeping, "your mom and dad had some huge fight about something. Keep in mind my parents were not thrilled about them getting married."

"How come?"

"Your mom . . . I mean, again, I don't want to sound rude or whatever . . ."

I shake my head. "Just the truth. You won't hurt my feelings."

Deirdre nods, but she waits a beat before she keeps talking.

Like she's trying to figure out how to say what she wants to tell me. "From what I heard, your mom just never adjusted to coming here. To being in America. I mean, look, I was a baby when she lived with us, so I have no memory of it. I think I can be objective about it. She was young. She came here not even knowing English. Then her parents died." Her eyes widen. "Wait, you knew all that, right?"

"Yeah," I say, reassuring her. "The Cuba stuff I know."

"Good," she says. "Anyway, you know, I guess she came from money. And we're, you know, working class." She shrugs, motioning at the living room for proof.

"Yeah, she came from money," I say. "She even had this debutante party back in Havana that was super fancy and in all the papers."

"Oh, my family heard about that party," Deirdre says, her voice rueful. "Anyway, you know, she just never fit in. She never got acclimated. But my brother—your dad—I guess he fell in love with her. From the pictures, you know, when she was young she was really pretty."

I think about Mami. Her birdlike body with bloodshot eyes. But there was a time when she had been pretty. I know that. She had been beautiful.

"So anyway, they got married," Deirdre continues, and I realize I'm settling into this story like it's about someone else, not me. Like it's the plot of one of those movies of the week that Mami and Elena watch on TV. "Your mom wanted to live by the ocean because it reminded her of Cuba, so they move down to Mariposa, my brother drops out of college . . ." She's interrupted by a cough from her father.

"You okay, Dad?" she asks. My grandfather opens his rheumy eyes and looks around like he's trying to remember where he is, then shuts them. We wait a moment until he's asleep again.

"He spends most of his time like that," Deirdre says, sighing. "I think he prefers sleeping to being awake." She takes a sip of her beer and continues her story. "So anyway, they move to Mariposa, they have you guys, and your mom . . . the way I understand it she just didn't want to have anything to do with us. She didn't even want to bring y'all up to visit or anything. The few times we saw you, it's because my brother brought you alone." She stops her story and looks at me. I wait for her to continue until I realize she's waiting for me, waiting for some sort of explanation.

"My mom is . . . I don't know," I say. "I think she just never got over Cuba, like you said. I think she's . . . something's not right about her." It's the first time I've ever said something like this out loud, and immediately I know it's the truth.

Deirdre nods, shakes her can of Lone Star to make sure it's empty, and sets it on the coffee table. "That's what it sounds like. Anyway, one weekend your dad came up here all by himself. He and your mom had some huge fight over something. He said he needed a break." She chews a thumbnail, just like I do when I'm thinking. Are habits genetic? "I was, like, ten years old, and I remember him and my parents sitting at the kitchen table, and my folks were telling him he had to go back down and get you two and bring you back here. That they could get a lawyer. Say your mom was unfit."

I take in that word. *Unfit.* We were never starved or locked in a closet or anything. Is Mami unfit? Was she unfit? I don't know. She's just Mami.

"So, you know, your dad was still in love with her, I think, despite all of it," Deirdre continues. "I think he still had hopes they could work it out. He would call down there and your mom wouldn't pick up. He sent the letters, obviously. Weird that she kept them, don't you think?"

"Yeah," I say. But was it? I just want to agree so Deirdre will keep talking.

"He was feeling really down about it. Not sure what to do, I guess. Depressed. One night I was asleep in my bedroom upstairs," she says. "I didn't even know he'd gone out. Anyway, I heard this screaming. I ran downstairs and the police were here." She motions her chin toward the front door. "Right there in the entryway, the police were telling my parents what had happened. My mom flipped out, of course." She pauses, looks over at her father. "Your dad was the oldest of all us kids and I was the youngest, so we were never really, you know . . . *close* or anything." She chews on her thumbnail, shifts her gaze to the front door again. "But he was still my big brother."

Outside I can hear a neighbor's dog barking. We don't speak for a moment or two.

"I'm sorry," I manage, finally.

"Oh, he was your dad," Deirdre says, coming out of her thoughts. "I really should say I'm sorry to you. Especially since you never really got to know him."

"Thanks," I say. It feels strange to say it, but how else do I respond?

"There's more, though," she says. "He was drunk. He was coming back from Caroline's Pub downtown and the guys at the bar said he'd had more than his share." There's a long pause. "He ran into a tree."

I don't know why she's pausing. Like there's something I'm supposed to understand but don't.

And then suddenly I see what she wants me to know but can't say herself.

"You think he . . . drove into the tree on purpose?"

Deirdre exhales long and loud. "Maybe," she says. "Of course we'll never know. My mother would never let anybody even bring up the possibility. But I believe some of my siblings think he did, yeah. Not sure what my dad thought. We never discussed it. But afterward . . . everyone was so broken over it. My parents were so crushed. And I think . . . I'm sorry, but I think they blamed your mom. And I think . . . I guess . . . they were happy with just letting her disappear."

"And us along with her," I add.

Deirdre nods and looks down at her hands. "Now I can see maybe that was wrong. You and your sister were their grandchildren. We could have fought for you. But . . ." she sighs.

"Hey, it's okay," I say. I look down at the open photo album.

At the picture of Elena and me in the sandbox. I imagine what our voices would have sounded like bouncing off these walls. I picture us playing tag in the front yard or spraying ourselves with a garden hose. I quickly construct a parallel universe where Deirdre feels more like an older sister than a long-lost aunt.

"You want another beer?" Deirdre asks, raising an eyebrow. "I mean, what I need to know is, did you earn your Irish genes?"

"Por supuesto," I tell her. "And the Cuban ones, too."

She cracks up and so do I, and then I say yes to the beer.

"Well come on back to the kitchen with me," she says. "You can see your mom's old room. I mean, if you want to."

Deirdre leads me into a tidy kitchen with white cabinets and a refrigerator covered with kooky magnets, and she opens up a door to a small but serviceable room with a view of the backyard. There are big cardboard boxes stacked up along the perimeter, one of them labeled XMAS DECORATIONS. An old sewing machine sits on a small table in the corner, facing out one of the windows.

"It obviously didn't look like this when your mom lived here," she says. "No matter what she told you, I promise. My mom and dad gave her a bed and a dresser and everything." She says it like she's half joking, but I can tell she wants to be sure I don't leave here thinking bad about her family. Which I guess is my family, too. Sort of.

"I'm sure they were good to her," I say, taking in the rest of the room. The walls are a cheerful yellow even though they're in desperate need of repainting. I touch the doorframe. Take in a little of the musty smell. When my mother was my age, she slept in this very room. Stared out these very windows. If she knew I was here right now, what would she do? What would she say? Nothing nice, I'm pretty sure. I can hear her voice in my head, sharp and biting.

"Look how they made me sleep off the kitchen like a maid. And I had a maid myself back in Cuba! My mother and father would have never let me go had they known I would be living like this."

Behind me I hear the sound of a can popping open.

"Here, nephew, drink up," Deirdre says, grinning, and I take the can in hand, grateful. I push my mother's voice out of my head. She hated this place like she hates all places that aren't Cuba. That's just how she is.

But there is nothing wrong with this place. No matter what she told us when we were little, I know that now. As I follow Deirdre back into the living room, I just keep thinking that this house would have been a really nice place to grow up.

CHAPTER SEVENTEEN

THE HOUSE IS DARK AND QUIET AS I CREEP IN, MY CON-
verse in hand so I avoid any extra noise. It's after ten o'clock.
Carlos's Chevette is parked down the street where Mami
won't see it. I'll return it tomorrow.

I stand in the middle of the living room, listening to the
hum of the refrigerator. The ticktock of the clock. My own
breathing.

I can't wait until tomorrow morning to tell Elena the
truth. She has to know right now. I tiptoe to her bedroom
door, rap on it lightly.

"Yeah? Joaquin, is that you?"

When I enter, Elena is already sitting up in bed, all lit up
from the streetlight that's streaming in through her bedroom
window. As a kid this was my bedroom, but the light kept me
up. Elena likes it. So we switched.

"Where *were* you?" she asks, indignant, but her face has relief written on it.

"I'm sorry," I say, my voice just above a whisper.

"Mami thought you were working," she says, curling her knees up under her chin, giving me a look that says she's not sure if she's forgiven me yet. "I didn't tell her any different. But where *were* you?"

I kick some clothes and magazines out of the way and clear a path to her bed before I sit at the foot. Elena scoots back, resting herself against the wall under that ridiculous Madonna poster.

"I have to tell you something. And it's pretty intense."

Elena frowns. Raises an eyebrow.

"Let me guess," she says. "Amy's pregnant. I'm going to be Tía Elena."

"Jesus," I say, rolling my eyes. "No. Now come on. I need you to be serious."

Elena sits up straighter and crosses her legs. She's wearing that old LBJ High track T-shirt of mine again. "Okay," she says. "What is it?"

In whispers punctuated by Elena's questions—which come out steady, sure of themselves, not at all hysterical like I imagined they'd be—I unfold the story of the weirdest day of my life, ending with Deirdre walking me out to my car and slipping me her phone number on a piece of paper.

"She told us to be in touch if we want to be," I say. "And if we want to meet the rest of our family."

Elena frowns. Her features twist up just a bit. "I don't know, are they really our family?"

I pull back, confused. "Well . . . yeah, aren't they?"

Elena shrugs. "They didn't want anything to do with us, did they? I mean, when they had the chance?"

My eyes widen. In the car on my way home from Healy, I imagined spilling everything to Elena as she shrieked in anger, paced under the glow of the streetlight, and cursed Mami for lying to us all our lives. But Elena seems *calm* about all of it.

"Yeah, I mean, I guess they could have fought harder to keep a relationship with us," I say. "But you have to admit that it doesn't sound like Mami made it very easy for them."

Elena absorbs that for a moment, then says, "Well, we're really only getting their side of the story."

"Seriously?" I ask my little sister. "Elena, she lied to us. She told us our father abandoned us. But our father is *dead*. He's been dead since you were a baby. This doesn't *bother* you?" I'm spitting out every word. My whispers are building up to full volume.

"Stop," Elena says, waving her hand in front of me. "You'll wake her up."

"Maybe she deserves to get woken up."

Elena sighs and leans over to the packed purse sitting by the side of her bed. She digs inside of it until she retrieves what she's looking for, a pack of Marlboro Lights. After cracking the window, she lights one up.

"Are you fucking serious?" I ask. "When did this start?"

Elena exhales a stream of smoke through the battered screen and ignores the question.

"Let me guess. J.C."

"No," Elena fires back. "I smoked sometimes before him."

"Well, you weren't buying packs."

Elena dumps the ashes into a glass with an inch or two of water that's sitting on her cluttered nightstand. I wonder if she keeps it for this very purpose.

"You'd better hope Mami doesn't smell it."

"I'll sleep with the windows open and take a shower first thing. And anyway, what do you even care what she thinks? Aren't you about to charge into her room and attack her for lying to us all our lives?"

She takes another puff. Elena probably thinks smoking makes her look older, but the reverse is true. She looks like a little girl faking it. It's dumb. Still, her question gnaws at me. What am I going to say to Mami? The whole drive I never thought about that part. Only about telling Elena.

"Just tell me if you're planning on waking her up, so I can put this out," Elena says, waving her cigarette in the air. Her voice has turned from neutral to hostile.

"What's going on with you?" I ask. "Why are you mad at me?"

"I'm not," she says.

"Liar."

"I'm not mad!"

Silence except for the *puff* and *sizzle* of Elena's smoke. I know if I wait her out long enough, she'll start talking. Finally, it works.

"Look, Joaquin, you come in here with your big news, expecting me to flip out," Elena starts, her big eyes staring me down. She shifts a bit and finally stabs her cigarette out on the inside rim of the glass before letting it drop into the water. "But the truth is, I don't really feel much one way or the other. From what you're telling me, our father kind of did abandon us. He went up to Healy and left us here."

"But he wanted us back," I argue, thinking of the big, two-story home where Deirdre and my grandfather are most likely fast asleep right now. I picture the family photo album. The rambling porch. The wide backyard.

"Maybe, but he still left us," Elena says. "Whether he went to California or back home, what does it matter?"

"But she *lied* to us," I insist. As usual when it comes to Mami, I'm the angry one. Elena is calm and collected. It pisses me off.

"Maybe she lied because she thought it would be easier than knowing he died," Elena says. And then she yawns. She actually fucking yawns.

"How are you tired?"

"Joaquin, I can't do this right now." She rubs the scar on her chin, her old, nervous habit. Deirdre's words run through my head. *They were going to say our mother was unfit.*

"How'd you get that scar on your chin?" I ask, going right for the jugular.

Elena lowers her hand slowly into her lap. "I got it hiking to Machu Picchu," she says, her voice soft and even, her gaze steady. "I got it skydiving in the Himalayas."

"Not now, Elena."

"You know how I got it," she says, her voice an accusation. "So why bother asking?"

"I just wish," I start, standing up, getting ready to storm out so she knows how mad I am, "that for once in your life you could stop making excuses for the situation we find ourselves in. That you could grasp the fact that she's going to control you for the rest of your life if you let her."

"Oh, *enough!*" Elena says, her voice louder than it's been all night. "You act like we live these super-fucking-horrible lives. If you hate it here so much, just leave."

I shake my head. I walk out of her bedroom and leave her sitting on her bed, staring at me. I shut the door before I can hear her start crying.

• • •

This is how Elena got her scar.

The summer she was twelve years old, she left the house to go to the Stop-N-Go while Mami was at work. I was out somewhere, riding bikes with Kevin Anderson. Heading down to the beach to see which girls in our class had started wearing bikinis. Some dumb shit. I was never subjected to Mami's check-in phone calls.

Mami called once, so Elena thought she was safe for a

while after that. But Mami must have been suspicious that day because I guess she called not long after. Only it was too late. At the moment the phone was ringing, Elena was making her way down to Mr. O'Rourke's store to buy a Coke and a magazine with some Christmas money she still had saved. As she walked, she was oblivious to the fact that Mami was calling and calling, and that the phone was ringing and ringing, and there was no one left to hear it but the walls.

By the time Mami got home from work that evening, I was back from wherever I'd been, and Elena and I were slumped on the couch watching the local news, bored out of our skulls.

"Shit, we should start dinner," I said, jumping up at the sound of the car door slamming in the driveway. I had just started cursing that summer, trying it out to see how tough it made me sound.

"Shit, shit, shit," Elena agreed, turning off the television and heading toward the kitchen.

We were pulling a pot out to fill with water so we could boil spaghetti when Mami stalked in, and immediately I knew that Elena and I were—to use a word I'd started using only recently—totally fucked.

"Where were you this afternoon, Elena?" Mami said, staring at us. Before Elena could answer, Mami marched over to the refrigerator and started making herself a drink. The ice cubes rattled a cold warning.

"I was here, Mami," Elena said, her hands still holding the pot.

"*Mentirosa*. I called and you didn't pick up."

Elena's face grew red. I stood between the two of them, my eyes jumping back and forth, anticipating the next move.

"Mami, I was here! Maybe I was just in the bathroom?"

Later on, Elena would get better at lying. But back then she was just an amateur. Mami stared her down, cocktail in hand. She took a sip from her drink and eyed us, her body blocking the front door. Waiting. She had already won and she knew it. It was just a matter of Elena officially declaring her surrender.

"Well," Elena started, her voice cracking, "I just went to the store down the street. I just wanted a Coke. I just . . . wanted to get out of the house." Elena could barely speak she was so anxious. Her voice trembled. Tears welled in her eyes. My heart was hammering hard inside my chest. She was my baby sister. I had to protect her somehow.

"Mami," I said, "calm down. It wasn't a big deal." Like swearing, standing up to our mother was something else that I'd recently started trying on for size.

Mami's face snapped toward me when she heard my voice. I sensed Elena shrinking back against the wall, the pot for spaghetti clutched in her hands, her knuckles white.

"What did you say to me?" Mami fired. The words were thick with fury.

"I said," I started in, enjoying the sound of my voice, newly deep and powerful, "that it wasn't a big deal. Let her leave the house every once in a while. It's ridiculous that you don't." Then, to punctuate my statement, I offered up a loud "Jesus

Christ!" in the same tired, world-weary way Kevin Anderson did whenever something pissed him off.

In one swift, explosive movement Mami was across our tiny kitchen with her hands out, coming for me. Reflexively, I ducked and she missed. In a microsecond she decided Elena would do, and as the pot clattered to the floor and I yelled for her to stop, Mami slammed Elena's face into the edge of the kitchen counter, leaving a dark red slice on Elena's chin as neat and straight as a ruler. A smear of Elena's blood marked the place where her face had hit, an angry explosion.

I shouldn't have moved, *hermanita*. I should have taken the hit for you.

But I didn't. I backed out like a coward.

Wordless, Mami stormed out of the house, dropping her drink on the porch where it shattered into pieces. The car engine started up. She didn't come back until very late that night, long after I had helped Elena clean out the cut and pick up the broken glass on the porch and hours after I'd worried she needed stitches. (She probably did.) By the time our mother returned, Elena was asleep in her bed, her pillow still damp from crying. I lay on a pile of blankets on the carpet next to her bed, a sheet over me, and every so often I sat up to check on her, my heart heavy with guilt.

Mami never spoke of the incident again.

For some time afterward, I tried to be more like Elena. Comply more with Mami's requests. Push her buttons less. I did it for my sister. The next summer Elena told me about her plan. I went along with it immediately. After all, I owed her. I helped her make the flyer that she allegedly found at Belden's. I picked out the names for the kids. I covered for her in every way possible. Together we invented the Callahans, and in doing so, Elena created a world where she could escape. A world where Mami no longer held such an influence. A world based on lies.

The Callahans lasted longer than I thought they would, and I grew to resent the fantasy they became for my sister. I guess because while Elena used them to fake obedience to Mami, I did the opposite, unable to stay compliant for very long. Unable to keep my mouth closed, even when it would have been smarter in some ways to do so. And as each summer trudged onward, as each year rolled past, as each evening at home filled with tension and anticipation of the next bad thing to come, I discovered more and more evidence of the real, hard truth of our lives.

And I stared into it like I was staring at the sun, until the pain of looking at it forced me to close my eyes and look away. But only for a moment.

CARRIE

1972

*Joaquin and Elena would never know it, but they had the hover-*ing ladies at the apartment complex to thank for what remained of any stability in their lives, at least during those early years. The women raised money for Carrie and her children and told their churches about their sad situation. They got Carrie a job as a receptionist at a local doctor's office—they even helped her find a babysitter for the kids. For a while, they made Carrie their little pet. And Carrie even enjoyed it. It had been so long since she'd been really taken care of.

She tried to ignore their home dye jobs, their working-class roughness, the way so many of them seemed to think wearing one size smaller than their actual sizes made them look thinner instead of like overstuffed sausages. So she smiled when they came over unannounced, forced herself to attend their boring bunco dice games, nodded with enthusiasm at whatever drippy, dumb stories they told. She was indebted to them. She knew this. And they were not unkind. But Carrie wasn't like them, and the more she spent time with them, the more she feared their commonness would rub off on her. Scrub away the last little bits of the part of her that she knew was special.

After almost a year she saved up enough money to rent a house in what she hoped was a slightly better neighborhood. She told the women she needed a fresh start, that the apartment complex was full of too many bad memories. But really she felt she needed to break away from them before she found herself twenty pounds overweight, smoking in the courtyard, and screaming at her children in front of the entire neighborhood.

On one of her last nights in the apartment, she forced herself to have the women over as a sort of thank-you and served them drinks and little cookies with *dulce de leche*. They thought the dessert was so exotic, and Carrie—warmed up a bit with a few rum and Cokes—regaled them with stories of Cuba and her perfect girlhood on a magical island. She felt like a princess with her ladies-in-waiting. It was almost fun. But when the last woman left, Carrie shut the door, exhausted, and later on, when the women would drop by her new house, Carrie would hustle the children into the bathroom. Turn out the lights. Pretend that no one was home until at last they left and, eventually, stopped trying to visit her altogether.

On the morning she moved into her new home, Carrie examined it with a careful eye. Her first thought: it was better than the apartment. Cleaner and newer, with kitchen cabinets that had recently been painted and three bedrooms instead of two. That the two smaller bedrooms—the ones for Joaquin and Elena—were actually the result of one bedroom being divided in half was something she was willing to overlook. The house was a tiny, almost infinitesimal step, but at least it was a step in the right direction. Certainly things would continue to improve.

Carrie even liked her job although she'd never thought she would like working. Dr. Sanders was an ophthalmologist and a serious, quiet man who expected a serious, quiet office. Carrie enjoyed keeping order and filing folders and using petty cash to buy fresh flowers and copies of *Bon Appétit* for the waiting room. She enjoyed the feeling of being gatekeeper to an important man because it made her feel important, too. Years later when Dr. Sanders retired and his son took over the practice, he changed Carrie's title to "office manager," which Carrie enjoyed writing down each year on her tax return. It had a weight to it, Carrie thought.

Sometimes, but not often, she missed Frank. She mostly missed their earlier years, which, like all things bathed in the passage of time, seemed almost sweet to her now. But she knew as the children grew that they would begin to ask questions about their father. Questions she didn't want to answer—she even thought Joaquin might have a few memories of him—so she was quick to hide photographs of Frank. To give away his clothes, shoes, knickknacks.

Still she worried. If she told the children Frank had died, and so tragically, too, they might want to know more about him. Maybe even more about his horrid family that had treated her like the hired help. If she told the children that Frank was gone forever, they might lionize him. Dream up a magical father so wonderful and good and perfect—how could she compete with a ghost?

As the children grew, she discovered it was easy for her to tell them Frank had abandoned them. And anyway, hadn't he? Hadn't he taken off, left her barely any cash for food, and never returned? She chose California as his destination—it was a place people ran off to, Carrie decided—and she was careful to offer up just the right pained expression to Joaquin and Elena whenever they pestered her about what had happened to their father. If she teared up when they questioned her, if she told them just how much he had hurt her, hurt *them*, they might stop asking. So she was sure to cry a little when talking about him. Sniffle and excuse herself. The crying was real, although it wasn't really over Frank. Soon Joaquin and Elena stopped asking about him altogether.

At night she would bathe the children and put them to bed and pour herself a drink and then sometimes another, and if she drank too much, she would let herself think about Cuba. About her mother and father and Juanita, too. She would pull out her old photographs. She would whisper old songs. She would conjure up an ending to her disastrous *quince* that involved kissing her neighbor Ricardo in the dusk next to the orchids that grew outside her home. And sometimes she could almost convince herself that this was really how it happened. And she would think of the sweet, sweet smell of *agua de violetas* and remember Varadero Beach and the blue, blue ocean.

Still tipsy from her drinking, Carrie liked to check on her children before she went to bed. She loved padding into their rooms late at night, adjusting their covers, pushing back soft hair from their sweaty heads. Joaquin always fell asleep with a book or a Lego piece clutched in his hand. Elena always ended up with her rear stuck in the air. Sometimes Carrie would simply stand there and stare at them until hot tears pricked at her eyes and a lump built inside her throat. Because of them she wasn't alone and she never would be. They would always be with her. They would never leave her. They were hers and hers alone. And as they grew they would come to trust her and love her and they would know—they would have to know—that she had done her best for them despite all the horrible things that had happened to her in her life.

And she promised herself this one thing. She would be a good mother.

JOAQUIN

CHAPTER EIGHTEEN

IN THE WEEKS FOLLOWING MY DRIVE OUT TO HEALY, Elena and I observe a frosty peace. I stay out of her way and she stays out of mine. I go to work at El Mirador. I spend time with Amy when she has the house to herself, and we take refuge in her bedroom and have sex and listen to music and in general block out the rest of the world. I tell Amy everything. She listens and kisses me and then tells me to hang in there. One more year. Technically it's less than a year, if we move to Austin next May. She spins dreams about the two of us heading up to New York City after college, of her becoming a famous novelist and both of us going to all the best punk shows. It's a beautiful vision, but I don't ask her what I'm supposed to be doing in New York besides going with her to hear bands play. I don't want to disrupt the illusion.

Is it enough to live your life as part of someone else's

dreams, if the dreams belong to someone like Amy? I don't know.

Elena schedules babysitting jobs and stays out too late and comes home tipsy and smelling of smoke. Not just cigarette smoke but weed sometimes, too. No more acid trips that I'm aware of, at least. August drones on. The days get shorter. The summer is saying goodbye.

Mami knows nothing about my trip to Healy. I find myself staring at her as she watches evening game shows or made-for-TV movies. I picture her in that yellow room off the kitchen. I imagine Deirdre's big smile. I recall my grandfather's hands clutching his stuffed puppy. I picture an entire parallel life for me and Elena playing out hours away in Healy.

One Saturday morning, Mami tells Elena and me to go to the grocery store. She's in a vicious mood for no reason I can figure, and I'm pretty sure she just wants to be alone. I don't fight it, instead taking the keys and sliding into the driver's seat of the Honda. Elena gets in next to me, Mami's list in her hand.

Halfway down Esperanza Boulevard, Elena says, "Joaquin, don't be mad at me anymore."

I glance over at her. How do I tell her that I'm not mad now? Not really. Only worried. I'm always worried about her.

"Okay," I say. "Just don't be mad at me."

Elena traces her index finger along the passenger-side window. She doesn't look at me when she says, "I've never been mad at you a minute in my entire life."

I take my eyes off the road for a moment to look at her, and when she looks back at me, it's like once again we are co-conspirators. Just my little sister and me.

At the store, we toss groceries into our cart. Elena chides me for picking overripe fruit. I roll my eyes at her choice of Frosted Flakes.

"Mami won't like that," I say.

"I'll put the bag of Frosted Flakes inside that old box of Cheerios, which she never eats," Elena answers. "Wouldn't be the first time."

"Clever, clever," I tell her. She laughs.

We anticipate each other's words. Choices. Gestures.

Is there anyone who knows you more than your own flesh and blood?

In the car on the way home, Elena lets me play my cassette of the Jesus and Mary Chain. She doesn't even make fun of it.

We get back to our house, and Elena and I haul as many bags out of the car as we can. When we get to the front door we find Mami standing there, leaning against the doorframe. She's watching us with narrow eyes. Sizing us up.

My stomach knots.

I pass her and go into the kitchen, but she stays focused on Elena, who approaches the house with a smile on her pretty, youthful face. Mami stares her down, the crow's feet around her eyes deepening as she scowls.

"We got everything on the list," Elena says, following me into the kitchen. She starts carefully taking a carton of eggs out of one of the bags and sliding it into the refrigerator. I go back outside and grab the last of the groceries. Just as I'm heading into the kitchen, Mami says, "I know you weren't babysitting last night, Elena."

My nerves turn electric. In my mind's eye I see the story Elena and I have built crashing down around us. I ease a paper bag onto the counter and stand next to my sister. Elena slowly hauls a plastic sack full of potatoes out of a bag.

"What are you talking about?" Elena says, not turning to look at Mami. Her voice is even. Relaxed. "Of course I was babysitting."

"You're a liar." I peer over my shoulder. Mami's eyes are hard and on Elena like a scope on a target. "I just got off the phone with Mrs. Callahan. She said you were supposed to babysit this morning and you didn't show up."

I can't move. *Mami just got off the phone with Mrs. Callahan.* But Elena turns around and leans against the kitchen counter. She absentmindedly touches the scar on her chin. The thin, rubbery line of white skin just as straight as the edge of the counter she now rests against.

"Oh, Mami, really?" she says. A smile slides onto her face. "Mrs. *Callahan* called?"

Mami bristles. She looks straight at Elena, and Elena stares straight back. "Yes, she called," Mami says, but some of the fight is out of her voice.

Elena says nothing, her eyes bright, cold, and steady. I don't move a muscle.

A beat or two later Mami opens her mouth again. "At least, I *think* it was her."

The stillness in the room shatters. I take two cans of baked beans out of the bag and walk toward the cabinets over the counter to put them away, trying to look nonchalant, but my heart is beating hard. My throat is dry.

Out of the side of my eye I watch as Elena drags her hands through her hair. She ties her dark locks into a lazy knot. "Mami," she says at last, patiently but firmly, like she's talking to a child. "I was babysitting last night. Where else would I be?" Then her voice turns playful. Light. "Don't be silly."

And at this she walks toward Mami and kisses her on the cheek. A simple peck. One fluid motion. Not a hint of anxiety. Not a flush of uncertainty. Elena has won the liars' showdown, hands down. She disappears into her bedroom, leaving me with the rest of the groceries.

Mami is frowning. She narrows her heavy-lidded eyes at Elena's door and mutters something under her breath that I can't catch. Then she turns toward me.

"Why are you just standing there, Joaquin?" she snaps. "Finish up in here."

"I'm almost done," I say, jumping into action. And as I put spaghetti boxes away, I watch as Mami heads into her bedroom, drink in hand.

The house is silent as I line up the cans. Stack the fruit in the bowl. In my mind's eye, the future rolls out before me like an endless sea: Elena's and Mami's lies go on forever and ever—each one manipulating the other until neither knows where the truth ends and the lies begin. They can't see any other way to be.

I close my eyes as panic swells up in my chest. I head outside onto the screened-in porch to get some air, but it's not enough. I go straight out onto the sidewalk. I resist the urge to run, to head nowhere in particular, and I force myself to just stand there for a minute. The humidity drapes itself over me like a wet, heavy blanket. In the background I hear the honk of a car horn. The sigh and shudder of a city bus coming to a stop. The shout of children in some neighboring backyard, playing tag.

I can hardly breathe.

"*You're it!*" a little boy's voice announces, victorious. "I got you! You're it!"

• • •

It takes me three days to work up the nerve to tell them.

After a dinner of chicken and rice, Elena clears the table and dumps the dishes into the sink.

"Joaquin, can you wash them?" she asks.

"Yeah," I say. My throat is dry. I look over at Mami, who is tracing the tip of her pinkie finger in her drink. "I need to tell you something though. I need to tell you both something."

Elena turns to look at me. Mami takes a sip of her cocktail, her eyes trained on the wall opposite her.

Do it, Joaquin.

"I've decided I'm moving to California," I say. "By the end of the summer."

My eyes are on Mami, but I hear Elena gasp. I can't look at her. I stare at Mami. Finally she turns her gaze toward me and squints her eyes. Peers at me.

"Is this because you think you'll find your father?" she says, her voice even. Cold.

She could tell me now. She could. She could admit the truth if she thought it might mean I'd stay in Mariposa Island. But that would mean admitting that she lied, admitting that she was wrong.

"Because I honestly doubt you'll ever track him down," she continues. "I can almost promise you that you won't."

It dawns on me that maybe she really believes Frank Finney is alive and living in Los Angeles.

"This isn't about my father," I say. "I just . . . I want to see what it's like. Before I figure out school or whatever comes next." It sounds stupid when I say it out loud. But what's the point of trying to explain? Mami and I could sit in this room talking for the rest of our lives and I could never make her understand.

She nods once, frowns slightly. Sips her drink. Turns her gaze to the window.

"Juanita had a saying," Mami announces, and she almost smiles. "*Ojos que no ven, corazón que no siente*," she says. "Perhaps I will understand that in the months to come."

Then she stands up, snatching her drink. "Good luck,

Joaquin," she says coldly as she walks toward her room, her back to me. "I hope it all works out for you there."

I look over toward my sister. Her face is red, splotchy, her neck is covered in hives. I open my mouth to speak, but Elena holds up her hand to stop me.

"No," she says, barely able to get the word out. I think she'll storm off, but she just sits there, making me take it. Making me witness her tears and her red eyes and her sobs.

"Elena, can't we talk about it?" I ask, moving toward her.

"No," she says again, pulling back. And then, "No, we cannot."

"Okay," I say, backing up. "Okay."

At last she gives up and walks out of the kitchen, slamming her bedroom door hard. I stand there listening to her muffled cries through the walls.

CHAPTER NINETEEN

THE DAY AFTER I TELL MAMI AND ELENA ABOUT MY decision to move to California, I get ready to go in and work the lunch shift, but my stomach knots up at the thought of it. El Mirador is usually an escape, but not today.

Because today I know I'll have to tell Amy.

I go through the motions. Smile and nod at the families trying to get in one last week of vacation. Babies and toddlers with sand in between their rolls of fat. Moms with tired expressions. Dads with sunburned noses.

"What can I get you to drink?"

"You need a minute? Take your time."

"Ready for the check?"

Amy has the later shift. Any minute she'll be here, and I'll have to tell her the truth. I think about the warmth of her body. Her kindness. Her dreams that aren't my dreams.

When she walks in she spots me by the bar. She comes over and hugs me, but she can tell something's wrong. When she asks what's up, I nod toward the employee break room. We head inside, and she shuts the door behind her and looks at me, her face full of concern.

"Joaquin, what's wrong?"

"Amy," I say, "I . . ." My breath catches. I haven't ever cried in front of her. But my voice cracks.

"Amy, I have to get out of here," I say, my voice dropping down to a whisper.

She frowns, confused. "You mean here, like the restaurant?"

I squeeze my eyes shut, trying to hold back the tears.

"No," I say. "Here . . . like my family. Here like this town."

When I open my eyes Amy's face is twisted with confusion. "What are you talking about?"

"I just can't be here anymore. I have to go away."

"Next year we're going to Austin," she says, gripping my hands in hers. "I thought that's what you wanted."

I pull my hands away, otherwise I'll never be able to do this. She winces.

"I know but . . ." I can't find the words to explain it to her but I still try, telling her what happened the day before when Mami and Elena engaged in their warped mind games. "I . . . I have to leave now," I say, finishing the story. "Like right now. I have to get out before I get sucked in."

"Hey, we can figure this out," she says, and now she is crying, tears streaming down her face. "Maybe you can stay with

319

Carlos? Or get your own apartment if you pick up more shifts at the restaurant?"

I close my eyes again and shake my head.

"Amy," I tell her, "if I don't leave Mariposa Island now I'll never get out."

When I open my eyes, her cheeks are red, and even though she is still crying, when she speaks her voice is fierce with anger.

"Are you breaking up with me?" she asks, incredulous. She sniffs and uses her free hand to wipe her eyes. "Is that what you're saying? We're just . . . done?"

The way she spits out the word *done* makes my heart sink. I give in to my own tears at last, letting them fall down my face.

"Amy . . ." I don't have the words.

"I can't believe this," she presses, crossing her arms over her chest. She looks away, but she doesn't move from in front of the door.

"Amy, I'm sorry," I mumble at last, crying hard now, barely able to see. I walk past her—it's the only way out—and I push open the break room door and race through the restaurant, still wearing my waiter's apron. When I get outside El Mirador, I head toward the side of the building where Amy and I used to talk and flirt when we first met. Now I stand there alone, gulping for air until the tears stop at last.

• • •

The week between my deciding I'm going to leave and the morning Carlos is supposed to give me a lift to the Greyhound station in Houston goes by in almost total silence—at least between Mami and Elena and me. Well, Mami and Elena still talk. I can hear their back-and-forth at night as they watch television.

A few days before I'm taking off, I'm busy digging through books and T-shirts and flyers from old punk shows and way too many cassettes, trying to figure out what I can part with and what I have to take. There are a few cassettes I'd like to leave Amy, but she's not talking to me anymore. She asked Carlos to schedule us on different shifts.

Suddenly, I hear the front door open. It's Elena, back from being out with J.C.

Her steps are loud and heavy. She drops her keys. Once. Again.

"*Damn*," she mutters. Then she appears, suddenly, at my bedroom door. "Hey. Hey, you."

I turn to look at her, tilt my head, and decide to make it light. "Did you break into the Callahans' liquor cabinet again, Elena?"

She rolls her eyes and falls back onto my unmade bed.

"I drank *allll* of their vodka," she answers, her face full of mock shame. "I'm the worst babysitter on the planet."

She's being like old times, silly. Goofy. I know it's because she's drunk, but at least she's talking to me.

"You packing?" she asks.

"Yeah," I tell her. I pull an old T-shirt from the closet, the one from my LBJ High track days. I toss it toward her and it lands on her face. She yanks it off and tries to focus her gaze on it.

"You can keep that one," I say. "You were always stealing it out of the laundry anyway."

Elena clutches the T-shirt to her chest, then curls up on her side. "Thank you, big brother," she whispers.

Like a knife is sliding through my chest.

"Elena," I say, taking advantage of the situation. It may be my only chance. "Elena, can we talk about why I'm moving? I mean, are we ever going to discuss it?"

Elena closes her eyes. "Joaquin?" she says.

"Yeah?"

"I don't want to have this talk right now, okay?" she tells me. "Okay? It's fine. You're going to California, not China. I'll see you again." She opens her eyes and stares at me, suddenly lucid. "I mean, I *will* see you again, right?"

"Yes," I say. "Yes, Elena, you'll see me again. Maybe you can come out and visit."

Elena laughs, roll over onto her back, my T-shirt still in her hands. "Not likely. Not unless the Callahans plan a trip to Disneyland and hire me as a mother's helper. But something tells me Mami won't buy it."

"Yeah, I guess," I say.

"You know what?"

"What?" I ask.

"The Callahans are going back to Houston this week. School's starting."

Tears start running down her face.

"Elena?"

"How can I see him if the Callahans are leaving?" she says, sitting up suddenly. "I don't want to *not* see him."

Maybe not seeing him wouldn't be the worst, I think to myself. But I need to tread lightly if I don't want her storming out on me, ignoring me and not saying goodbye.

"Hey," I say, sitting on the bed next to her. "Hey, you'll figure it out." What shitty advice. But I don't know what else to say.

Elena shrugs. Sniffles. "I guess," she says. "I guess I wish the Callahans could just move here permanently. But he has this amazing job in Houston, so . . ."

"Maybe you can find another family to babysit for," I suggest. "Or get some sort of real job."

Elena blinks back her tears and nods. "Maybe she'll let me. Shit. I am almost seventeen."

"You're almost an adult," I remind her. The statement is laughable, but I say it anyway.

Elena yawns, falls on her back. A moment passes and then I hear her snoring lightly. I dim the lights in my bedroom, cover her with my blanket, and keep packing. When the clock makes it past midnight, I head into Elena's bedroom and collapse onto her bed, trying to block out the streetlight shining through the window and the smell of cigarette smoke on her sheets.

. . .

The night before I leave I barely sleep at all. It's still dark when I finally get up, shower, dress, and haul my bags to the porch. I open the front door slowly, but it still creaks. The morning humidity is thick as a milkshake already.

After I set down my bags, I come back inside and head toward Mami's door. I open it an inch.

"Mami," I say into the dark room. "Mami, I'm leaving now." Silence.

Hell. She's my mother and I'm leaving. What can happen to me now? I go ahead and walk in, crossing the floor to her bed. She's wide awake and lying on her side, her head on the pillow, her eyes staring out at the wall. She looks so much older without makeup and with her hair a morning mess.

"Mami, I'm leaving, okay?" I say.

She nods wordlessly.

"I'll call when I get there, all right?"

Again she says nothing, just nods. No eye contact. I stand there, not sure what to do next. I can't remember the last time we hugged.

The eyes of my Cuban grandparents look down on us from photographs, strangers to me.

"Mami," I say. Because I must. Because it really is true. "I love you."

At this Mami curls up, pushes her face into the pillow.

"Be safe," she murmurs.

I close the bedroom door behind her and discover Elena

waiting for me in her long white nightgown, her arms crossed in front of her. She yawns.

"It's so early," she whispers.

"I know, but Carlos is picking me up at six. I want to get the bulk of the trip out of the way today. Tonight I'll be in Phoenix and then tomorrow I'll be there." Elena knows this already. It's just talk to fill the moment.

"Well, call when you get there," she says. "Call collect if you have to."

I nod. I open the front door and peer outside. Carlos has just pulled up and parked, the engine of the Chevette idling.

"Well," I say, "looks like I have to go."

"You don't *have* to," Elena says, but she says it gently. Like a joke.

Once, when we were small, Elena and I had played hide-and-seek in this house and I'd hidden in my bedroom closet and fallen asleep. When Elena finally found me, she was sobbing and mad. So mad she'd shoved me hard in the chest.

"Don't you ever do that to me again!" she'd yelled. "Promise!"

I had promised. But this isn't hiding. She knows where I'll be. She knows how to find me.

I find myself praying to God—something I never do. *God, please watch out for Elena.*

Carlos honks his horn—two short, little staccato beats.

"Don't make him wait," Elena says, and she's not even crying. She's keeping her face nice and calm. Even.

"Elena . . ." I say.

"Just hug me and go, Joaquin." She opens her arms wide and I do hug her, but it's light and quick. We're not in the practice of hugging much, either.

When it's over, she offers me a smile and steps back, almost pushing me out the door.

"Elena, I love you."

"I love you, too," she says, still smiling.

And then the door shuts.

I head down the front steps and toss my bags into the back of the Chevette and get in the front passenger seat.

"You ready, man?" asks Carlos. He scratches the back of his neck and yawns.

"Yeah," I answer. He pulls the car out onto Esperanza Boulevard.

I don't look back.

JOAQUIN FINNEY

LOS ANGELES

1987

THE AWFUL SONG WAS RIGHT. IT NEVER RAINED IN southern California. In fact, it was always sunny with a chance of sun. And the beach was glorious. Wide and sugar-white, bordering a deep blue ocean that made the waters off Mariposa Island seem like God's joke version of the sea. Back in Texas, Joaquin never cared one way or another about living by the water, but in his new home when he had an afternoon off he often found himself sinking into the sand, staring out at the waves crashing one on top of the other. It was easy to be there alone. He liked it, like he liked his new life in L.A.

He had an apartment, an efficiency the size of a postage stamp, and a job, at a Mexican restaurant that Carlos hooked him up with because his cousin worked there. Joaquin looked forward to coming home after work to an empty apartment, playing his favorite music as loud as he could, eating whatever he wanted. He enjoyed the feeling of waking up in the morning and knowing there was no one in the apartment whose complicated personality he had to navigate. No one whose day-to-day life he had to worry about. He stopped biting his nails.

On the weekends, Joaquin went exploring. Even though it was touristy, the Griffith Observatory became a favorite spot. He'd people watch and stare out at the Hollywood sign, which was still weird to see in actual, real life. He had no intention of becoming an actor or a musician. He had no idea what he wanted to become here in Los Angeles, but he didn't mind being an anomaly. And anyway, there were a million possibilities in this world.

On Sunday nights Joaquin called home, but on the rare chance his mother was the one to pick up the phone she refused to talk to him, passing the phone over to his sister Elena, who questioned Joaquin about the weather, his apartment, his job. He answered carefully, trying to picture where Elena stood in the house as she took his call. The beat-up couch in the den. The screened-in porch. Joaquin was keenly aware of the fact that his mother was listening in on everything being said, but truth be told this didn't even anger him. "How's your year going?" Joaquin would ask Elena, eager to keep the spotlight on her.

"It's fine," she would answer, her voice tight.

One Sunday evening he asked, "Is J.C. still around?" He lowered his voice just in case their mother was too near the receiver.

"Yeah," Elena answered after a beat. Her voice grew more strained. Joaquin didn't ask about the Callahans or how Elena was managing to get out of the house. Instead, he talked about superficial things and paced in his microscopic kitchen for as far as the cord stretched. When he said goodbye, his stomach hurt, and even though his heart broke a little each time, he was so happy he could hang up the phone and be alone in California.

He wrote letters to Elena. It was the only way Joaquin could think to tell her what was really on his mind, at least in a way he couldn't during the phone calls monitored by their mother. He knew the mail always came during the day, and Elena was always the first one to get to it. So Joaquin took his spiral notebook and found a comfortable spot on the cheap carpet and settled in, his back pressed against the bare wall, his fingers gripped around a ballpoint pen whose ink ran spotty and rough. He wrote without stopping or censoring himself. He told his little sister about what was going on in his life, of course, but he also wrote to tell her he was worried about her and about what was going on with J.C. He told her he was anxious about how she was being treated, not just by J.C., but by their own mother. He told her he could understand if she was mad at him for leaving, but he tried to explain why it was something he had to do.

Joaquin asked Elena if the Callahans would be back next summer.

When he could afford it, he slipped a five-dollar bill from

his tip money in with his letters, and he mailed them on his days off from the restaurant. Grinning politely at the women working behind the counter at the post office, he licked his stamps and centered them carefully, officially, like the last piece of a puzzle. Then he slid the slim envelopes across the counter and hoped for the best. Because in all those many months of settling in, finding a job, renting an apartment, Joaquin had never gotten a letter back from Elena. Not even once.

Sometimes, in the still of the night or while standing on his balcony overlooking the parking lot, Joaquin liked to imagine Elena climbing the front porch steps to the mailbox when she came home from school, her beat-up red backpack slung low off one shoulder. Her hair in a messy ponytail. He pictured her standing on the porch that needed painting and flipping through bills and glossy circulars and finding his letter in the thick of it all. Her name in his most careful print. Joaquin could see her holding the letter up to her face, right near the thin, straight scar on her chin, as she opened the envelope carefully so she didn't tear the paper inside. He visualized her tugging at his letter, unfolding it right there on the porch and reading it over and over again. Maybe she even breathed the letter in, anxious to catch a bit of the Los Angeles air that traveled with it. Maybe she was happy to hear from him.

God, he hoped she was.

In Joaquin's mind's eye, Elena clutched the letter for as long as she could, contemplating it, and even after she folded it up and placed it in the back pocket of her jeans, it thumped like a heartbeat there. It beckoned like a talisman. Or a promise. And then, he hoped she'd take a moment to glance back at the streets of Mariposa Island and consider all that was around her, all that was waiting for her—both there and elsewhere—before she opened the door of her childhood home and went inside.

AUTHOR'S NOTE

Like Elena and Joaquin's mother, Caridad, many Cuban children were spirited out of Cuba after Fidel Castro and his followers officially took power on January 1, 1959. The Peter Pan movement, known as Operation Pedro Pan, was a real, mass exodus of 14,000 children out of Cuba to the United States in the early 1960s. The program was run by the Catholic Welfare Bureau, and as part of the program Cuban children were placed in private homes and orphanages all over the U.S. Most, but not all, were eventually reunited with their families. Like Caridad, many children who came to the United States through the Pedro Pan program can recall *la pecera*, or fishbowl—a glass enclosure that separated children from their parents in the moments leading up to their departure.

During the Cuban Revolution and the time shortly before Castro's control of the country, there were several bombings that took place on the island during the years 1953 through 1958. The bombing of Caridad's *quince* is wholly fictional.

Elena refers to herself as Hispanic in this novel. While this word is still in use today and was a commonly used term in the 1980s, *Latino*, *Latina*, or *Latinx* are often preferred today.

This book is inspired by an episode of the radio program *This American Life* titled, "Yes, There Is a Baby," which originally aired on January 5, 2001.

ACKNOWLEDGMENTS

This book would not have been possible without the generosity afforded to me by my mother and her three sisters, all Cuban-born women who fled their homeland after Fidel Castro took power. While my mother was not part of Pedro Pan, she, too, left Cuba as as an unaccompanied minor and remembers the painful experience of saying goodbye to her parents through the glass wall of *la pecera*. It took two years for my mother to be fully reunited with all of her sisters and both parents. My mother's openness in discussing this period in her life as well as her memories of the Cuba of her childhood helped to shape this book. It is my wish that one day she will visit a free Cuba. Thank you to my maternal aunts for their willingness to answer questions about their memories on the island and to my mother and father for their assistance with the Spanish language portions of this book.

I would also like to thank Olivia Gonzalez for taking the time to speak with me about her experiences as part of Pedro Pan. Her detailed memories, while certainly painful to recall, contributed to this book in so many important and meaningful ways. Thank you to my Cuban *hermana* and fellow writer Christina Diaz Gonzalez for putting us in touch. Christina's novel *The Red Umbrella* is a beautifully written story about a young girl leaving

Cuba as part of Pedro Pan, and I cannot recommend it highly enough.

To my editor, Katherine Jacobs, thank you for the seed that became this book and for your care as you shepherded it to conclusion.

To my agent, Kerry Sparks, and to the entire amazing team at Levine Greenberg Rostan, especially Beth Fisher, thank you always for being on my side.

To everyone at Macmillan, including Mary Van Akin, Jo Kirby, Elizabeth Clark, Lucy Del Priore, Katie Halata, Molly Ellis, Allison Verost, Brittany Pearlman, and everyone associated with getting my books out into the world—thank you a million times over for your support and encouragement.

Thank you to Cathy Power for answering all my questions about being an '80s punk in Texas and for being such a cheerleader of my work. *Un abrazo fuerte* for the wonderful Domino Perez for reading over some critical scenes. Thanks also to Claire Barnhart for answering my Los Angeles inquiries, and to my brother, Chris Mathieu, for taking me to the Griffith Observatory more than once.

To my YA community, including Jessica Taylor, Julie Murphy, Kate Sowa, Christa Desir, Katie Cotugno, Jeff Zentner, Liara Tamani, Leigh Bardugo, Mitali Perkins, Caleb Roehrig, Anna-Marie McLemore, Emmy Laybourne, the YAHous, the good folks at Blue Willow Bookshop in Houston, and so many others who take the time to support me and each other—thank you!

Much love to my second family at Bellaire High School for

your ongoing support of my second career, especially Michael McDonough and Carl Casteel. I am Cardinal Proud!

To the Jesus and Mary Chain, whose gorgeous and heart-breaking music served as my writing soundtrack for this novel.

And finally, to my biggest fan, my husband, Kevin. What would I do without you? I never want to know. Texas-sized love to you and Elliott forever.

GO FISH

JENNIFER MATHIEU

When did you realize you wanted to be a writer?
When I was in the fifth grade, I won a fiction writing competition at my school. I wrote a mystery titled "Mystery at Grandma's" (titles have never been easy for me), and it won! The prize was that the book was housed in my school library for one school year. It was such a rush to know other kids were checking out my work and reading it. I think that's when I realized I wanted to be a writer.

What's your most embarrassing childhood memory?
I was constantly embarrassed even though most of the time what I was going through was not that embarrassing. I remember I had a weird habit of eating paper in middle school. My teacher called me out in front of the class, and I just about died. It did break me of the habit!

What's your favorite childhood memory?
I have several, but when I think about my childhood, I smile when I remember the solitude. I loved shutting myself up in my bedroom, creating stories with my dollhouse characters, drawing, writing poetry, reading, and listening to the

radio. I still crave and need solitude, and as a child, I felt I had quite a bit of it. It recharges me.

What book is on your nightstand now?

Right now I am reading the diaries of Dawn Powell. Dawn Powell was a novelist and critic who worked and published from the 1930s until the very early 1960s. She had such a keen eye and sharp wit and in many ways was ahead of her time. She was definitely a writer's writer. Her diaries are a true goldmine of funny anecdotes and insight into the creative process and the world of publishing. More people need to know about her!

What sparked your imagination for *The Liars of Mariposa Island*?

This novel was sparked by two things: my mother's own journey to the United States from Cuba as a young girl and an episode of the *This American Life* radio program about babysitting.

What challenges do you face in the writing process, and how do you overcome them?

By biggest challenge is time, and I try to overcome that by setting specific, achievable, measurable writing goals for myself.

What's the best advice you have ever received about writing?

Figure out what works for you and do it that way. There is not one set of writing rules that works for everyone. It's okay if you're a careful outliner and someone else writes without an outline. It's okay if you write to music and another writer has to have absolute silence. Just figure out what works for you.

What advice do you wish someone had given you when you were younger?
Stop being in such a hurry. Stop trying to be perfect. Give yourself some grace. Of course, I doubt I would have listened. It's likely someone did give me this advice and I ignored it!

Do you ever get writer's block? What do you do to get back on track?
Sometimes I do, yes. It's fairly rare, but when it happens, I know it's because something big isn't working in the story. That's when I call my brilliant editor or talk it out with a friend. Once I've addressed the problem, I'm usually able to get back on track.

What would you do if you ever stopped writing?
Read more. And watch more Netflix, Hulu, and Amazon Prime!

What are you working on right now?
I am working on *Bad Girls Never Say Die*, a novel set in 1964 Houston that I pitched as a sort of feminist homage to *The Outsiders*. It's about a gang of girls from the wrong side of the tracks and what happens when they befriend a rich girl from the right neighborhood. I'm having a lot of fun with it!

An unlikely teenager starts a
feminist revolution in this novel for all the
young women fighting the good fight.

Keep reading for an excerpt.

CHAPTER ONE

MY ENGLISH TEACHER, MR. DAVIES, RUBS A HAND OVER HIS MILITARY buzz cut. There's sweat beading at his hairline, and he puffs out his ruddy cheeks. He looks like a drunk porcupine.

The drunk part may be true. Even if it is before lunch on a Tuesday.

"Let's discuss the symbolism in line 12 of the poem," he announces, and I pick up my pen so I can copy down exactly what he says when he tells us what the gold light behind the blue curtains really means. Mr. Davies says he wants to *discuss* the symbolism, but that's not true. When we have our unit test, he'll expect us to write down what he told us in class word for word.

I blink and try to stay awake. Half the kids are messing with their phones, grinning faintly into their groins. I can sense my brain liquefying.

"Vivian, what are your thoughts?" Mr. Davies asks me. Of course.

"Well," I say, folding in on myself and staring at the Xeroxed copy of the poem on my desk. "Uh . . ." My cheeks turn scarlet. Why does Mr. Davies have to call on me? Why not mess with one of the groin grinners? At least I'm pretending to pay attention.

Neither of us says anything for what feels like a third of my life span. I shift in my seat. Mr. Davies stares. I chew my bottom lip uncertainly. Mr. Davies stares. I search my brain for an answer, any answer, but with everyone's eyes on me I can't think straight. Finally, Mr. Davies gives up.

"Lucy?" he says, calling on the new girl, Lucy Hernandez, who's had her hand up since he asked the question. He stares at her blankly and waits.

"Well," Lucy starts, and you can tell she's excited to get going, even sitting up a little straighter in her chair, "if you think about the reference the speaker makes in line 8, what I'm wondering is if the light doesn't indicate, a, um, what would you call it . . . like a *shift* in the speaker's understanding of . . ."

There's a cough that interrupts her from the back of the room. At the tail end of the cough slip out the words, "Make me a sandwich."

And then there's a collection of snickers and laughs, like a smattering of applause.

I don't have to turn around to know it's Mitchell Wilson being an asshole, cheered on by his douche bag football friends.

Lucy takes in a sharp breath. "Wait, what did you just say?" she asks, turning in her seat, her dark eyes wide with surprise.

Mitchell just smirks at her from his desk, his blue eyes peering out from under his auburn hair. He would actually be kind of cute if he never spoke or walked around or breathed or anything.

"I said," Mitchell begins, enjoying himself, "make . . . me . . . a . . . sandwich." His fellow football-player minions laugh like it's the freshest, most original bit of comedy ever, even though all of them have been using this line since last spring.

Lucy turns back in her seat, rolling her eyes. Little red hives are burning up her chest. "That's not funny," she manages softly. She slips her long black hair over her shoulders, like she's trying to hide. Standing at the front of the room, Mr. Davies shakes his head and frowns.

"If we can't have a reasonable discussion in this classroom, then I'm going to have to end this lesson right now," he tells us. "I want all of you to take out your grammar textbooks and start the exercises on pages 25 and 26. They're due tomorrow." I swear he picks those pages blind. Who knows if we've even gone over the material.

As my classmates offer up a collective groan and I fish around in my backpack for my book, Lucy regains some sort of courage and pipes up. "Mr. Davies, that's not fair. We *were* having a reasonable discussion. But they"—she nods her head over her shoulder, unable to look in Mitchell's direction again—"are the ones who ruined it. I don't understand why you're punishing all of us." I cringe. Lucy is new to East Rockport High. She doesn't know what's coming.

"Lucy, did I or did I not just announce to the class that it should begin the grammar exercises on pages 25 and 26 of the grammar textbook?" Mr. Davies spits, more enthusiastic about disciplining Lucy than he ever seemed to be about the gold light behind the blue curtains.

"Yes, but . . . ," Lucy begins.

"No, stop," Mr. Davies interrupts. "Stop talking. You can add page 27 to your assignment."

Mitchell and his friends collapse into laughter, and Lucy sits there, stunned, her eyes widening as she stares at Mr. Davies. Like no teacher has ever talked to her like that in her life.

A beat or two later Mitchell and his friends get bored and settle down and all of us are opening our textbooks, surrendering ourselves to the assignment. My head is turned toward the words *subordinate clauses*, but my gaze makes its way toward Lucy. I wince a little as I watch her staring at her still-closed textbook like somebody smacked her across the face with it and she's still getting her breath back. It's obvious she's trying not to cry.

When the bell finally rings, I grab my stuff and head out as fast as I can. Lucy is still in her seat, her head down as she slides her stuff into her backpack.

I spot Claudia making her way down the hall toward me.

"Hey," I say, pulling my backpack over my shoulders.

"Hey," she answers, shooting me the same grin she's had since we became best friends in kindergarten, bonding over our shared love of stickers and chocolate ice cream. "What's happening?"

I sneak a look to make sure Mitchell or one of his friends isn't near me to overhear. "We just got all this grammar homework. Mitchell was bugging that new girl, Lucy, and instead of dealing with him, Mr. Davies just assigned the entire class all these extra pages of homework."

"Let me guess," Claudia says as we head down the hall, "make me a sandwich?"

"Oh my God, however did you figure that one out?" I answer, my voice thick with mock surprise.

"Just a wild guess," says Claudia with a roll of her eyes. She's tinier than me, the top of her head only reaching my shoulder, and I have to lean in to hear her. At 5'10" and a junior in high school, I'm afraid I might still be growing, but Claudia's been the size of a coffee-table tchotchke since the sixth grade.

"It's such bullshit," I mutter as we stop at my locker. "And it's not even original humor. Make me a sandwich. I mean, dude, you could at least come up with something that hasn't been all over the Internet since we were in middle school."

"I know," Claudia agrees, waiting as I find my sack lunch in the cavernous recesses of my messy locker. "But cheer up. I'm sure he'll grow up sooner or later."

I give Claudia a look and she smirks back. Way back when, Mitchell was just another kid in our class at East Rockport Middle and his dad was just an annoying seventh-grade Texas history teacher who liked to waste time in class by showing us infamous football injuries on YouTube, complete with bone breaking through skin. Mitchell was like a mosquito bite back then. Irritating, but easy to forget if you just ignored him.

Fast forward five years and Mr. Wilson managed to climb the Byzantine ranks of the East Rockport public school hierarchy to become principal of East Rockport High School, and Mitchell gained thirty pounds and the town discovered he could throw a perfect spiral. And now it's totally acceptable that Mitchell Wilson and his friends interrupt girls in class to instruct them to make sandwiches.

Once we get to the cafeteria, Claudia and I navigate our way through the tables to sit with the girls we eat lunch with every day—Kaitlyn Price and Sara Gomez and Meg McCrone. Like us, they're sweet, mostly normal girls, and we've known each other since forever. They're girls who've never lived anywhere but East Rockport, population 6,000. Girls who try not to stand out. Girls who have secret crushes that they'll never act on. Girls who sit quietly in class and earn decent grades and hope they won't be called on to explain the symbolism in line 12 of a poem.

So, like, nice girls.

We sit there talking about classes and random gossip, and as I take a bite of my apple I see Lucy Hernandez at a table with a few other lone wolves who regularly join forces in an effort to appear less lonely. Her table is surrounded by the jock table and the popular table and the stoner table and every-other-variety-of-East-Rockport-kid table. Lucy's table is the most depressing. She's not talking to anyone, just jamming a plastic fork into some supremely sad-looking pasta dish sitting inside of a beat-up Tupperware container.

I think about going over to invite her to sit with us, but then

I think about the fact that Mitchell and his dumb-ass friends are sitting smack in the center of the cafeteria, hooting it up, looking for any chance to pelt one of us with more of their lady-hating garbage. And Lucy Hernandez has to be a prime target given what just happened in class.

So I don't invite her to sit with us.

Maybe I'm not so nice after all.

DON'T MISS THESE OTHER EMPOWERING, THOUGHT-PROVOKING BOOKS BY JENNIFER MATHIEU.